Bad Boys
Down Under

Bad Boys Down Under

Nancy Warren

BRAVA

KENSINGTON PUBLISHING CORP.
http://www.kensingtonbooks.com

BRAVA BOOKS are published by

Kensington Publishing Corp.
850 Third Avenue
New York, NY 10022

All Kensington titles, imprints and distributed lines are available at special quantity discounts for bulk purchases for sales promotion, premiums, fund raising, educational or institutional use.

Special book excerpts or customized printings can also be created to fit specific needs. For details, write or phone the office of the Kensington Special Sales Manager: Kensington Publishing Corp., 850 Third Avenue, New York, NY, 10022. Attn. Special Sales Department. Phone: 1-800-221-2647.

Brava and the B logo Reg. U.S. Pat. & TM Off.

ISBN 0-7582-0585-6

First Kensington Trade Paperback Printing: July 2004
10 9 8 7 6 5 4 3 2 1

Printed in the United States of America

Acknowledgments

Bad Boys Down Under owes a great deal to the *Best Girls Down Under*. Those are: my patient and brilliant Sydney-sider sister-in-law Wendy Warren; the creative, globe-trotting and fun-loving Anne Brettingham-Moore; and a wonderful online friend Karen Horeau. These three Australian women read my manuscript, offered advice, and set me right on all things Aussie. Thank you all so much!

For a Canadian to write a book that featured Australians and Americans was a challenge, but it was one of the most fun projects I've ever worked on. It gave me a chance to re-live my best memories of visiting Australia, as well as in-stilling a burning urge to go back. Soon.

The idea for *Bad Boys Down Under* came from my incredible editor Kate Duffy and, of course, the inspiration came from Aussie men themselves. There's just something about those sexy, rugged men . . .

While researching *Bad Boys Down Under,* I read a lot of books about Australia. Two that are particularly fun are: Bill Bryson's *In a Sunburned Country* and a little book my sister-in-law sent me called *Aussie Slang: Great Australian Slang and Phrases Explained in Basic English* by John Blackman.

Thanks as always to my wonderful supportive agent, Robin Rue, to the team at Kensington who take a big, sloppy manuscript and somehow make a book, and to my family who put up with me insisting that watching and re-watching Hugh Jackman movies is research!

Contents

Sizzling in Sydney

Chapter One

What Jennifer Talbot hated most about business travel was the business of traveling—and the unpleasant surprises that cropped up from time to time when she was too tired, jet-lagged, and far from home to deal with them.

The man lounging in the outdoor spa appeared to be one of those unpleasant surprises.

Not that he wasn't gorgeous with that barely civilized, raw-sex Aussie appeal, and she wasn't displeased that the CEO of Crane Surf and Boogie Boards wanted to see her so soon after her arrival in Australia.

It was just that Jen had stumbled out of the cab from Sydney Airport believing the address she'd been given was a hotel. Her suit was rumpled, her feet seemed to have swelled inside her pumps, her eyelids were scratchy from lack of sleep, and her temper was seriously frayed. What she needed was a very large bottle of Perrier, an even larger bed, and about fourteen hours of uninterrupted sleep.

What she had was her client, Cameron Crane, whom she'd come a very long way to do business with, gazing at her like she was one of those prawns they always talked about *putting on the barbie:* as though she were some luscious bit of food he was contemplating devouring in a couple of bites.

"G'day. Welcome to Australia," he said, steam wafting

back and forth across his face giving him a dreamy, fantasy quality. His dirty-blond hair was much longer than necessary and curled roguishly at the ends. He sported a tough-guy jaw, a not-very-successful boxer's nose, and eyes that were both lazy and penetrating at the same time.

"I thought this was a hotel," she said. It was certainly large enough—a sleekly modern house set back off the street in barely tamed tropical gardens. The house was right across the street from the beach but if its owner didn't want to walk that far for a swim, there was a good-sized swimming pool at her feet so cool and inviting her feet throbbed just looking at it. And beside it, the spa, steaming silently without its jets on.

Since she'd done her homework, she knew that Crane was a financial wunderkind with a lot of fingers in a lot of very lucrative pies. She'd flown from San Francisco to help him add the USA to his pie collection.

She tried to keep her voice pleasant; he was the client, after all, but even she could hear the edge of irritation. "If you'd told me you wanted to meet right away, I'd have come better prepared."

"You should have let me send a car for you."

"It's just as well you didn't, since the plane was delayed several hours." A fact that only added to her fatigue.

"I don't want you to work tonight. You're staying here as my guest. I thought you'd be more comfortable in my house than in a hotel."

In a pig's eye. She wasn't entirely sure why he wanted her under his roof, but she doubted it was for her comfort. "I see. I'm Jennifer Talbot."

She thought his eyes were a smoky gray-green, but it was hard to tell in the steam. What she could certainly see was the cocky grin that revealed I-could-eat-you-all-up even white teeth. "Thought you might be. Come on in. Water's great."

She managed a frigid smile. "I didn't bring my bathing suit."

The grin intensified. "Neither did I."

She refused to gasp or blush. She had a pretty good idea he'd be only too pleased if she did either, or, preferably, both. She'd met his type before. "All I want to do is go to bed." Before he could say a word, she added, "Alone."

He laughed outright at that. "I'm Cam."

"Nice to meet you." Though it would have been a lot nicer in an office when she had her wits about her. She eased an aching foot out of a pump and rubbed it against the back of her calf.

"Sit down and take a load off. Like a beer? I think I've got another one in the esky." He gestured behind him to a small cooler.

She sank into a teak lounger with a green and white striped cushion, unable to resist putting her feet up. "I don't suppose you have a Perrier?"

He scratched his chin, where darkish stubble shadowed a dimple. "Might, I suppose. I'll ring through to the kitchen." He started to rise, water sluicing down muscular shoulders and a dark-haired chest. As he turned to climb out, she caught a glimpse of the white bulge of his backside and realized he hadn't been joking about being naked.

As hot and cold shivers chased themselves up and down her spine, she opened her mouth to say, "No. Please don't bother. A beer's fine." But she caught the glance he shot her over his shoulder. He paused for a second, waiting for her to stop him. She closed her mouth and sank back into the lounger. *He wanted to play chicken? Fine.*

She wouldn't even look away. In truth, she couldn't have if she'd tried. He emerged from that bubbling water like a Greek god out of the steam of creation. Even in her dehydrated condition, she felt her mouth go dry. His body was muscular and solid, tanned to a rugged bronze, his paler buttocks rounded, but just as solid and muscular as the rest of him. She was accustomed to working with men who appeared better in their business suits than out of them. She had a feeling Cameron Crane looked better in the buff.

There was a smallish dark patch up high on one cheek that she took to be a bruise until the curtain of wafting steam parted and she recognized the company logo. A small crane.

Anybody who had their company logo tattooed on their butt was either way too arrogant, or a complete workaholic.

If he were a subtle sort of man she'd concede a certain ironic humor in the location of the tattoo, but based on five minutes acquaintance, she doubted Cameron Crane kept much subtlety in stock.

Cam watched blondie watching him.

She looked, he thought, like one of those American film and telly stars: tense, tight-arsed, and anorexic.

He hated for anyone to have the upper hand over him, especially a woman. In this case, he had to admit, Jennifer Talbot did. She was here because she was a brilliant marketer with an intimate knowledge of the California market, and since she'd be a key player in introducing Crane products in the U.S., she had a lot of clout.

Which meant he needed to make absolutely certain he had more. Luckily, he had a foolproof plan for maintaining control of their relationship. He'd sleep with her. He'd already decided to seduce her before she even got on the plane.

If she'd gained a few stones, or lost her teeth since her Harvard photo, he still would have bedded her for the sake of his company. But in the flesh she was even nicer than the eight-year-old photo had led him to believe. He'd seduce her all right, for the sake of his company, and his own pleasure.

He used the intercom to alert Marg that company was here and asked for a sparkling water. Then he turned back and found blondie still gazing straight at him.

Beneath a gaze of icy reserve, he caught the gleam of hot intelligence in her eyes. She didn't blush or remove her eyes as he gave her his best view and slowly returned to the spa. She didn't look him up and down like she was going to measure him for a suit, either. He could have been fully dressed for all the reaction he'd caused.

Her eyes locked with his and her eyebrows rose in a challenge. He sank a bit quicker into the swirling water than he'd planned, as something else raised itself. There was nothing he enjoyed more than a challenge.

He reckoned seducing this one, with her hot intelligence and cool beauty, was going to be more fun than he'd imagined. Hell, he might even do the world a favor and loosen her up a bit. In any case, the next few weeks promised to be interesting.

There were two things Cameron Crane was really good at. One of them was making money.

Chapter Two

At least he has hired help, Jen thought, relaxing marginally when a leather-skinned woman who obviously hadn't heard the word sunscreen appeared with a tray holding a bottle of sparkling water, the bottle covered with condensation, which she hoped meant it had been refrigerated since the accompanying glass held no ice. There was also a can of beer.

"You must be Jennifer." It came out as *Jinnifer,* and Jen was momentarily startled to be addressed so casually. "I'm Marg. Cam said you'd be arriving today. If you need anything, give me a hoy."

Whatever a *hoy* was, Jen doubted she'd be giving it to anyone. "Thank you, but I don't think I'll be staying—"

"I know." The woman threw up one hand and nearly knocked the can of beer over. "That's what I told Cam. She'll want to stay in a hotel, I told him. Not stuck out here with the likes of you. She doesn't need the aggro. But he never listens. You might as well know that straightaway. Cam always does exactly as he pleases."

Jen blinked slowly, feeling not so much jet-lagged as time-warped. If she didn't know from her dossier that Cameron Crane was single, she might have thought this woman was his wife, even though she was clearly much older. Could she be his mother? Since reticence didn't seem to be part of this woman's makeup, she felt safe asking. "Are you a relative of Mr. Crane's?"

The woman emitted a hoot of laughter that caused an unknown bird to squawk in the dark rustle of leafy green trees Jen couldn't yet identify. "Not bloody likely. I only stay because he pays me."

"If I double your salary, will you keep your mouth shut?" asked the man who paid her salary from his private spa, where he'd sunk back in the water, his arms outstretched and gripping the sides of the Jacuzzi in a casual way that annoyed Jen. She'd come a long way to do a job. She didn't appreciate being toyed with.

Marg's laugh came again, but good-natured, as though she and her employer acted like this all the time. She walked around the pool with an unhurried, flat-footed gait and plonked the fresh can down beside Crane, who winked at her and said, "Cheers."

Rising and turning back to Jen, she asked, "Are you hungry?"

"No. Just thirsty." Jen sipped from her drink. "And tired." Beyond tired.

"Did you sleep on the plane?"

"I never sleep on planes." It was a curse. Other travelers snoozed and snored. She could fly around the world and not manage a doze. Mostly, she worked.

In the eighteen or so hours it had taken her to fly from San Francisco, California, to Sydney, New South Wales, she'd re-read her material on Crane Surf and Boogie Boards and reviewed the report she'd prepared on the already tight California market. Of course, California was just a start. Mr. Crane, she'd realized as she read up on him, was an ambitious man.

He'd made his first million a decade ago, by the time he was twenty-four. He'd had no family leg up in the business world. His father was a sheep farmer and his mother a homemaker. Cameron had left the sheep station at a young age, it seemed, because the next anyone had heard of him, he was making a name for himself as a surfie, as they called them here. He'd won some competitions, started designing and building his own boards, and soon he'd made a small fortune.

He'd parlayed that into a business empire in the next decade of his life, going from self-made man to self-made mogul.

She'd been prepared to find this man admirable, driven, aggressive—she knew the type well. But to find herself manipulated into sharing his home, met with nakedness and sultry challenges, was more than she'd bargained for.

If she'd been the client, she'd be hailing herself another taxi in a heartbeat and speeding out of here. But *he* was the client, and, within reason, it was her job to give him what he wanted. But, if the naked man in the hot tub thought she was part of the package, he was going to find he'd mistaken his woman.

As a marketer, she knew all about stereotypes, played with them or against them in advertising campaigns, and used them to help place product in the marketplace. However, because she knew how misleading they could be, she always made a conscious effort not to fall into the trap of judging people by stereotypes.

But Cameron Crane was the quintessential Aussie bloke. Right now, she was just tired enough to snap unwisely at a lucrative client she'd come halfway around the world to work with; antagonizing him because she was dead-tired and he was a chauvinistic, beer-swilling, naked womanizer, was not going to start them off on the path to a harmonious working relationship.

Having downed most of the water, she rose from the blissfully comfy lounger and said, "I'll go to bed now, if you don't mind. I'll want to be fresh and ready to work tomorrow morning."

"It's still early. A quick dip in here'll set you right up," he promised.

She sent him a smile so frigid it should have put a layer of ice over his spa. And his libido. "I doubt it. Good night."

"Oh, stop it, Cam. You can see the girl's dead on her feet. Come on then. I'll show you your room," Marg said.

Jen took a step and remembered her heavy suitcase. She hadn't been certain what the weather would be like in Sydney in September—it was their spring, which meant what exactly? The Internet weather guides weren't much help. It seemed anything could happen in the spring: summer heat or cold, damp days. So she'd packed for both, and her case was heavy.

"Oh." She turned and gestured vaguely at the beast.

"Don't worry about your bag. I'll see to it," said Crane.

He didn't jump right out to help, though, did he? He must know her night things were in there, but he shook his beer can and clearly hearing it slosh in his ear, settled back and sipped.

"Don't trouble yourself," she snapped.

His eyes gleamed wickedly through the steam. "I won't. I'll have Roger do it. He's my gardener and odd-job man."

Too irritated to speak, and too fuzzy-headed to think of anything annihilating enough anyway, she picked up her briefcase and followed Marg, who said as soon as they entered the house, "Don't bother yourself about Cam. He acts like an arse, but it's only an act."

"Well, he's damn good at it."

A low chuckle shook the older woman. "I think the next couple of weeks are going to be beaut."

She was more than a little surprised when a soft knock a few minutes later had her opening her bedroom door to find not the odd-job man Roger but big-shot Cameron Crane himself, hefting her suitcase as though it weighed nothing.

And he wasn't naked, thank God.

"This is a surprise," she said, stepping back so he could bring the suitcase into her bedroom.

"Marg said I was being an arse," he told her, his hazel eyes twinkling at her in a way that suggested there was more to him than she'd suspected.

"Marg is a very intelligent woman."

He laughed, big and easy. Now that he was closer and there was no mist between them she noticed the way his eyes crinkled when he was amused, and she imagined him squinting into the sun, gazing over red-soiled land. Sure he was a Sydney-dwelling surfer, but it was the Outback that had bred him.

"Let's start over, shall we?" He stuck out his hand. "I'm Cameron Crane. Call me Cam."

She took his hand and shook it. His palm was warm and firm and tough-skinned. She let him hold on a moment too long and told herself she was amused by him, and not feeling the tug of attraction.

"So," she said, pulling back. "Arrogant didn't work, now you've moved to charming?"

Once more his big chest rumbled with laughter. "Glad you noticed." He glanced around the guest room as though checking up. "Got everything you need?"

"Yes, thanks." This had to be the strangest introduction she'd ever had to a client. She'd seen him naked and they'd been alone together in her bedroom within the first hour of meeting.

Tomorrow, when she'd had some sleep, she was going to get them on a professional footing. Tomorrow.

As she stifled a yawn, Cameron Crane walked to the door. "Sleep well," he said, and he was gone.

While she dragged out her night things, she couldn't help wondering about him. He'd struck her as an arrogant beer-swilling jerk on their first meeting, but when he'd brought the suitcase he'd exuded warmth, almost teddy-bearish in this rather hairy man. Contrasts like that intrigued her, and she didn't want to be intrigued by Cameron Crane—just paid well.

Thinking the next few weeks were going to be quite the

challenge, she fell into bed and wondered if cool, crisp sheets had ever felt so good.

Jen awoke with a start, momentarily disoriented. She blinked a few times in the darkness, feeling tired, wide-awake, and starving hungry all at once. As memory returned about where she was and why, she scowled and rolled over, searching out the clock by her bedside. Three A.M. The green fluorescent dots broadcast the time as though it were good news. She groaned, rolled over, and squeezed her eyes shut, but who could sleep with the racket coming from her stomach?

It was hopeless. She flipped on the bedside light, illuminating walls of a pale Wedgewood blue, a couple of paintings on the wall—one of tropical flowers and one of a sailboat floating over blue-green water—typical guest-room fare except that when she'd examined them last night she'd discovered they were originals. Good ones, too, although she'd never heard of the artists. Australian probably.

The blue and green batik bedspread and the rattan furniture in the room continued the tropical theme. She got out of bed and thought she'd prefer amateur prints on the walls and the floral polyester bedspreads of a hotel. At least if she were in a hotel she could raid the mini bar. In a private home she was going to have to put up and shut up until it was morning.

Since she was wide awake, she pulled out her laptop. Might as well do something useful, she decided.

But in the next heartbeat, stomach pangs attacked her again. She wondered why she should be polite about being a guest in Cameron Crane's home when she was an unwilling guest. Her stomach rumbled again. She was so hungry she was starting to feel nauseous.

She snapped the laptop closed.

If there was food on these premises, she was going to find it. She shrugged into her robe and the terry slippers she never traveled without and pushed her hair out of her face. Quietly, she eased open the door and stepped into the hall.

The house slept soundly, so she padded down the stairs then through a hallway that led to the back of the house where the kitchen must be.

She found it without trouble. There were dim nightlights in all the hallways, which struck her as useful for the jet-lagged, but odd otherwise.

The kitchen matched the dimensions of the rest of the house and was predictably huge: restaurant-sized, sleek, and industrial. She flipped on the light and was nearly blinded by the gleam of stainless steel appliances and black counters. It looked like he'd taken his decorating palate from a carving knife. Everything was sharp and cold.

She shivered as she made her way to the refrigerator, where she found orange juice and yogurt. A little more snooping in the cupboards uncovered muesli, which looked like plain old granola to her. She was happily chowing down until the thing she dreaded most—and at three in the morning wouldn't have believed possible—happened.

"You're up early," said the twangy voice with its subtle teasing note she'd hoped to avoid until the sun rose.

"Jet lag," she said, not bothering to turn around.

She sipped her orange juice, wondering if she could pretend to being already full and dash back to her room—except she wasn't full. She was still hungry.

He padded past her and leaned against a counter, pausing to look her up and down. *God, did the man have a single good manner?*

She wore a robe, but Crane had a way of gazing at her that reminded her she wore no underwear. She was two not very sturdy garments shy of naked.

At least her host was still fully dressed in jeans and a T-shirt, though his feet were bare.

"I hope I didn't wake you?" she asked politely.

"No. I was working in my study."

Her eyebrows rose. "In the middle of the night?"

He shrugged. "I don't need much sleep." He glanced at her shrewdly. "I'd say you're done sleeping for the night, darl. Come on back when you've finished your brekkie. I've got some reading material for you."

"I'm sure I'll go straight back to sleep," she lied, thinking endless games of solitaire on her laptop were preferable to a meeting with Crane's CEO in the wee hours.

"Take it up with you anyway. It'll bore you to sleep."

What could she say? "All right."

He walked to the sink with an easy grace that forced her to remember how he'd looked with nothing covering him but a little steam and a few bubbles.

He grabbed a glass of water. "I'll leave you to it, then. My study's back there." He pointed through a doorway at the opposite end of the kitchen, and then he was gone.

She finished her food but, as Crane had smugly prophesied, she wasn't remotely sleepy. She'd deliberately set her watch to Sydney time, but that didn't prevent her from calculating that it was only nine in the morning yesterday in San Francisco.

After tidying up and putting everything away, she ran back upstairs. Cameron Crane might be able to dictate her actions, but no way in hell was she going into his study to talk business in her nightclothes.

Besides, her calculations reminded her that her fiancé, Mark Forsythe, would be wide awake and dying to hear that she'd arrived safely. He was such a sweetheart—steady, reliable, good-hearted, and he worried about her.

She called and he answered on the first ring, as though he'd been sitting by the phone waiting. Sure enough, his first words were, "I'm so glad you called. I was wondering if you made it okay. How was the flight?"

"Long and boring."

"Don't forget to drink lots of water. Jet lag can be a killer."

"I know. It's three in the morning and I just ate breakfast."

He chuckled. "Give me your hotel and room number before I forget."

She hesitated. She loved Mark and sometime in the next year or so was going to marry him, but he could be a little old-fashioned. He'd blow a gasket if he knew where she was currently staying. She hadn't finished blowing her own gasket so she didn't need any extra aggravation.

"My schedule's going to be so hectic, it's probably easier if I call you. I've got my cell. I'll keep it with me at all times."

"Okay." He was so trusting and so dear. She called up his face: good-looking in a clean-cut, all-American way, with his clear blue eyes and crisp black hair. So different from Cameron Crane with his dirty-blond hair, eyes so shifty they couldn't decide between gray, brown, and green and had settled on a murky hazel. Mark was always clean-shaven. Crane looked as though he had five o'clock shadow twenty-four, seven.

As though divining her thoughts, Mark asked, "Have you seen the client yet?"

"Yes. Briefly." And all of him there was to see, but she kept that information to herself.

"First impressions?" Since Mark was not only her fiancé, but a tax accountant who often did work for her marketing firm, they tended to talk business a lot. It helped her to bounce ideas off him, for he was as logical as she was creative. That's what made them such a great team. So, she sighed and said, "I'd say dynamic, driven, mercurial . . . and domineering." *Great bod.*

"You don't like him."

She laughed. "You know me too well. Not unless my first impression changes drastically. He's the client. I'll hide my feelings, naturally. But no, I don't like Cameron Crane."

Chapter Three

She hates my guts, Cam thought to himself, perfectly aware that Jennifer Talbot wasn't still in the kitchen eating. He'd expected her to come and see him when she was done, but it looked as though she'd bolted—not that he entirely blamed her. He had been a pig.

He rolled his chair back from the computer and contemplated why. Since he planned to get her into bed as soon as possible, alienating the woman was stupid. But there was something about the coolness in those big blue eyes and the carefully sleek blond hair that made him want to mess her up a little.

Stupid, since he'd just made the task of seducing her tougher. Still, he hadn't made an outrageous success of himself by avoiding challenge. Quite the opposite. And when the challenge looked like the cover of a glossy dollie magazine, smelled like peaches, and gazed at him as though she saw right through him, he had no choice but to seduce her.

Ah, who was he kidding? If she was anyone at all and he'd met her anywhere, she'd have drawn him. She was everything he wasn't but secretly admired: tidy, cool, careful, and well-educated.

Footsteps sounded in the hall, and he was delighted that his first assessment had been right. Jennifer Talbot didn't avoid challenges any more than he did. She had the look in her china-doll blue eyes of a fighter. He recognized that look. It stared back at him every morning in the mirror.

When she knocked on his open door and entered, he stifled an appreciative grin. *Oh, yeah. She was a fighter all right.* She was fully dressed right down to shoes. She hadn't come to him in a bathrobe, nor had she slipped into jeans and a shirt, like him. No. She was wearing navy slacks with a crease you could cut yourself on, a silky white top that covered her but still tantalized with a hint of her shape, and dressy looking white sandals. Her hair gleamed smooth and blond and, based on the sheen to her lips, she wore makeup. In case he was in any doubt that her visit to him in the wee hours was strictly business, she carried a slim corporate-woman briefcase in one hand.

It was three-forty in the morning, and she looked as though she were ready for his company's annual meeting.

He liked her better in her nightie and mussed hair, and he bet she knew it.

"I'm glad to have this opportunity to talk to you," she said in that accent even he could recognize as quintessentially Californian. Soft, a little breathy, and full of sunshine and bottled water. "I think it would be better for both of us if I moved to a hotel."

He was a little surprised she was charging into battle only hours after she'd arrived—and on precious little sleep. He admired her for it. He leaned forward a little and motioned her into a chair. "I work at home a lot of the time. This is more efficient. You seem like a woman who appreciates not wasting time."

"Certainly, but—"

"As you'll find, I've a lot of demands on my time during the day. You'll hardly see me. Here, you've got full access." *And how.* Not only could she do business with him at any hour, but she was welcome to jump all over him. He almost laughed at her pinched expression. *Yeah, that was going to happen.*

Oh, but it was, he decided. His love life had been too much of the same recently. He dated women who were young, fun, and looked good on his arm. Maybe he was getting on a bit, but sometimes he yearned for more. Jennifer Talbot was definitely in the "more" category. She wasn't as young as his usual fare, and while she looked good—fantastic, really—it was a different kind of gorgeous. He usually dated chicks who were pictured in the gossip columns. Jennifer Talbot's picture was usually in the business section.

And fun? Did she know how to have fun? Probably, but it looked as though she were on the road to forgetting how. *Damn it.* Seducing this one was going to be more exciting than surfing Bells Beach on his newest board.

"I appreciate your position, Mr. Crane, however, my *fiancé* is rather old-fashioned. It would make him uncomfortable to know I was staying in your home."

So she had some bloke on the string, did she? That didn't surprise him, and now that he bothered to look, there was a flash of diamond on her engagement finger.

"I'm not the village pervert, darl. If you sleep with me it will be because you can't help yourself." He held back a chuckle as she visibly fought down a hasty response.

"No. Don't do that. Don't stifle whatever you were going to say. I always say what's on my mind, and I appreciate it in people I'm close to."

"Work with," she snapped. "We're not close."

"You see? Don't you feel better for saying that?" he asked approvingly.

"All right. Since you asked. In my background research, I've discovered you have a reputation for wild behavior."

He knew his reputation perfectly well and did everything he could to enhance it. He was convinced his rep helped sell his products. "Right. You mean drinking, hell-raising, and womanizing?"

She nodded. "And brawling."

"I hit a pushy cameraman who got in my face once too

often. Highly exaggerated," he assured her, noticing how fine her skin was and that the blue irises had tiny flecks of black.

"And the drinking, carousing, and womanizing?"

"Those are my hobbies," he explained.

"Well, I'm not so worried about the first two, but . . ." She cleared her throat. "If I were to stay here, would I have your promise that you wouldn't . . . that there'd be no . . ."

Once more her words petered to silence. Once more he helped her out. "That I won't try to seduce you?"

Her color was up, but she nodded. This was going to be more fun than he'd imagined.

"Darl, you have my promise that I *will* seduce you."

Challenge flashed back at him as clear and blue as a wall of water building behind him and his surfboard, daring him to try it. He might end up flipped on his arse, but he'd have a ride to remember.

"You can try," she said crisply.

"I play fair. I'm telling you in advance. You're beautiful, interesting, and smart, and I'm a red-blooded bloke who likes women. But it will be up to you, you know. If you're so in love with your man at home, you're in no danger of falling for me, now are you?"

Her eyes snapped to his and he read everything in them he needed to know. She was feeling the sexual sizzle between them just as he was. She was confused. And she wasn't in love with her bloke at home.

He wondered how long it was going to take her to work that out for herself.

"I've pulled together the latest report on our sales figures in Australia and New Zealand and the budget we've tentatively allocated to the California expansion." He held it out. "Some light reading."

She received the report with her fingertips, keeping as much of the eight-by-eleven inches of paper between them as she could. She slipped it into the silver metal briefcase, snapped the lid, then rose and headed for the door.

"Oh, Jennifer?"

She turned back, brows raised.

"Pleasant dreams."

She rolled her gaze at him as though he were a chippie on a construction site who'd whistled at her, and left.

Crane Enterprises was located in a restored Victorian warehouse in an area down by the harbor known as the Rocks. Jen had expected something in the Central Business District, or CBD to the Australians who seemed to her to have a mania for shortening or abreviating everything. But no, Crane was located in the most historic part of Sydney. The faded and smudged red brick actually looked hip with the light wood and glass that were the main building materials for Crane's front offices.

The woman at reception was young and buxom, with one extra button open at her throat than Jen thought was necessary. And she didn't look older than twenty.

Still, she knew who Jen was and immediately led her to an empty office.

"Cam said you were to have this one. The phone works, there are some supplies in the drawers, and I'm to act as your assistant if you need anything." She grinned, her face at once sexy and impish, and Jen had the idea that Cameron Crane hired his support staff based on bra size not typing speed. "I'm Fiona," the girl said.

"Thanks, Fiona. Can you see if all the people on this list would be available for a meeting today at," she glanced at her watch, "shall we say eleven o'clock?"

"Sure."

"If you're going to be assisting me, can you come in and take notes? Is there someone who can cover for you on the front desk?"

"Oh, yeah. No worries," Fiona said, taking the list that Jen had culled from the organization chart.

When Jen got to the boardroom right at eleven, it was packed. From a quick head count, not only were the people she'd requested present, but a few extras. She guessed that was better than sparse attendance. It argued an interest in what she was trying to achieve.

The only way she knew it was a boardroom was because the sign on the door said so. Transport that group around the table to a different setting, and they could be playing beach volleyball or hanging out at a bar somewhere or—no, she had it now. Surfing. They all looked like surfers, from the sales manager to Fiona taking minutes. Toned, tanned, young, and buff, she doubted there was anyone in the room over thirty. Well, apart from her—the grandmother of the bunch at thirty-one. And Cameron Crane, of course, who'd taken his place at the end of the pale wooden board table. He had a couple of years on her.

She was pleased he'd shown up. He had a lot of business interests, so she figured he was a busy guy. It didn't matter that he probably came to the meeting to check up on her; his action still sent a message to his staff that she was to be taken seriously.

Jen hadn't expected Crane's executives to dress like Wall Street bankers, but neither had she expected them to look like they had damp sand in their shorts from catching a few waves before work.

Board shorts, loud shirts, khakis, mini skirts—it seemed anything was acceptable. Cam wore the loudest shirt of all. The red was so bright her eyeballs hurt to look at him, and was relieved with neon yellow flowers with purple centers.

She'd assumed the office would be reasonably casual, so she'd dressed in a sleeveless white blouse and a royal blue skirt and dress sandals, but she was totally overdressed for this crowd.

"Like the shirt?" Cam grinned at her as she stared at it, half-hypnotized.

"I can't begin to describe what I feel for that shirt."

He chuckled. "It's from our clothing line. Crane Casuals." Like there might be Crane Formal Wear?

He rose and came round to greet her, and she discovered

he was wearing baggy black cargo pants with that shirt. "Everybody, this is Jennifer Talbot from the States. You can all introduce yourselves in a bit," he said.

"Yes, I'd like that."

"Here. Welcome to Crane and to Australia." He handed her a cellophane bag. Inside were two tank tops made of lycra and cotton, she suspected; one in fuchsia, and one in aquamarine. A baggy shirt in a floral pattern—not quite as bright as Cam's, but sunglasses-preferred bright—went with each of them. And, to complete the ensemble, there was a pair of drawstring surfer shorts in aquamarine, trimmed with the same pattern as the shirt.

"Like the boardies?" Cam asked with a grin as she inspected the shorts.

"Yes. Thank you," she said holding up the shorts. Everyone was grinning at her, so she decided to show them she could be part of their team, or at least try to fit in. She slipped the shirt from the bag and put it on over her outfit. When in Rome. "I'll never have to worry about getting lost at sea," she joked weakly, wishing she were feeling as wide awake now as she had at three in the morning. Right now, she wanted to crawl off for a nap.

She glanced at Cam Crane. Yep, that shirt jolted her awake faster than a double espresso—a short black, as she'd discovered when she stopped at a café on her way into Crane's building when the cab let her off. Cameron Crane had told her she was certifiable when she insisted on taking a cab to his office when he was driving that way in his car. But if he didn't know that his employees would get the wrong impression of her if she arrived at nine in the morning with him in tow, she—whose entire career was about creating image—knew.

Taking her own place at the other end of the long oval table, she listened carefully as everyone introduced themselves. Because she knew image and reality didn't always coincide, she refused to take these surfer kids at face value. There had to be some smarts in the room. Cameron Crane hadn't built the number one surf and boogie board company in the southern hemisphere all on his own.

"Okay," she said, once the introductions were done. She gestured around the room, feeling the new cotton on the wow-your-eyes-out shirt scrape her upper arm. Hanging on the walls were glossy posters and magazine ads, pictures of Crane surf and boogie boards and the clothing line, each with the tiny black crane logo.

Their ad campaigns tended to be straight up. The people in those photographs were defying waves, cresting breakers that made her—a born-and-bred Californian—shudder. As far as she could tell, the photos weren't studio-shot or airbrushed to perfection; they were as raw as the powerful waves, and they packed quite a punch.

These were surf products for honest-to-God surfers. But if she was going to help them launch in the U.S., they were going to need a different approach.

She turned back to the group eyeing her with expressions from curious, blank-eyed, and possibly hungover, to the man at the end of the table whose expression read *come to bed*. She did her best to telegraph back, *forget it*, and then tried to ignore his presence.

"Crane Enterprises has saturated the Australian and New Zealand markets. Am I right?"

Nods all around the table.

"So, you think, they surf in California, they surf in Hawaii, we'll take over those markets."

More nodding.

"How are we going to do that?"

They gazed at her collectively as if to say, *What do you think we hired you for?*

"The vast majority of foreign products that try to sell into the American market fail. Not because they aren't good, but because people don't buy them."

There was more nodding, but some frown lines appeared in those unlined faces.

"Now I know the California market, where we'll begin.

But you guys know the product. So tell me, why should a kid in California, who's never heard the word Crane, except at a construction site, buy one of your boards?"

"Best-made boards in the world," a young male voice piped up.

"Can you back up that claim?" She'd read all the bumph that the Crane people had sent her, but she wanted to know how the people making the products felt.

"Too right. I'm the chief engineer, I should know. We design and build for speed, planing, maneuverability, and sensitivity. I was a surfboard glasser when I met Cam, and he was the shaper. We're best known for our longboards, but we build a full range of long and short boards, knee boards, and learner boards. They're tops."

The kid didn't look old enough to shave and he was the chief engineer, and had obviously worked with Cam for quite a while. She'd read up enough to know that a shaper actually shaped the surfboards, sometimes to the specific requirements of a particular surfer, and a glasser applied the covering and finish.

"How do you know your boards are the best in the world?" she challenged him.

The kid gave her a smile so broad she wanted to laugh. " 'Cause I've tried 'em all."

She blinked. "You have personally surfed on every surfboard in the world?"

"Yeah, I reckon. Every competitor's, anyway. Their top-of-the-line boards, and usually a few others. After I test them, I let the others 'round the office have a go."

There was more nodding. "We're all surfers."

Of course they were. Well, it was an unorthodox way to choose staff, but who was she to argue with success?

"Okay, so you've got a quality product. Give me another reason for your success."

"We've got great colors," said a twenty-something woman with long dirty-blond hair who ought to be modeling. She reminded Jen of a young Elle MacPherson.

"Would you come off it with the colors?" the chief engineer scoffed.

"Color is important, especially for girls," the Elle clone informed him. Her name was Bronwyn Spencer, Jen remembered from the introductions.

"She likes her surfboards to match her nail polish." There was general laughter, but the young woman merely tossed her cascade of wavy hair over her shoulder.

"Not just surfboards, but wet suits, board bags, even wax and sunscreens. Sure, we only sell the best, but why shouldn't the best have some decent color to it?"

"She's my little sister. I have to give her something to do," Cam teased.

The girl didn't get huffy, merely tossed that mane of sun-licked hair once more and reminded him that without her, there would be no clothing line and hadn't Crane Casuals boosted their profits by eighteen percent last year?

Jen assumed Bronwyn was used to the teasing and full enough of self-esteem that it didn't bother her. She couldn't imagine a woman that gorgeous not oozing self-esteem. So she was Cameron Crane's younger sister. They had the same hair color, she saw, and a similar arrogant sexuality.

Pulling herself back to the discussion at hand, she nodded. "Great. We've got quality, designer colors, what else?"

"We can go in at a competitive price point, especially with the Australian dollar so weak against the greenback," said another young man with a goatee and sun- or wind-reddened cheeks.

By the end of an hour, she had a great deal of information, but better, a sense of who these people were and how they operated. Cam himself hadn't contributed a lot, but he'd listened and he'd watched. Mostly, he'd watched her. She tried not to let her gaze get caught up with his—even across a packed boardroom table, the impact was too much of a jolt.

"Good," she said when things wound down. "I think you've hit our strengths very well. It's not going to be easy.

It's going to be a real challenge, but I think we can have a lot of fun, especially based on the energy and commitment in this room."

She smiled. "I've got a temporary office here, so please drop in any time if you have any ideas. We're going to design a marketing strategy, an advertising campaign, and some targets. I'm hoping we can take over five to ten percent of the California surf and boogie board market within twelve months from the launch."

"I'm after market domination," Cameron Crane said.

Like that was a surprise. He struck her as a guy who wanted to dominate everything and everyone. And, of course, that was why he'd wanted to show up with her this morning. She knew the American market, which gave her the edge. But he'd wanted his staff to see that she was still under him. In bed and in business.

The man was as obvious as that shirt. Still, she'd been hustled by smoother operators than he and never succumbed. She didn't think she was in much danger from Cameron Crane and his caveman tactics, although she had to give him credit for a certain animal magnetism.

She'd enjoy watching him try to get her into bed and failing spectacularly. She wondered if he thought for one second he was being subtle.

Chapter Four

"I see you're not one to waste time," Cam said, walking out with her after the meeting and accompanying her to her temporary office.

"I'm only here for three weeks. We have a lot to accomplish."

"I think a person can accomplish anything they set their mind to," he told her in a tone that had nothing to do with target markets and surfboards.

She wished this hairy, loud-dressing, barely civilized man didn't . . . affect her, but she was too honest not to admit that he did. He was sexy in an earthy way, completely opposite to the type of man she went for, so it surprised her to find that her erogenous zones seemed to perk up when he was around. She must have worse jet lag than she'd thought.

"My phone works, I've got a desk, supplies, and an assistant. Thank you."

"No worries. You're going to have to get to see a bit of Oz and get to know a few Sydney-siders while you're here."

"Yes. I know."

"Start by getting to know me. Have dinner with me tonight."

She smiled. So he was back to trying on the charm, was he? "By dinnertime I'll be sound asleep." Still, they had to work together and she was determined to get them on a friendly professional footing. And two could play at power games. "Why don't *you* have lunch with *me?*"

Lunch was much safer and she did want to get to know one particular Sydney-sider better. His own dynamic personality and boundless energy had a lot to do with his success, but she needed to know if he could bring that same level of intensity to a U.S. expansion. She also needed to know if there were any skeletons hiding in his closet.

She slapped a hand to her mouth too late to stifle a yawn.

"All right," he said, grinning at her in a very unsettling way. "I'll take you down the street to the touristy part of the Rocks. It's noisy enough there to keep anybody awake."

The Rocks was the oldest part of Sydney, a place of refurbished warehouses, museums, and quaint shops. They sat outside in one of a string of restaurants, and she was charmed to find the arch of the Harbour Bridge on one side of her and the famous white sails of the Sydney Opera House on the other.

"On the weekend there's a great market here if you want to pick up some things to take home," he informed her. "Over there is the oldest pub in Sydney, serves a very nice home brew."

Since he'd acted perfectly normal since they'd left the office, offering her a running commentary on the city as they'd walked here, she let herself relax.

The restaurant was abustle with tourists, business people, and regular people, she supposed, having a meal out. She opened her menu and noted that Cameron Crane didn't bother to open his. He must eat here a lot.

"Do you like seafood?"

"Sure."

"You must try Moreton Bay Bugs."

"You have got to be kidding me."

"Trust me."

"I'm not that stupid."

He gave a diabolical chuckle, then ordered them anyway. She ordered a chef's salad.

When the bugs arrived, they turned out to resemble tiny lobsters.

"Come on," he said, "try one." He forked up some of the white meat, dipped it in butter, and offered her the dripping morsel.

Of course she could say no and push it back at him, but she could see that's what he expected of her. Somehow she didn't feel like giving him the satisfaction of being predictable, so she opened her mouth and let him feed her in a gesture she pretended she found neither tantalizing or intimate.

Then her taste buds started getting blissed out and she almost moaned. "This is fantastic."

"You see? It's good to try new things." He leaned closer, and his eyes crinkled at her. "You can discover all kinds of pleasures you didn't know existed." Her heart banged against her ribs and for a second she couldn't pull her gaze away from his.

"Everything all right?" asked their waiter, and she had a moment to pull herself back together.

While Cam answered, she turned to look at the harbor. When the waiter had moved on, he slipped back into casual mode. "This is where they used to let the convicts off."

"Is that how your family came to Australia?" she asked in her blandest tone.

He grinned at her. "No. The law-breaking in my family is more recent."

And that was something personal she *did* want to discuss. "If your temper is an issue in any way, I need to know it ahead of time."

"What? You want to know if I'm a drunken lout?"

"I wouldn't have put it in quite those terms, but you did clock that photographer. If you come to the States I need to know—"

"That I won't get pissed, trash my hotel room, and drop my dacks in public?"

She nodded. "Pretty much."

"Well, I won't."

She toyed with her sparkling water. "Since we're on the subject, there are some holes in your resume. I wonder—"

"Christ, I thought this was a date, not a bloody job interview."

"It's a working lunch," she said, holding on to her even tone with difficulty. "As I believe I mentioned, I'm engaged to be married."

"When's the wedding?" he asked so abruptly she blinked.

"We haven't set a date yet, but—"

He snorted. "If you were mine, I wouldn't let you traipse off halfway 'round the world without even having a date set to tie the knot."

"I can't believe you're the kind of man who chases married women."

"I'm not. You're single, darl. Fair game."

"As flattered as I am," she said glaring at him to make it clear she was anything but, "I am not game to be hunted. I'm here to do a job." She slipped a notebook and her solid gold Mont Blanc pen from her bag. She hadn't intended to conduct business so blatantly but he needed constant reminders, and, besides, Mark had given her the pen. She twiddled it to be certain the Aussie game hunter could see the engraved script.

"Nice pen," he said as though cued.

"Thanks. It was a gift."

"From a grateful client?"

"No. From my fiancé, Mark. For my birthday."

Instead of backing off as she'd expected when faced with this proof of her fiancé's thoughtfulness, he threw his head back and laughed, white hunter's teeth gleaming in the sunshine.

She put down the pen, picked up her fork, and stabbed a

piece of lettuce viciously, but couldn't restrain herself from asking him, "What is so funny?"

"Darl, a man who buys his woman a pen is looking for a business merger, not a wife."

He was trying to rile her. She knew it, so why did she want to use her pen to stab him somewhere soft and full of nerve endings? She drew a breath. "Mark is practical. It's one of the traits we have in common."

"A man doesn't buy practical gifts for the woman he's bedding. He buys jewelry, champagne, black sexy things you put on in order to tear them off." His gaze moved to hers and there was a sexual intensity that had her forcing herself not to lick her lips.

She didn't have the same control over her heart, which pounded as though she were some kind of game animal staring into a loaded rifle.

"As I was saying . . ." What the hell had she been saying? *Oh, yes.* "There are some holes in your resumé."

"What holes?" he said, his gaze still fixed on her with clearly carnal intent. He could probably sell those damn surfboards on sex appeal alone. "Your eyes are the most amazing color. Like the water up in Queensland when you get near the reef. It's not green, or blue, but something that's both." He touched her fingers with his. "Your eyes were the first thing I noticed about you."

She felt the sun, warm against her face, heard the sounds of people at other tables, muted traffic sounds from somewhere, the bustle of the harbor. She felt the curious buzz of sensation as his fingers toyed with hers, then reality hit her like a slap.

"There are places in the world where your behavior could be construed as sexual harassment," she informed him, pulling her fingers away.

"This is Australia, mate."

"And what would you call what you're doing—in Australian?"

His eyes both laughed at her and undressed her. "Your lucky day."

"I suppose you subjugate women, too," she muttered half to herself.

The look he sent her was potent sexuality. "Ah, now that depends on the woman."

With such arrogance, what could she do?

She rolled her gaze and gave an annoyed *tsk*. "Holes," she said, "in your resumé, such as your education. I can't find any mention of your schooling in any of the biographical material about you."

"Do you think a bloody surfie cares whether I did the *HSC?*"

"*HSC?*"

"Higher School Certificate." When he saw her raised brows he said, "Whether I finished school."

She blinked, unable to hide her shock. "Didn't you finish high school?"

"No."

"Why not?"

He shrugged his shoulders, then stared into his beer as though thinking. "I was bored. I had to, I don't know, see the world. Make my own mark."

He was still doing that, she realized, merely extending the reach of his marker. She wondered when he'd feel he'd made enough of himself, or if he ever would. She walked him through his business from when he'd moved to Sydney to work in a surfboard shop at the world famous Bondi Beach, become a surfer and instructor and then, with the overconfidence she'd already discovered was a big part of his nature, decided he could design a better board.

"That's right. I won enough surfing competitions to get some money together, plus saved my pittance from working in a surfing shop, got a good mate to help me build my board—he's now the chief engineer at Crane; you met him."

She nodded, amazed that he'd come so far so fast.

"Then we strapped the board on my old bomb of a car and drove it 'round to all the shops and the shows. I also surfed on it and won more competitions with the new board. People started to take notice." He shrugged as if to say *and the rest is history.*

She nodded again, knowing the rest of his story probably as well as he did himself. From that early success, he'd branched out. Bought a lot of real estate, a sizable interest in two television stations and a newspaper. He even owned a small commercial airline. Now, he was so diversified she doubted anyone knew his exact wealth, including himself. But the surfboard company was where he kept his office, and obviously the business he most loved.

"You're also the spokesman for Crane products here in Australia. Do you intend to do the same in the States?"

He shook his head. "I was thinking you'd find a Hollywood star or one of those California surfie chicks in a string bikini to sell the things."

She rolled her eyes. "I see you've given this a lot of thought."

"I hired you to think for me."

"Then you'll agree to be guided by my advice as regards the California market?"

He sipped his beer, which sparkled gold in the sun. "I promise to listen to you. I make all the decisions."

Control freak. A solid gold, no excuses, no exceptions, control freak. It wasn't a big surprise to have her suspicions confirmed, right down to the fact he was trying to seduce her in order to control her.

"You were smart enough to hire me. Be smart enough to take my advice."

"Let's hear what it is first."

She tapped her birthday-present pen against her notebook, then frowned and dropped it. Had Mark ever bought her the kind of sexy lingerie that was meant to be torn off?

Of course he hadn't. She bought her own underwear. Some of it was quite sexy, thank you very much. She didn't need a man to choose her underthings for her.

"My initial idea is not to hide the fact that we're Australian, but to promote the hell out of it."

He held up a hand. "No koalas or kangaroos, or I'll lose my lunch."

"No," she agreed with a grin. "No cute animals. Well, a cute guy."

"Guy?" His glass hit the tabletop with a thunk. "What about my string bikini?"

"No string bikini," she said with a small, smug smile. "I'm thinking a handsome young sun god. He has to be Australian. A model with some verbal ability or an actor with model looks. We put him into your clothes, on your boards. I'm thinking about giving the boards Australian surf beach names: Bondi, Byron, Surfer's Paradise. We'll even put a tiny Australian flag on each one."

"Why?"

"Because you've got to stand out in an already crowded marketplace."

"No. Why the fellow?"

"He needs to be the kind of guy who women drool over and other guys want to be like. Trust me on this one."

He looked at her for a minute, and she wondered what it was about him that pulled at her. Especially when he didn't answer her, as though trust was not an option. "If you've finished chasing that bit of lettuce around your plate, let's go."

As they walked back toward the office, he said, "You should take some holiday while you're here and let me show you around Oz."

Did this guy ever give up? "Thanks, but I don't really have the time."

"You need to get to know Australia in order to sell the boards."

"No. I don't. I need to know California. That's where I'm marketing the boards."

"Are you always a pain in the arse?"

She thought about it. "To men like you? Probably."

A man was coming straight toward her on the sidewalk. She stepped to the right to give him berth, and he stepped to the left; they crashed into each other.

"I'm so sorry," she muttered.

"No worries."

"We walk on the footpath the same way we drive. On the left-hand side," Cameron explained helpfully.

"Thanks, I got it. I need to get back to work." She only had three weeks here, and a great deal to do.

"You surf?"

"No."

"Never?"

"No."

He stopped dead and stared at her. "You live in California and you've never surfed?"

"That's right."

"Why not?"

"I've been busy."

"Too busy to surf?"

"I tried windsurfing once." She shook her head at the memory. "I ended up with a strained wrist and my back in spasm. I'm not the athletic type."

"You just haven't had the right teacher."

"Let me take a wild guess. That would be you?"

"Best in the business." He said it with a perfectly straight face. "I'll teach you."

She let a woman in a hurry pass between them to give herself a minute to think. She had to admit, the man had a point. She'd sell his products a lot better if she'd actually been on one. Strained wrist, pulled back, she tried to be philosophical. That was part of the business she was in—temporarily.

Except the idea of spending any time in a wet bathing suit with Cameron Crane had all her warning bells clanging. "I'll think about it," she said, pretty sure she could find plenty of excuses in the three weeks she'd be here.

"Great. Oh, and can you keep Friday night free? There are some people I want you to meet."

"What kind of people?"

"Experts in the field. You can listen to what they say about Crane boards."

"A focus group, you mean?" Wow. She was delighted he was thinking strategically about the marketing.

"Yeah. Exactly. A focus group."

Chapter Five

"You conned me!" she yelled over the din of drinking songs, pickup mating calls, and some drunks in the corner playing pool. Someone was going to get a pool cue–induced black eye any minute, she was certain.

"You wanted a focus group, darl. This is it. We can focus better if we sink a few tubes of Tooheys."

Drinking in a pub at Cam's old haunt, Bondi Beach, with a bunch of his "mates," wasn't exactly what she'd expected. Most focus groups didn't involve mass consumption of alcohol and didn't take place in a noisy bar, but this wasn't the time to be picky. These guys were young, obviously surfing crazy, and, so far, reasonably sober.

"So," she shouted above the music, "tell me about Crane surfboards."

"Beaut," said one. Although he could have been referring to the cute girl he was trying to make eye contact with. He'd said he was certain he'd seen her topless on the beach earlier and he was clearly anxious to renew the acquaintance.

"Best boards in the world," said another.

"Why?"

"Dunno," said a tall redheaded guy with an earring. "Well, okay, I was surfing Margaret River in W.A., and—"

"W.A.?"

"Western Australia."

"Right."

"And I purled off the top of the wave, another surfie rode right over my board. And the board didn't break. Didn't even crack. The other fellow's snapped in two. Well," he said, "goes to show."

"Oh, and remember that time up at Noosa," another eagerly broke in, and they were off.

Poetic, they weren't, but these surfies were certainly committed to Crane products. Pretty much everyone in the bar looked like a surfer to her. She kept her eye peeled for the sort of man who'd be a perfect spokesman for the U.S. market, but none of these guys was right somehow.

Cameron Crane disappeared, leaving her alone while she asked her questions. She assumed it was so none of the surfers would feel coerced into saying nice things about his products when he was around, but soon he returned with two glasses of beer, one of which he placed in front of her.

"I don't normally drink when I'm working."

"It's camouflage, so you can blend in with the natives."

"And I don't drink—"

"Well, you can't drink sparkling water here."

"I would have ordered dry white wine."

The snort he gave her in reply made white wine sound worse than water. Whoever said Americans and Australians spoke the same language had obviously never met Cameron Crane.

He then took up his post beside her, close enough that she could feel the heat coming off his skin, feel the skin itself whenever he leaned in to explain in plain English some jargon she couldn't work out. Since he didn't do anything really stupid like put a hand on her knee, she ignored the "accidental" arm contact, and tried to convince herself those shudders she felt every time they touched meant she was cold.

Talking to all those surfers was thirsty work, and she

was probably still dehydrated from the plane and the hot climate. Plus, she had to shout over the noise and the "footie" match on the TV and the "pokies," poker machines that seemed to be a big draw. So she drank more than she meant to, not disliking the beer as much as she'd thought she would.

When they left the pub it was after one and she felt great, with a sheaf full of notes, a head full of impressions and a few ideas for the campaign that at one in the morning after a couple of beers sounded pretty darn good.

"You did all right in there," Cameron said, putting a friendly arm around her shoulders. "You asked the right questions and they talked to you."

"I'm good at what I do," she said.

"I could be wrong, but it looked to me—just for a second—like you were having fun."

"It was fun. And what are you suggesting? That I'm not a fun person?"

"I think you could have a lot of fun. You need to let go now and then, that's all."

Even in the dark she could hear the busy ocean with its crashing waves, feel the ever-present breeze against her cheeks. It was a little chilly after the warm atmosphere of the pub, and she shivered. Cam rubbed up and down her arms and pulled her in tighter.

It was cold, she told herself, that's why she stayed snuggled against him.

"You're a long, cool drink of water, aren't you?"

He'd said that to her before and she'd ignored him, but after a couple of beers and the suggestion that she wasn't any fun, she suddenly needed to know. "What is that supposed to mean? I'm cold? Wet? Colorless?"

Cameron chuckled, a low rumbling sound. "Is that what you think?"

"No. It seems to be what you think."

"A long, cool drink of water . . . well, it's what you want on a hot day, after you've worked hard and you're tired."

"I thought that was a beer."

"Too right. But you can't call a woman a beer. She might get the wrong impression."

"I'm not convinced I got the right impression by being called a glass of water."

"This is what I mean." Before she had time to realize his intent, he pulled her up against him and kissed her.

If the impact of his gaze had affected her, the feel of his mouth on hers had her staggering: warm, strong, faintly beer-flavored, and devastatingly sexy.

Oh, no. No and no and no and no! Her head was clamoring denial but her body seemed to cut off all communication with her brain the minute their lips met.

She'd never believed all that malarkey about fireworks and rockets. To her, kissing had always just been kissing. Enjoyable, mildly arousing, a nice prelude to easy pleasure. But this was something different. The minute he kissed her, something went pop. Kind of like a champagne bottle, and then everything inside her seemed to foam and fizz.

Cameron kissed the way he did everything. Head-on, aggressive, no holds barred. There wasn't a subtle bone in his body or, she imagined, an unobtrusive move in his repertoire. His tongue swept into her mouth without permission or apology and swept all her polite refusals away. His power was raw and earthy and something inside her responded. A part of her she hadn't realized existed, calling up a wild urge to kiss him back.

He tasted of beer and hungry man and his body against hers felt tough and strong. He wasn't a particularly tall man, but he was solid and hard. His unshaven face scraped across hers as he changed the angle and deepened the kiss.

Her fingers were in his hair before she'd known she planned to put them there, plunging in and enjoying the feel of the thick strands against her fingers, pulling him closer, trying to deepen the kiss even more.

He licked at her, teased and played at her mouth, his hands running possessively over her back and finally grasping her hips to pull her in tight against the bulging fly of his jeans.

Oh, how she wanted this and more. But as the lights of a car strobed over them, she came back to her senses.

"No," she cried, pulling away from him. "Stop it. I can't do this."

"Yes," he said, his eyes wild and compelling in the night, "you can."

But she was already out of his arms and striding for the car.

They were silent on the drive home to Cam's place. He obviously wasn't going to apologize for his appalling behavior, and she simply wanted to forget hers.

What had she been thinking? She was practically married—she had the tasteful diamond solitaire to prove it—and she'd indulged in wild kissing with another man. She twisted the ring around on her finger like a talisman all the way home.

Once more she regretted not moving to a hotel. She'd meant to, but somehow she'd been so busy with work and then fallen into bed dead tired for the three nights she'd been here, until it was easier simply to stay.

Cam had acted like a perfect gentleman, his busy schedule taking him out two of the three nights she'd been in his house, and on the one night they'd dined in together, Marg had stayed to serve dinner and clean up, and they'd talked business, adding a couple of his associates by conference call so she hadn't felt she was alone with a determined seducer.

Not until tonight.

Once they reached home she mumbled an incoherent explanation of why she had to get straight to bed and left him gazing at her with a mixture of amusement and frustration.

"Hey," he said from the bottom of the stairs, forcing her to turn and regard him from her position halfway up. She waited for an apology, but he said, "I've got a surprise planned for tomorrow."

"What kind of surprise?" If she had to bet money, she'd wager his surprise involved getting naked and maybe introducing whipped cream.

"We're going surfing."

"Oh, but I . . ." She what? "I'd planned to work tomorrow."

"That's what I reckoned. Darl, you've got to surf to sell the boards."

He was right. And besides, she'd have a whole day to prove to him that it was the beer that had kissed him, not her.

"All right."

"Can you be ready by six?"

She nodded.

"Night."

"Good night."

"Hey," he called again.

Once more she turned.

"If you get lonely in the night, you know where to find me."

Not until she was safely in her room with the door closed did she drop her head in her hands and groan. Cameron Crane, the man she'd kissed so passionately, wasn't just a man, but her client. And she was an engaged woman.

Worse, she could still taste him on her lips, still feel the imprint of him on her nerve endings—which clearly didn't follow the same moral standard as the rest of her.

She made her way to the ensuite bathroom and stood under a hot shower, then brushed her teeth furiously.

As she looked at that big empty bed, aware in every cell of her body of one sexually overheated male somewhere in this house who would doubtless provide the antidote for her own sexually overheated body, Mark had never seemed so far away.

She picked up the phone, not bothering to calculate the time back home—not even caring. She had to talk to Mark. The sound of his voice would bring her back to her senses and dull the wild clamoring in her body to finish what her reprobate client had begun.

Mark answered. Steady, reliable Mark. He wasn't off kissing other women. He was right by his phone so she could get through to him.

"Hi. Good thing I woke up early this morning. Is everything okay?" He sounded surprised to hear from her. Then she realized she'd called only a few hours earlier, before he went to bed.

"I just wanted to hear your voice."

"Homesick?"

No, that wasn't the term she'd use. Heartsick maybe. Guilt-ridden for sure. "Not really. It's beautiful here and the work's challenging." She sighed, "I wish you were here."

"You won't need a tax accountant until the deal's signed," he reminded her. "Which reminds me, can you ask their comptroller—"

"I don't want to talk about business," she wailed, half-desperate for she wasn't sure what. "Do you love me?" she asked, sounding pathetic and needy.

"What kind of a question is that? We're getting married, aren't we?"

"But do you really love me?" Maybe that's what was wrong with her. She was getting cold feet, having last minute jitters about the wedding. All she needed was reassurance, a vow of undying love and she'd be fine.

"I spent yesterday evening calculating how expensive a home we can afford after the wedding. I'll show you my spreadsheet of our incomes, household expenses, taxes, and so on when you get home."

"I ask for undying love and you give me a spreadsheet?" Her voice rose all on its own, like a helium balloon from a toddler's grasp.

"I thought it would make you happy that I'm working on our future."

"But do you love me?"

"Isn't that what I'm telling you?" He sounded as frustrated as she felt. "Would I plan a thirty-year mortgage with a woman I didn't love?"

It was hopeless. If she didn't get off the phone quick, he was going to explain his long-range projection of mortgage interest rates, the real estate trends in the Bay area, and then she wouldn't be held responsible for her reaction.

"We'll talk more when I get home. I only wanted to check in and say good night."

"Get a good night's sleep. That jet lag can be a killer."

"Jet lag, right. Good night."

"Night."

But jet lag had nothing to do with the jumpiness she was experiencing, as though she'd hit a pocket of turbulence and couldn't get clear. Her stomach was jittery, her skin hot, the ground didn't feel solid under her feet.

And the entire experience intensified when Cameron Crane was in the vicinity. Which he was, too damn much.

She wasn't stupid; she knew why he was trying to seduce her. He wanted to maintain the upper hand in the most basic way. Many men had tried to pull that stunt. None had ever succeeded.

So why, now, when she was planning her wedding to another man, should she be almost as eager to use his boardroom table for illicit purposes as he was to take her there?

Last minute pre-wedding jitters.

It had to be.

She pulled on a cotton nightgown, the kind she always wore. They were comfortable and easy to launder. Mark had never complained.

And all she could see was her in something black and absurd, and Cameron Crane staring at her with that look in his eyes that informed her he was about to tear her little bit of outrageously expensive black silk and lace right off her body. Probably with his teeth.

She shuddered as she climbed into bed. A big lonely bed where the sheets were as cool and sensible as her nightgown. A mortgage affordability spreadsheet was a good thing, a sensible thing. In Mark's masculine brain, she knew it was his way of telling her he loved her.

But a bit of flowery nonsense about how much he missed her would have gone a long way to easing her jumpiness. He could even have started his day by giving her some earthy suggestions on exactly what he was going to do to her when she got back.

Her smile went a little lopsided as she imagined crisp, businesslike Mark Forsythe talking dirty on a long distance call. He was a good man, and they were compatible. She had to accept he wasn't always going to sweep her off her feet.

In fact, Cameron Crane was exactly suited to display all the qualities Mark lacked. That's why he was starting to look so good. He was all raw sex appeal and casual attitudes. If he were in love with a woman, he wouldn't waste a long distance phone conversation on mortgage rates. He'd be having phone sex. Of course, he was such a troglodyte he likely wouldn't ever need to have phone sex long distance. He wouldn't let his woman out of his sight.

Mark was a modern man. He respected her. She had to remember that respect was a lot more lasting than blood-simmering sex.

She punched her pillow and placed her head back on it. *Right. Long-term.*

But in the short-term, she had a problem.

She wanted blood-simmering sex. And she wanted it with her client.

Chapter Six

"Can you be ready for surfing by six?" Cam had asked her before she raced up the stairs to escape the memories of his kiss.

"Not a problem," she'd assured him. She wasn't being polite. It wasn't a problem, unfortunately. Her inner clock was still so whacked that she was in pretty good shape at six in the morning. Wide awake and alert. Sadly, the same could not be said of her by six P.M. Still, she knew she'd adjust eventually. Probably the day she flew back home.

Sure enough, when six rolled around, she was ready to go. She'd had time for a shower, had written up some ideas from last night's focus group, and gone for a light makeup. No doubt she'd soon be smeared in sand and salt water, but at least she'd start the day fresh and looking her best.

She wore her new Crane duds, mainly to flatter her client, but when she got them on she really liked how they fit and felt. A woman wearing clothes this easy-wearing and brightly colored couldn't take herself too seriously. Or the man she was with. They'd surf, get back on the businesslike, friendly terms they'd been on before last night, and she would, on no account, drink a beer. Now that she thought about it, she was pretty sure Mark had warned her that Australian beer had a higher alcohol content than its U.S. counterpart.

She'd lied to Cam the first day here. Of course she'd brought her bathing suit. A couple actually, and the one she put into a beach bag along with her sunscreen, a cotton hat, and a sarong wrap was the one she used for swimming lengths at home. It covered as much of her as any bathing suit could. Mr. String Bikini was going to be out of luck. In fact, if she had a choice, she'd take her lesson in a full wet-suit.

She was ready in plenty of time, and if she felt a slight blush rise when she encountered Cam, he was so absolutely the same as always that she could almost have imagined their passionate embrace of the previous night.

This early on a Saturday, the streets were all but empty, so she took in the Victorian architecture, mostly terrace houses, some neat and tidy, with a brightly painted door and updated windows, some sagging in Dickensian squalor. She recalled seeing streets like this on her trip in from the airport.

Wait a minute, this looked exactly like the road to the airport.

"Where are we going?"

"Surfing."

"Which beach?"

"Nice little place called Byron Bay."

"Byron Bay? Isn't that in Queensland?"

"Somebody's been reading their Lonely Planet guide. Well done. Byron Bay is in the northern part of New South Wales. But you can drive to Queensland from there in about ten minutes," he said, as though pleased with her grasp of Australian geography. "Excellent surfing."

"But—but so does Bondi Beach."

"Not as good. And it's too crowded."

"But how—" She bit down on her own question, having a strong intuition that the answer was going to irritate her. So she shut up.

Wisely, he stayed silent and since she wasn't looking at him she didn't have to know if he was smirking.

"Here we go."

They were in a private airfield. Naturally. And he had his own plane. Naturally.

When he climbed into the cockpit, she stilled. She'd go pretty far to keep a client happy, but getting herself killed by an overconfident womanizer was a little too far.

"What's the matter? Scared?" He shot her a grin of pure challenge.

"Not scared. Prudent."

"Tell her, Ernie," he said to an official-looking older man in a uniform who stood ready to slam the doors shut. "I don't like to boast."

Her eye-roll was a thing of beauty; too bad he was fiddling with instruments and didn't see it.

"Mr. Crane's a very good pilot."

"Have you flown with him?"

The man grinned at her. "I taught him. Really, he's a lot better than he looks."

There was prudence, and then there was stubbornness. Besides, she wasn't usually risk-averse, and she *did* know how to have fun. From a plane, she would get more sightseeing done than she'd believed possible.

"All right. But if we crash, I'm going to be seriously disappointed."

Cam laughed shortly. "I won't crash. I've got precious cargo on board." He waited a bit and grinned. He jerked a thumb toward the back of the plane. "The new long board demo. I'm trying it out this weekend."

Ha, ha. Weekend? He hadn't mentioned anything about a weekend. "Is this an overnight surfing trip?"

The engine roared, and she swiftly fastened her seat belt. "Did I forget to tell you?" he shouted over the noise of propellers.

"Yes, you did."

"Don't worry, I've got everything you'll need."

He was just egotistical enough that he probably believed that, too.

Still, it was a beautiful day, and she literally had a bird's-eye view—once she stopped watching Cam at the controls, deciding he seemed to be doing what pilots usually did, and they were staying airborne. So, she gazed down at dry fields, farms, green leafy trees, and the sparkling blue waves.

Cam brought the small plane down with barely a bump; naturally, there was a car waiting. Some kind of Australian SUV. They drove down a winding road with an amazing view of the bay on one side and the lush green hills on the other. Byron Bay was postcard-pretty, a big smiley-face curve of white sand and blue water. She tried not to notice how white the whitecaps were and concentrated on the smooth crescent of sand.

"Where are we going?" she asked when they didn't take the posted road to the public parking.

"My house."

She swiveled in her seat to stare at him. "You have a house here?"

"I have a lot of houses. I don't like hotels. They're too cold and unfriendly. Besides, real estate is a good investment."

Sure, she was a big land mogul herself, her with her one apartment in San Francisco.

His house was more of a large, ocean-front cottage and was all clean angles and modern lines. It had clearly been designed around the view and there were windows everywhere.

Hardwood floors, cool colors, modern, sleek furniture. Two bedrooms and a loft. He'd made it his, though. He'd hung old surfboards on the walls like artwork along with surfing photos, tide charts, and ocean maps.

"Want something to eat or drink before we go?"

She shook her head. "I'm a little nervous about the surfing. I want to get it over with."

"All right, then. Get your cossy on and let's go."

"Okay." She took a deep breath. Surfing wasn't going to kill her. Unless a shark got her, or the riptide, or one of those stone fish she'd read about . . . "Um, which bed-room?"

"I use that one," he pointed to the beachside room. "You're welcome to join me, or take the other."

She didn't even bother to answer, but strode to the other room. At the doorway, she asked, "Do I wear a wet suit?"

He looked at her like she was crazy. "Naah."

So much for that idea. In a couple of minutes she was back out with her bathing suit on and her sarong, her sun-hat, and glasses. She'd already lathered herself up with sun-screen. She was as ready as she was ever going to be.

Cam was already outside with a couple of surfboards. They both looked enormous. Didn't he know she'd never done this? She wanted something the size of a skateboard, not the monstrosity he was hauling around.

When she raised this excellent point with him, he said, "Naah," once more in that poetic way of his. "This is a learner board. Made of foam. You can't hurt it."

"Very reassuring."

He only grinned at her, and then carried both boards to the beach. She followed, thinking if he was going to carry that big heavy board around for her he wasn't all bad.

He put the boards side by side and told her to lie on hers on her stomach and practice paddling in the sand. He threw himself onto his own board and demonstrated. She tried to concentrate on his technique and not on the tawny skin bulging with nicely defined muscles, or the way the sun caught highlights in his unruly hair, or the little patch of sand that had stuck to his chin.

When he was focused on something other than getting her into bed, he could be a lot of fun, she decided, as they flapped their arms around and pretended they were perched on waves rather than sand-bound. "Okay," he said, pad-dling his muscular arms while her own were already tiring, "you're paddling for shore, right?"

"Right."

"When you feel the wave grab the back of your board, jump to your feet and squat. Like this." He jumped and crouched there, looking like the real thing with the balanced stance, feet moving like a fencer's, arms out to the sides.

"Okay," he said, "you try."

It wasn't so hard, except she didn't feel like a surfer in control of her board; she felt dork-like and tippy. It was bad enough on the sand—she couldn't imagine doing this with water wobbling away beneath her.

"All right," he said after they'd practiced about fifteen minutes. "Ready to have a go?"

"What, already?"

"Sure."

With a deep breath she rose and removed her sarong, the glasses, the hat, even the shoes.

There was a leash that attached her board to her ankle, which she hung onto as she pushed and dragged her board, fighting the waves and the "soup," the white choppy water after the break of a wave. By the time he told her to stop, she was soaked and the salt stung her eyes, but the water was warm and she was out of the office and doing something she'd always secretly dreamed of trying.

"Right," he said after they'd let a few waves go by and she thought she could let quite a few more go. "Here comes a wave. Ready? Up you get."

She scrambled to her feet and was tossed off the board like the cork out of a pop gun. Before she knew it, she was underwater, gargling salt water. When she dragged herself to the surface the tip of her board emerged, looking like the ocean was sticking out its tongue at her.

She felt like making a rude gesture back.

Cam didn't laugh. Merely grinned. He made her try again.

And again. Her arms were sore, her knees were scraped raw by the board, everything ached, but she was absolutely determined she was going to lick this thing.

She set her jaw and listened to every word of advice Cam had for her.

When she finally caught a wave and managed to ride it from her squat position she felt as though she were flying. The exhilaration had her whooping for joy, until she was dumped once more. But she didn't care.

"I did it," she yelled at Cam, "I surfed."

"You did," he yelled back, looking almost as pleased with his student as she was with herself.

She jumped back on her board and paddled back out. "Getting tired?" he asked.

"No. I want to go again."

Three more times she managed to squat-surf, out of about twenty attempts. She was exhausted, and this time when the surf spit her out, she let it. Dragging herself and the board to the sand, she collapsed on her back and closed her eyes.

Her chest heaved, her skin felt crispy with drying salt, her throat and nose were salt-sore, every muscle ached.

She let the sun warm her, breathed the balmy, sweet-smelling air, and decided she wasn't moving for a very long time.

A shadow fell across her face, and, knowing it was probably Cam, she ignored it.

Harder to ignore was the full body kiss, when he laid himself right over top of her and kissed her softly, and with surprising sweetness.

She opened one eye a slit. "What was that?"

"Kiss of life."

"I'm not dead."

He grinned at her, devilish and silly and lovable. "See? I did a good job."

He kissed her again, at the junction of throat and neck, and she felt his stubbled chin, the firm, surprisingly warm lips, and the wet lick of his tongue. "You taste like someone took the salt shaker to you," he said.

"I feel like they took a meat mallet to me. What do you think you're doing?"

"Tasting you." He moved slowly down to where her breasts swelled above the top of the suit, kissing her, giving her those crazy little licks.

She was tired, she was weak, and she wanted to touch him so badly she couldn't keep her arms at her sides but wrapped them around his torso, ran her hands up his powerful back. His skin was still damp, but warm. So warm. He'd surprised her by not showing off today. He'd caught a couple of waves and looked so graceful she'd held her breath, but he'd been awfully low-key about his own prowess and spent hours coaching her.

"Thanks for teaching me," she said, pulling him away when his lips started nudging aside her bathing suit.

"You're welcome. I could teach you a lot more, you know," he said, running his palms lightly over the nipple-sized bulges in her suit. "You're freezing, let me warm you up."

He must have been able to tell it was already working; warmth was stealing through her, from his body which was on top of hers, from his hands, his lips, and from the devil lights in his eyes. She felt like she was in the famous scene in *From Here to Eternity.* Any minute now the tide was going to wash over them, and that would be the end of her virtue.

"I'm going to marry Mark Forsythe," she reminded them both.

His eyes glittered down at her. "Are you?"

Chapter Seven

"We did it!" Jen raised her glass in a toast to Bronwyn and Fiona, who'd helped her pull together a complete marketing plan and proposal in record time.

They clinked glasses and sipped champagne, though in truth Jen didn't feel much like celebrating. Since the trip to Byron Bay, when she'd had to admit to herself that her feelings for her client were a lot warmer than was appropriate, she'd worked day and night—especially night, to avoid her host whenever possible. And the result was that she was very close to being ready to leave Australia. Ahead of schedule.

The three women shared a booth in a trendy Thai restaurant in Sydney, relaxing after another hard day. "I couldn't have done it without you two. Thanks."

"Does this mean you'll be leaving soon?" Fiona asked.

"Yes. I've . . ." She thought of the way her body had responded when Cam touched her on the beach, thought of the sleepless night she'd endured after he'd surprised her by backing right off when she'd told him she was marrying Mark. That was the trouble with Cam; he wouldn't stay in the mold she'd stuffed him into. He kept surprising her. "I've got to get back."

"We'll miss you," Bron said. She hesitated, then looked straight at Jen. "Cam will be a bear when you go."

Fiona nodded vigorously. "He's dead-keen on you."

"You can tell?" Jen asked, horrified.

"Yeah," they said in unison. "His eyes follow you whenever you're around," Fiona added.

"He asks me how I like you and how you're getting on every time I see him. He's got it bad," Bron added. "Of course, it's good for him to lose once in a while. Usually the women are all over him."

"Mmm," Fiona agreed. "Sickening. They're always gorgeous model types. You're the first one who's not—" She gasped and clapped a hand over her mouth while Jen laughed.

"It's okay. I'm not the model type. I've always been the girl next door."

"The cute girl next door," Bron said. "And Cam's crazy about you."

It was difficult to be completely frank with the woman who was his half-sister, but she needed to try. "I think he only wants me in his bed to prove he's in control."

Bron snorted with laughter. "I knew you'd see right through him. He's such a dickhead sometimes," she said with affection. "That was how it was when you first arrived. Not anymore. I've never seen him like this."

"He's used to getting his own way, that's all," said Jen.

"Maybe."

She'd meant him to remember her as the woman who'd said no, but she'd never intended to hurt him, she thought as she drove home after the dinner, the printed proposal in her briefcase.

Could he be hurt? He was a man of the world. Of course he wanted an affair with her—he'd as good as told her so— but he'd never hinted at warmer feelings. No, she decided, Bron and Fiona were young romantics. He wasn't serious about her.

Although there was a warmth in his eyes when he gazed at her that hadn't been there in the beginning. Since he'd laid off the constant attempts to get her into bed, she'd assumed he'd come to respect her as a business equal, and like her as a friend.

She bit her lip as she pulled into his garage and noted with a tiny spurt of pleasure that his car was there, so presumably he was home.

If Bron and Fiona were right, then it was definitely time for her to leave the country. And what about her, she mused as she got out of the car and headed inside. Did she like him only as a friend?

From the way she felt jittery every time she imagined getting on the plane and leaving, she thought she couldn't do it soon enough. Nothing but trouble could result if she let herself fall for Cameron Crane.

She could wait until tomorrow to give him the report, but Cam handled his paperwork at night here in the house. It was logical and sensible to take the proposal to him now.

When she got to his study, he was behind his desk, his computer on and papers spread around him, just like she'd seen him so many nights. For all his big reputation as a drinker, carouser, and womanizer, he hadn't been doing a whole lot of that while she'd been here.

Sure, he had fun while he was out, but it was clear that he hadn't built a multimillion-dollar empire in his thirties by being a playboy.

The man was a workaholic.

"How ya goin'?" he asked as she appeared in his doorway. The warmth leapt into his eyes, and she recalled what his sister had said. Was he "dead-keen" on her?

Since she felt her own warmth kindle, she had to ask herself the same question about him. "I'm all right," she said. "And you?"

"Couldn't be better. Is that what I think it is?"

"My preliminary marketing plan and proposal, yes." She handed him the bound document. He put it beside him on the desk and raised his gaze back to her face. "I'll read it later. Give me the highlights."

She sank to the chair in front of his desk, thinking he

looked like a kid playing at being a grown-up with his scruffy, tanned face, mop of sun-streaked unruly hair, and the surfing clothes.

"I've finished the initial research and I think you're ready for the California market. I'm suggesting the product launch for next spring. It's aggressive, but," she stopped to smile at him, "aggressive seems to be your style."

He grinned back. "Too right."

"You've got a wonderful product, but you know that. However, the competition's fierce in California. Frankly, I think the key will be the product spokesman and the advertising campaign."

"You just said we've got great products."

"That's right. The ad campaign gets them on the boards and into the clothes in the first place. After that, the products have to do their job. And word of mouth." She frowned as worry assailed her. This was the hard part of her job. Giving the green light or red light when all she had to go on was research and instinct. If she was wrong, the downside was heavy. "You're taking a big risk, you have to know that."

He grinned at her and leaned back from the heavy desk with his hands clasped behind his neck. "Taking risks, that's where the fun is, darlin'."

He looked at her long and steady and she heard the ticking of his bright red surfboard clock on the wall. "You might try it sometime."

"I—" She was as much a risk-taker as anyone. Wasn't she? So her fiancé was home putting together flow charts of their combined incomes and poring over amortization schedules for a thirty-year mortgage. That didn't mean they couldn't take risks. But her gaze faltered. "We're here to talk about Crane Enterprises. Not me."

"I've got a creative mind. I can think about two things at once. Three, even. Do you want to know what else I'm thinking about?"

His gaze wandered lazily from her face to her feet and

she felt a swath of heat follow the same path. Oh, she knew what he was thinking all right. *Damn him.* If only she could stop herself thinking the same thoughts.

"A spokesman," she said. "We need to focus on a spokesman."

"Do you want a big name? An actor who's known on your side of the world?"

She'd thought about it. Long and hard. She shook her head. "An established name will certainly get attention quickly, but the risk you run is that people will be more interested in them than the product."

"That makes sense, I suppose."

"I thought about you." More than she should have. "You've got the kind of charisma and a certain animal magnetism that will score well with . . . women."

He grinned at her. "I didn't think you'd noticed. Animal magnetism, hmmm?"

And he knew it. She ignored the obvious opening to sidetrack the conversation from the professional to the personal. "But with your schedule, I'm not sure you've got the time. And you'll be on camera a lot with the product launch. I think we need someone unknown outside Australia. Remember what Paul Hogan did for Foster's beer sales in the States?"

He nodded vigorously.

"We need someone who can do that for your products. Could be a model, a surfer, an actor, someone without ties who can spend a significant amount of time in California."

Cam nodded. "Everyone who works for Crane is surfing mad. They're young, some of them good looking, I s'pose, and they do know their stuff. What about one of them?"

"I've been keeping my eyes open, but none of them has rung my bells." Except the annoyingly sexy Crane himself, but she was doing her best to muffle those bells.

"What are we going to do?"

"If you approve the concept and budget, I'll get agencies here and at home working on it." She shrugged. "You never know. There may be an Australian waiting tables at this moment somewhere in Manhattan or Vail who'd be perfect."

"They don't have to be a trained actor then?"

"No. They need a certain look, the right build, and the right . . . attitude. I can't explain it, but I'll know him when I see him." She rose. "Trust my instincts on this. It's why you pay me the big bucks."

He nodded slowly. "All right. I'll read this tonight and we'll talk again tomorrow."

"Good night then."

He stared at her and rose, too, stepping closer. She was aware that it was after midnight and they were alone in the house. There was nothing holding them back but her morals.

Cam might as well have read her mind. "You've only got a week left. Are you really going to go on home like a good girl? To your man and your predictable life?"

"Yes," she said fiercely, hanging onto her sense of what was right. "I am."

"You'll always wonder, you know. You'll always wonder what it would have been like."

She knew. Even now, she was wondering. She tried to breathe calmly but her lungs were acting strangely, as though they'd forgotten their primary function. "I'm engaged," she said softly, almost desperately. It was her last defense, and it seemed to be crumbling.

"That's no-man's land," he scoffed. "You're not hitched yet. I don't mess with married women, but you're not married, and if you're looking at me the way you're looking at me right now and kissing me back when I—"

"I don't—"

"Don't bother to deny it; we both know you do. Then you should at least take the trouble to find out what you'll be missing for the rest of your life."

"And for what? What's the point? Maybe I haven't spoken wedding vows, but I promised Mark I'd marry him. He deserves my loyalty."

"He deserves better than a woman who doesn't love him."

"Who says I don't—"

"If you loved him, would you seriously consider coming to bed with me?"

"Well, that just proves it, because I'm not considering going to bed with you. I'll admit you're attractive—or you could be if you shaved a little more often. And I like your mind and your . . . business acumen—"

His laughter cut through her tirade like a blowtorch through a snowbank. "It's not my business acumen putting the dark circles under your eyes, love. You're not sleeping. And I know why." He reached out to touch her hair, to push a lock behind her ear, which sent shivers of reaction to her toes.

"You want me. I want you." He was close enough that she could feel his warmth, count every individual whisker that shadowed his jaw, smell him—the warm male, soap, and T-shirt smell of him.

"I don't," she groaned.

"You do." And he pulled her gently toward him and kissed her. How could a pair of lips undo her like this, she wondered as she kissed him back, feeling the fever pound in her blood.

Maybe he was right. If she was contemplating making love with another man, her future with Mark was shaky at best. But to be here, kissing him, knowing that tonight she'd take this wild attraction to its logical conclusion, made her acknowledge that she wasn't the woman she'd believed herself to be. And for some reason, Cameron Crane was the man to help her find her true self.

So she wrapped herself around him, leaning up to kiss him deeply, running her hands up and down the muscles and bones of his back, happy to finally be doing what she'd longed to from the start.

"I want to make love with you," she admitted, rubbing herself against him, wanting him so badly she could barely stand still.

"Mmm." He pushed her back against the wall and took her mouth as though he owned it, letting his hands roam quick and hot over her.

As she let herself go, she refused to think about how much she might regret this. What was happening seemed too important to ignore. His hands weren't entirely steady as they slipped the buttons from her cotton shirt, unsnapping her bra and pushing the cups out of the way so he could get to her breasts. Chills and fever chased each other across her skin as he palmed her breasts, rubbing and kneading them lightly.

She heard the quiet hum of the computer, the ticking of that foolish surfboard clock, and the murmured words of pleasure from her companion.

He reached for the zipper on her navy capris and she realized dimly they were going to end up making love in his study, because she wanted him too much to waste time going upstairs. Already she was tugging at his T-shirt, anxious to feel his chest naked against hers.

He helped her yank his shirt off and then he tossed it so it landed who knew where? He pulled her against him and she loved the heat of him, and the roughness of hair on his chest, the pounding of his heart, the pounding of hers. She reached up eagerly to kiss him again.

"We'll see in the morning about having your flight moved back," he said.

A strange noise came out of her mouth as she pulled away and stepped back, grabbing her shirt and shoving buttons through holes. "Oh, what am I thinking?" she said in fury. "All you want to do, all you've ever wanted to do since I got here, is control me."

His eyes narrowed, and she saw the passion head to anger. "I want some time with you. You think a week's enough? Not for what I've got in mind, it isn't."

"I am not some company ripe for takeover. If I sleep with you, I'll sleep with you because I want to. If I leave in a week, I leave in a week."

His eyes had grown hard. "I don't think I'm the only one who likes control. Face it, darl, you like to call the shots. What's your plan? Shag me for a week and then run home to your tame boyfriend whose idea of an intimate gift is a bloody pen?"

"He doesn't own me. And neither do you. Forget it," she said. "Just forget it."

"Fine."

Chapter Eight

All the millions in the bank, his photo on the cover of *Business Review Weekly*—even an honorary degree from Macquarie University—and Cam couldn't figure out how to bring one stubborn woman to her senses.

After downing one beer, he cracked open another.

She was probably packing right now. Running home scared, to the man she could control and the life that would bore her senseless.

And because he couldn't keep his bloody great mouth shut, she'd bolted. The morning would have been the time to mention about putting off her flight. Yeah. He saw that now. *Brilliant. Bloody brilliant.* He'd all but had her and then made her bolt.

"God damn it," he said to himself.

Well, it wasn't in his nature to give up easily, not give up something he really wanted, and he wanted Jennifer Bloody Talbot more than he'd ever wanted anything. What he needed was a plan of attack.

He tapped the bottle lightly against his teeth, thinking. Bron, he decided, was the next person he needed to enlist in his campaign. He'd seen her and Jen hanging about together. She might have some ideas.

So the next day, when Bron wandered in late as usual, he was waiting for her in her office.

"Don't start," she said, raising her hands. "I've been working like a maniac on swimwear all week. I can't get the right fabric, and the right color, and the right price. You do not want to give me any aggro."

"Partying late again, I see. You've still got some of that sparkly makeup stuff on your shoulders." But he said it mildly. He needed her help.

Since she'd known him all her life, she put her hands on her hips and stared down at him. "All right. What do you want?"

"Jennifer Talbot."

Bron's impish grin dawned and she threw herself onto the bright pink sofa she kept in her office. "I knew it. You're mad for her, aren't you?"

He nodded. "And now she's pissed off with me."

Once more she threw her hands in the air. "I'm not acting as a go-between." She shuffled among the piles of paper on the long counter behind the sofa which, in theory, was her work area. In reality, it was where she stored all her rubbish. How she produced anything in such chaos he could never work out. "But while you're here, I'll show you the color samples for the new wet suits. If I can bloody find them."

"I don't want you for a go-between," he said, fairly certain, given the mess, that he wasn't going to be looking at color samples any time soon. "I want your advice."

She stopped mid-pile. "You do?"

"Yeah. What does she like? How can I make her stay?"

"She's a woman, you great git. She wants romance."

He wished he hadn't bothered asking Bron. "Romance."

"Yes. Flowers, chocolates, champagne, moonlight." She laughed at him. "I know you can do it. You've got a real soft spot; you just hide it mostly."

"Do you think?" He stopped and put her desktop calendar to today's date, updating it a couple of months. "Does she say anything about me?"

"No." Then she laughed again. "It's what she doesn't say

that's important. You ask me, she's crazy about you, but she doesn't know how to give in. She's like you. She doesn't know how to say she's made a mistake."

"She says she's leaving in a week. And I don't know how to make her stay."

Bron looked at him like he was stupid. "Have you told her how you feel?"

"God, I never should have asked you anything. You want to turn my life into one of those stupid soap operas."

"I didn't think you had." She tsked at him as he headed for the door. "Tell her you love her, you great stupid."

Jen was tapping away at a spreadsheet on her computer when Cam stuck his head around her office door.

Though she hadn't moved to a hotel, she had rented herself a car so she could come and go as she pleased. And she'd never been more pleased to travel on her own to the office than this morning.

"Got a minute?" he asked.

"Of course," she said in a manner she hoped combined cool professionalism with personal detachment. "I have a week of minutes." As if she'd change her return date because Cameron Crane figured if she slept with him she'd follow him around like a lovesick fool until he decided it was time for her to go.

He stood there, staring at her, and if there was a lovesick fool around, she sort of thought it was him. She didn't want to soften toward him, but when he looked at her that way, she was lost.

"What can I do for you?" she asked, hoping her professional tone hid the crazy hammering of her heart.

"I wanted to apologize. I . . . ." He seemed to be in pain, as though the words hurt as they came out of his mouth.

"You?"

"I'm sorry about last night."

Jen picked up a stapler and put it down. "Probably it's a good thing last night didn't go any further than it did. I wasn't thinking clearly. Sleeping together would be a terrible mistake."

"Have dinner with me tonight."

"I'm not sure—"

"I finished your report last night."

Her heartbeat quickened. "And?"

He grinned at her. "Wear something swish. We're celebrating."

Okay, it was a little high-handed, she thought as he left her office, but she was prepared to let a lot go when the man was accepting a marketing proposal that was both aggressive and expensive.

Because she wanted to prove to him that his decision was the right one, and she and her company were worth every one of the considerable number of pennies he was about to fork out, she got on the phone immediately to get started implementing a plan as focused and forceful as the man behind the company. If she could get a line on a spokesman in the next week, she could do everything else from her office in San Francisco.

She called every ad agency in town and asked for portfolios. Then she called her office back home and got Lise Atwater, who'd handle the advertising, working on locating any suitable Australian actors or models already in the States.

Cam had told her to wear something swish. While she showered she reviewed her options. Since she was living out of a suitcase, they weren't limitless, but she had brought a soft, blue-green silk chiffon halter dress that she loved. She slipped it on and tried to imagine Cam doing "swish." She spent extra time on her hair and makeup and wondered if she really knew what she was doing. Cameron Crane was a man who could explode her ordered existence, and her conception of herself and her life. Did she want that?

Mark was a good man, she reminded herself, but was he

the right man? If she was so easily attracted to another, how could she be ready to marry?

She grabbed the silk wrap that went with the dress and decided to trust her instincts.

She left her room and made it to the bottom of the stairs when her heart almost stopped. Cam was wearing evening dress. He glanced up at where she'd stalled about five stairs from the bottom and sent her a crooked grin. "You look beautiful."

How did he know that a man in a tuxedo was her greatest weakness? Oh, and he filled his out so nicely. Under the smooth, urbane tuxedo she saw the play of powerful muscle. He was smoothly shaven, he'd had his hair cut—not very short, but shorter and neater than before. It was even freshly combed, but he still wore the thug's nose and the eyes were far from civilized.

"Is my tie crooked?" he asked, fingering the bow tie that was, in fact, perfect.

"I have a thing for men in black tie," she admitted, thrilled to her toes that he'd dressed up for her.

"Head waiters must love you."

"Oh, and don't let me near a supper club band."

"Don't worry," he said. "I won't." The possessive way he spoke had her thinking that last night hadn't permanently changed his mind about wanting to sleep with her.

"Car's outside." He held out his hand, and she made her way to the bottom of the stairs feeling his gaze on her the entire trip. He took her hand and at the touch of his skin against hers she felt little quivers jump to life deep in her belly.

"A limousine?" she asked when she saw the driver open the rear door of the long black car.

"I told you. We're celebrating."

She slid into the back and he slid in beside her. He even smelled good, she thought, as she settled back for the ride. She knew him well enough to know he loved everything casual, from his clothes to his lifestyle. Trussing himself in a tuxedo, shaving, combing, organizing a limo that left him in a vehicle he didn't control must be stressing him right out. And he'd done all this for her. She turned to him, liking the smooth-shaven look of him, but realizing she sort of loved him scruffy, too.

His eyes seemed to burn right into hers as he leaned closer, not saying a word. He kissed her the way a man in a tuxedo ought to kiss a woman—smooth, lips only, drawing back before he made a nuisance of himself.

Without knowing she did it, she leaned in for more and with an animal sound that was out of place coming from a guy in a tuxedo, but very Cameron Crane, he pulled her in and kissed her with everything he had.

She responded with everything she had, until desire grew, budded, and bloomed, all in under two minutes.

"Christ," he muttered, pulling away from her and hauling his body out of touching range. "I promised myself I wouldn't act like an animal around you for one evening. To prove I can be a gentleman." He thought about that for a moment. "If I put my mind to it." He shoved his hands in his trouser pockets and glared ahead. "Sorry."

"I mussed your hair," she said, thinking how much more familiar he was to her with his hair tossed all over the place, and how glad she was that he was overcome with lust when in her company.

Chapter Nine

They drove through the darkened streets, and she let herself feel like a tourist for a change. Sydney Harbour Bridge rose before them in a graceful curve and, in front of it, the famous white sails of the Opera House, which grew larger as they approached.

"We're going to the ballet," he said. "This is a gala opening."

"I'd pegged you as more comfortable watching Aussie Rules football or something."

"In Sydney, rugby league football is the major code. And you're not giving me enough credit for worldliness," he said, sounding mildly piqued.

"You're right. I'm sorry. Do you see a lot of ballet?"

That grin flashed in the dark. "I think this is my second time."

"How did you know I love it?"

"You're not the only one who can do market research, you know. You're on the board of the San Francisco Ballet Society."

Okay, so he'd put a lot of thought into a romantic gesture for her. She couldn't help but be flattered.

She also couldn't help the thrill at actually stepping inside the famous opera house that had appeared on practically every postcard she'd ever received from this country.

Inside, the windows offered a spectacular view of the harbor she'd come to love. She stood staring out at the lights while Cam fetched her a drink from the bar.

They watched the inaugural performance of the Australian Ballet Company's newest production from a private box, and she enjoyed the first few minutes just gazing around the Opera Theatre, the second largest of the center's venues. The walls and ceiling were black; the floor, according to Cam was made of brushbox timber. The seats were white birch and upholstered in red so the whole place felt both earthy and opulent.

Then the dance started, and she was lost in one of her great loves. She shot the odd sideways glance at her companion, but if he wished he were in a noisy bar somewhere with his beer and his mates, he hid it well.

"Oh, that was wonderful," she said, still feeling blissful and starry-eyed as they left. Cam might not frequent the Opera House, but he was well-known and had been stopped many times for hellos and back-slapping. He'd introduced her to politicians, other business people, and a couple of Olympic medal-winning swimmers. In each case, he'd made it clear that she was a visiting professional acquaintance from the States rather than his main squeeze.

It was the first time she'd seen him act like the big shot multimillionaire, and she thought maybe he was doing it to impress her. The idea was so sweet she felt gooey all over.

As they walked around Circular Quay they passed a tight group of crisply uniformed Korean sailors, two men holding hands, a group of giggling teenaged girls, and scores of others: families, backpackers, strolling lovers who must look just like them.

She thought maybe they were going to eat in one of the restaurants that surrounded the Opera House, but instead he walked her to a waiting water taxi.

"I thought we were going for dinner," she said.

"We are. This will take us to the Finger Wharf at Wooloomooloo, where my boat's moored. I had the crew fix us something. I hate restaurants," he shot her a look. "Too impersonal."

She wasn't buying that excuse for a second, but she liked the idea of being alone with him enough that she allowed him to hand her into the water taxi and they sped out to the yacht.

"This is like something out of a James Bond movie," she said after they'd been welcomed aboard the enormous white ship by a man in some sort of uniform and led from the wooden deck through teak doors and down into a living area that seemed as big as her first apartment—and a whole lot more luxurious.

"I keep it to impress clients, mostly."

In the combo living, dining area was white upholstered furniture, and a round glass table with a bouquet of yellow roses in its center. She could be in a ritzy penthouse, apart from the fact that everything but the flowers was built in.

The dining area held a round table covered in a damask cloth and set for two. A single yellow rose sat in a crystal vase. The evening took on a certain fantasy quality. There was a uniformed waiter and an exquisite four-course meal with a different wine for each course. There was soft classical music coming from hidden speakers and the tiniest movement to remind her she was on a boat.

She barely tasted the food or distinguished one wine from another. Who knew what music they heard?

All she knew was that tonight, everything was different. She was being seduced in the most opulent, bazillionaire-tycoon-woos-female-from-lower-economic-bracket manner possible.

She should be rolling her eyes and gagging at this obvious effort to woo her, but it was so sweet she wanted to hug him.

She loved every romance-on-the-high-seas minute of it. They talked about business, they talked about the ballet, but the real communication was in the burning eye contact and the back-and-forth intimacy of body language. She knew all about body language; it was incredibly useful for her business. So when she caught herself flicking her hair, she knew she was broadcasting that she wanted him.

When he fed her from his fork, she knew they were playing the oldest mating game known to man. She'd forget she was even on a boat, and then she'd hear the quiet hum of the engine and feel the odd roll of the swell beneath them.

"What I should have said last night, what I meant to say, was, I don't want you to leave so soon."

He reached across the table and took her hand, and her pulse jumped as though he'd pushed a button. The waiter returned with a frothy looking white dessert and placed it before them. Cam didn't release her hand and she didn't make a move to pull away.

"Why?" she asked softly, hoping he had the answer for both of them, since she was tired of feeling torn.

"Because there's something here. When I touch you, it's . . . oh, hell. Are you going to eat that?"

She glanced at the dessert she'd forgotten was in front of her. She shook her head.

He came around the table, and her heart picked up speed. He knelt beside her so their faces were even and put his hand on her cheek, the leathery palm warm against her skin. "There's something special when I touch you," he said softly. Leaning closer, he kissed her.

Oh, she'd been kissed by him when he was trying to make a point, trying to get her into bed on the force of his will and sexual heat alone, but she'd never been kissed by him when he was letting her know she was special.

He was right, too, damn it. Somehow, they connected.

He didn't bludgeon her with his tongue, but teased her a little. His hands didn't grab and dominate, but stroked her bare shoulders and arms. Her breasts were unrestricted beneath the halter bodice, but as much as they ached for his touch, it didn't come. He slid both warm hands down her arms and held her hands. Then he looked the question he didn't have to ask.

It was decision time. If she wanted to go home, he'd take her there.

If she wanted to make love to him, she was pretty damned certain there was some kind of ridiculously opulent master suite on board.

Since he didn't ask with words, she didn't answer with them. She merely leaned forward and kissed him back, then rose from her seat, taking him with her.

Still not speaking, they turned and he led her to the aft cabin.

If she hadn't been so keyed up, she would have laughed when he opened the door. It was practically all bed. A kind of headboard upholstered in grays and blacks that matched the duvet went around three sides of the built-in bed. You could stay in bed through a typhoon and never get a bruise. Or have some pretty acrobatic sex just as safely.

When he would have taken them both straight to the bed, she excused herself and slipped into the adjoining washroom. Head, she supposed she ought to call it.

While she was in there, she took a good look at herself in the mirror, knowing that what she was about to do would change her destiny.

For she couldn't sleep with Cam and then marry Mark. She had no idea what she was getting into, but this wasn't a last fling before settling down.

Sadness squeezed her throat as she twisted the engagement ring off her finger. It clung stubbornly—probably because her fingers had swelled in the heat—but it still gave her a bad moment as she pondered the significance of an engagement ring that refused to let go.

She ran warm water and lathered her hand with soap until finally, after more twisting and tugging, the ring came off, but with enough protest that she was left with a red indentation on her ring finger and probably a bruised knuckle. She didn't even want to think about what Mark would be left with, but she had the dubious consolation of knowing that he was better off without her. She wiped the ring carefully and wrapped it in a tissue, knowing she'd return it to Mark, then placed it inside her purse.

Smoothing the now-ringless hand across her stomach, she drew a breath and opened the door.

The minute Cam looked up she could tell he was wondering if she'd changed her mind. He wasn't the tough guy standing there, but the teddy bear she glimpsed from time to time. The one with all the vulnerability and the big heart. At this moment she could see he was trying to hide how much he wanted her behind a quizzical expression. He wasn't fooling her, though.

He'd removed his jacket and the tie, and unfastened his shirt, then he'd stopped, probably in case she changed her mind.

She caught an enticing glimpse of tanned belly when he turned to look at her and the shirt shifted. She walked toward the face that fascinated her with its tough, pugnacious nose and the eyes so full of yearning, the rough stubble of his cheeks, and the soft warmth of his mouth. She walked right into the arms that opened for her and then she put her head against his shoulder and just held on.

It felt weird to go to him for comfort when she'd just made the decision to end her engagement to another man, but right now she needed the simple warmth of a hug.

He seemed to understand, and when she wrapped her arms around him and tucked her head under his chin, he pulled her in tight and held her.

She was tucked under his chin and she was either going to stay there for all eternity, or, now that she'd finally and irrevocably made her decision, she was going to give in to the attraction that had pulled them together from the first moment.

Enough of being serious and sensible. It was time for the fun to begin.

Even as the word *fun* played around in her mind, she recalled all the times Cameron had thrown at her that she didn't know how to have fun, was no fun, wouldn't know fun if it bit her in the ass . . .

Well, maybe it was time to show the man that she was as much fun as the next young, healthy and sexually-excited woman.

And if there was ever a place for fun and games it was in a floating bedroom that was all bed and padded walls. Cam's boat was nothing but a playpen for adults.

So she stepped back to give herself some room.

"What's the matter?" Cam asked.

That was the trouble when a man thought you were no fun. The minute you got silly he thought there was something wrong. Time to show Mr. Cameron Too Sexy for his Own Good Crane that there was absolutely nothing the matter with her.

She felt fabulous. Free, sexy, and as fun as a woman about to have sex with a business client could be.

Okay, forget the words *client* and *business,* she warned herself. Those were not fun words.

No. And she was about to show Cam so much fun he'd never dare to criticize her again for lack of spirit.

"Do you have any music?"

"You want to listen to music?" he asked in half panic, half confusion.

"Yes." It was really hard not to smirk, but he had no idea what he'd unleashed. Fun was throbbing through her veins—well, that might have been sexual excitement, it was getting hard to separate the two.

"Okay." He looked disappointed but game. He walked to a built-in cupboard and opened it to reveal a sound system, including a nicely crowded rack of CDs. "What are you in the mood for?"

She walked up beside him and nudged him out of the way. "Settle yourself on the bed. I'll choose my own."

"Will you be joining me?" He sounded so completely bewildered she wanted to kiss him and reassure him that everything was going to be fine. But telling was too easy. She decided to show him.

"Yes," she crowed, when she came across a CD she was amazed to find in his collection. It was too perfect. She wanted something with a very nice bump and grind beat to it. And there was David Lee Roth's version of *California Girls*.

"In a minute," she said, and flapped her hand at him until he was leaning back against the padded headboard, looking a little confused, half-dressed and inexpressibly sexy.

"Did I ever tell you I used to dance?"

"No."

"Ten years of jazz and ballet. I'll show you."

"You want to dance? Now?"

"Yes. It will be fun." Hah, would it ever. She put the CD on and moved to the foot of the bed, tipped her head back, closed her eyes, and let her own sexuality out.

She hadn't danced for a long time, she realized. Once she got serious about her career, she'd let it go. But the impulses were still there. The way her muscles and bones responded to the beat, oh, that was still there. Amazing.

She'd forgotten how much she loved to dance.

Okay, so maybe he was a teensy bit right when he said she was no fun. But she *had been* fun once upon a time, and she was pretty sure she could be fun again.

Now seemed to be the moment to test that theory. Listen to the music. That's what she had to do. Listen and move. And have fun!

When he heard the music she'd chosen he started to laugh. And when she began to move he abruptly stopped laughing. She was a bit rusty, but she'd never felt as in tune with her own body. And if things got a little rocky, she could always blame the ocean swell.

The music spilled out, kind of funky, kind of rock and roll, totally upbeat, and very catchy. She wondered if she could do this without screwing up.

And decided that if she screwed up she'd deal with it. That was what fun was all about she realized: the unexpected. The surprise. The thrill of being alive, crazy over some guy she barely knew on a boat in the middle of one of the world's greatest harbors.

That man made every cell in her body turn into a cheerleader. She spun. She leapt, she posed for a second, one leg extended, her back arched and her hands thrown back. She held her scarf above her like a parachute.

And realized she wasn't as flexible as she'd been at eighteen.

But then, Cam wasn't going to judge her on agility or flexibility. All that mattered was showmanship. And the more she showed, the less he was going to figure out her best dancing years were a decade behind her. She made up a routine based on some half-remembered moves from dance school combined with a few stripper routines she'd witnessed over the years until she figured she was about two steps away from back spasm, immobility and physiotherapy.

Time for plan B.

She did the last leap she had in her, then turned and gave the old bump and grind her best, thrusting her hips back in his direction and rotating. While she was there, she placed her hands behind her neck and played with the bow that held her halter in place.

There was no sound from behind her but David Lee Roth reminding her of her roots. She was from the Fun Girl state for God's sake; what had happened to her?

She felt Cam's concentrated focus on her as though it were a laser beam. And her body began to heat.

She pulled the bow with a flourish, felt it release, until the silk bodice was sliding down her chest leaving goosebumps in its wake.

She caught the silk in one hand, turned in time to the music, and kept it going, though her step faltered momentarily when she encountered Cam's gaze and almost swallowed her tongue.

If she'd wondered whether her jazz striptease was working—it was.

His eyes scorched her skin with a glance. She felt paths of heat trail from her head to her toes. Neither of them could stand much more of this. They'd wanted each other too much. Denied it too long.

"I wish they all could be California Girls," David Lee Roth belted out. She lifted her arms, arched and swayed, while the silk bodice sighed in surrender and slipped until her breasts were naked and danced right along with her.

There was a sound from the bed. The sound of a man at the end of his rope.

She smiled at her hold over him and kept dancing. Never had she felt so powerful, so alluring, so utterly sexy.

There was a bit of a zipper holding the skirt in place, and she made it last, pulling so slowly that she felt every tooth of the zipper disconnect, and she had a pretty good idea that Cam felt every tooth also.

She held his gaze, her body moving by instinct to the music since she'd long since given up any formal steps, and simply let the thing drop. The silk licked its way down her bare legs, ending with a sigh of blue silk at her feet.

Now she wore heels, pretty peach silk bikinis, and her scarf.

Oh, yes. Her scarf.

She smiled at him, and got the impression that he was trying to smile back but his lips were numb. She licked her mouth glossy, tossed her hair and kept her hips moving as though they twirled a hula hoop she was never going to drop.

She toyed with the scarf, and now understood why peelers always had props. She could be coy with a scarf, draping it just so to hide her breasts, or she could be bold, wrapping it around his ankle like a restraint, just enough to make his eyes widen before pulling it free and draping it boa-style.

"You're killing me," he finally managed.

"Do you still think I don't know how to have fun?"

"I can't believe I ever thought that."

"Do you now?"

He shook his head, slow and definite.

"Good." She rewarded his common sense by peeling off her panties, slowly, still moving with the music and the gentle rocking of the boat.

She'd never before considered what it would feel like to be a stripper, but now she had an inkling of what it must be like. She felt power of the most elemental kind. The sort of power that has a man begging at your feet, unable to tear his gaze away.

She was used to corporate power, and basic, attractive young woman power, but this was new, and heady stuff. This was sexual power.

She saw his hands clench against his thighs and knew he wanted her so much it was testing his willpower to remain a passive spectator. And she loved him for his struggle.

But enough was enough. Her own heat was building relentlessly. So, she planted one heel on the bed, threw her scarf out like a lasso and caught her man around the neck, pulling him forward.

She felt the heat coming off him in waves, caught the sizzle of his gaze, and then closed her eyes and touched her lips to his, feeling electricity pump and sizzle between them. She pulled him in closer and hoisted her other foot, ready to seduce him with a dancer's grace.

The boat lurched. Whether it hit the wake of another vessel, banged into a wharf or beached itself, she didn't much know or care. She tumbled, naked on top of Cam.

So much for her smooth, coy routine.

She was plastered on top of him, naked and heaving like a sexually desperate woman. Oh, the hell with coy, she decided, and attacked him.

She yanked at his clothes, and he helped. They kissed while they wrestled with sleeves, belt, socks, and a pair of cotton boxers that had naval flags all over them. Later she'd tease him about them, she was certain. Now she only wanted them off.

He clicked a discreet cupboard open and pulled out a handy box of condoms and donned one while she waited, half-impatient and half-ready to postpone. For her, this was it. Once he entered her body, her life would never be the same.

But she'd come to realize in the last couple of weeks that somehow she'd been on the wrong course. Now, amazingly, on the other side of the world, she'd discovered she wasn't the person she'd thought she was, and the man she'd planned to marry was the wrong man.

As Cam settled himself between her thighs, the possibility flashed that he was the right man. She trembled beneath him.

Cam didn't plunge inside her as she'd suspected, but kissed her softly and gazed down into her eyes.

He entered her slowly and even through her intense excitement she felt the emotional pull. She'd seen him tough, she'd seen him vulnerable, and tonight she'd seen him tender. Under her stroking hands the muscles of his back rolled like the swells beneath them while his hips thrust in a rhythm that suited her perfectly. Not too fast, not too slow, each slide pulling her deeper into bliss.

It was so easy and so sweet that a wave of pleasure caught her and carried her off without her even realizing she was about to come.

Every bit of her clutched at him, wanting, giving, loving. His response was a long, grunting groan, but it was quite eloquent enough for her as she felt him jerk and shudder inside her and she held him through to the end.

They still didn't have any words. Didn't really need them. They kissed slowly and deeply, and she realized they'd only just begun.

"You in a hurry to get home?" he asked her.

He meant back to his house, she knew that, but she realized she was in no hurry to get back to San Francisco either and leave the most interesting man she'd ever met. He was still inside her body, as though he belonged there, and in that moment she realized he did belong there.

She loved him. The thought made her blink rapidly and bury her face in his neck. "No," she said, kissing the warm skin. "I'm in no hurry."

"We'll stay overnight then."

"All right." The night couldn't last long enough.

Someday it would be tomorrow, and she would have to face the fact that she'd fallen in love with a man who was completely foreign to her in every way.

But, she decided, wrapping her arms around her new lover, she'd deal with it when tomorrow dawned.

Chapter Ten

"That's him!"

Jen grabbed Cam's arm and blinked and blinked again at the man who'd walked into the front reception area of Crane, hardly daring to believe her eyes.

No. The man didn't walk. Swagger was closer, but that wasn't right either. He had the loose, confident stride of an athlete and something about the easy roll of his hips suggested a potent sexuality.

He stood around six two or three, she guessed, and his open shirt revealed a nicely bronzed chest and a hint of copper hair. He wore jeans and the kind of plaid shirt worn by road crews and cowboys everywhere. His hair was sunkissed brown, his skin weather-beaten, and his smile both boyish and knowing.

"I have to have him," she said when her heart remembered to beat.

"You just had me," Cam reminded her in an aggrieved tone.

She smiled at him, thinking the early bout of sex before work this morning seemed to have boosted her creativity. She was full of great ideas. "Don't worry. I don't want him for sex. I don't have the energy." Since their time was running out, she and Cam spent every possible second together, usually naked. They couldn't seem to get enough of each other. He hadn't mentioned putting off her trip again, but she knew it was on both their minds. She'd never been so happy. Or so terrified. Would she give up everything from her citizenship to her job for this man?

Would he even ask her?

She wanted to kiss Cam but since that was grossly inappropriate, she squeezed his arm and let go. "I'll see you later."

Then she turned back to the paragon, pleased to see he was just as perfect as he'd been twenty seconds ago. He glanced around as though he might have the wrong address and the idea he might leave again had her almost racing across the foyer, intercepting him before he could vanish.

"Hello," she said, extending her hand and giving him a warm smile. "I'm Jennifer Talbot."

"Steve Jackson," he said, shaking her hand and giving her a smile that could melt chocolate. Strong, masculine hand. Nice hint of callous. Up close he was as utterly perfect as he had been from twenty feet away. Maybe even more so, for from here she could see that his eyes were a stunning blend of gray and green, that he handled himself with innate confidence, and that his voice was incredible. Deep and rich, but also approachable. If she didn't sit down soon, she thought she might swoon.

"Are you here to see me?" she asked. One of the agencies must have sent him. Whichever it was they were going to get a fat bonus along with their fee.

"I suppose," he said. "I'm here about the job."

"Wonderful."

He followed when she led the way to her office.

"Did you bring a portfolio?" she asked when they were sitting. She couldn't wait to see how he photographed.

"A portfolio? You mean like a CV? Didn't think of it. Sorry."

Okay, no portfolio. She could live with that. Somehow she knew the camera would love him as much as she did. "Do you have any television or film experience?"

"Television?" He was even gorgeous when he wrinkled his forehead in a puzzled frown. "I'm a steelworker. Just finished up a bridge."

"But you are here about the job?" she asked in dismay. He was the perfect image she was searching for, the spokesman for Crane.

"Sure, I'm here about the job. I'll be laid off for the next couple of months, so I'm here about temporary work in the packing plant. It was advertised in the paper."

He was between jobs and had a couple of months to spare. That was all she needed to know. She smiled and opened her drawer to find her digital camera.

"I'd like to interview you for a different job. Something I think you'll find much more exciting than packing surfboards."

"What is it?" He eyed her and her camera with suspicion.

"We're searching for a spokesman for the new product launch into California. You'd become the face, body, and voice associated with Crane Surf and Boogie Boards in North America. You'll travel, shoot commercials, and make public appearances, promotional videos, and print ads." While she became more enthused with each word, she wasn't getting the same reaction from the man sitting across from her. If anything, he was looking more and more revolted.

"You're looking for a male model?" He made it sound as though she were asking him to star in a gay porn flick.

"Not exactly. More a product spokesman, though a little acting may be required. I'd like to take a few pictures of you and a bit of video just to get a feel for how you come across on film."

He raised a hand in front of his face and rose to his impressive height. "Sorry, lady. I'm not your man. I'll be right packing boxes. I'll find my way back to the front."

He was walking away. Vanity, fame, and travel hadn't hooked him. She tried filthy lucre. "If you get the job, you can expect to earn at least fifty thousand dollars for a couple of months' work."

He stopped mid-stride and turned to her, his eyes widening. "Fifty grand? To parade around with a surfboard for a couple of months?"

"At least fifty. Probably more. You'll travel all expenses paid, naturally. And I did mention the pay is in U.S. dollars?" With the exchange rate, that was a hefty bonus right there.

"Fifty grand." He rubbed the back of his neck. Thank goodness he wasn't immune to the lure of filthy lucre.

She held up the camera. "Can I take a couple of shots?"

"You did say U.S. dollars?"

"I did."

He sent her a smile that she suspected would make women the world over take up surfing because he was so sexy. She bet men would rush to buy products he endorsed because he was so confidently virile. If her initial instinct turned out to be right, he was Crane's dream come true.

"Take your photograph," he said.

"Oh, he's perfect," Jen gushed, slapping photos of the cocky looking bastard she'd fallen all over herself running after this morning.

"Perfect for what?" Cam wasn't feeling quite so thrilled to stare at photos of another man pushed under his nose by the woman who'd just become his lover.

"The spokesman!" she said, as though he were being incredibly dim. "For your California launch. He's exactly, wonderfully perfect. He's got the build." She shuffled through until she found one of the guy shirtless, and looking less than pleased. Couldn't blame him. The background was Jen's office. She could persuade men into the damnedest things.

"He's got the look of a hard-playing, rugged surfer, a man who braves the tallest waves and triumphs. Tough, manly, but something in his eyes says he's got a soft spot for women." She sighed. "Even his voice is right. Low and sexy, his accent's not so strong you can't understand what he's saying. Like I said, perfect."

"If he's so perfect, why haven't I ever seen him in a film or on telly? Or advertising some fruity men's cologne in a magazine?"

She glanced at him and, if anything, the sparkle intensified. "That's what makes him even more perfect. He's not an actor. He's a laid-off steelworker. He came here about some packing job."

Had she gone completely off her rocker? "You want to hire an unemployed steelworker to promote my boards?"

"Yes. My instincts are almost never wrong. I think he can do it. Look at the way his masculinity and sexual appeal come across in a few casual snaps."

But he wasn't looking at the photos, he was narrowing his eyes and staring at her face. She'd said her instincts were almost never wrong. "Define almost."

She grinned at him. "Trust me. I won't use him until we're certain. I'm going to send him to Lise Atwater. She'll train and groom him until he's perfect."

"You said he was already perfect."

"He's perfect raw material. Lise will refine him into the epitome of the Crane man. This is a huge breakthrough for us." She slipped a hand to his shoulder in a gesture that would look casual to anyone who popped their head round the door, but her fingertips on the back of his neck were an intimate caress. "This makes me feel like celebrating."

Since he knew what she had in mind by celebrating, he squelched his unreasonable jealousy over the bloke in the photos.

"Just one question," he said, when she gathered up her pictures and was on her way out the door.

"Yes?" she turned her head.

"Can he surf?"

Her eyes widened and a smile played over her mouth. "I have no idea. If not, somebody's going to have to teach him."

He couldn't stop the laugh that shook him. He'd never understand marketing people. She was raving about a fellow as the perfect spokesman for a product he might not know how to use.

And somehow, he was certain, even if the poor bugger couldn't swim, that Jen would have him looking like an Olympic freestyler given a weekend and a wading pool.

"Hey," he said stopping her in mid-skip.

She turned her head. "What?"

"Speaking of surfing lessons, you're due another. How about coming up to Byron this weekend?"

"It's my last weekend," she said, and he felt her voice falter even as his belly tightened.

"Only if you want it to be," he reminded her. They'd not spoken of her delaying her trip since she got so pissed off the first time, and he'd finally realized she had to be the one to make this decision. It drove him insane, but he couldn't make this stubborn-arsed woman do anything. He could persuade her, though, and he'd damn near exhausted both of them with his physical attempts at persuasion.

A funny little smile played over her lips. "Okay."

He'd find a way to make her stay longer. He had to.

Chapter Eleven

She had to tell him.

Jen stared at the phone in her hand, drew yet another calming breath—she'd drawn so many she was starting to hyperventilate—and punched Mark's home number. It was late at night and the house slept, so she knew she'd have the privacy she needed for this, the most dreaded conversation of her life.

Mark answered on the second ring, dashing her craven hope that the service would pick up. "Hi," he said, sounding the same as always. "What's up?"

I'm sleeping with someone else and am about to shatter your world. She'd liked Mark for being so straight and honest and dependable. Now she wished he had some skeletons in his closet, an unpaid parking fine, a library book a decade overdue, anything that would help him comprehend that nice people sometimes did horrible things to each other.

She drew in a breath and said, "Mark, I have to talk to you about something serious." Her voice trembled a little, and she hated hearing it.

"What's the matter?" he sounded worried, not suspicious. Of course.

"I don't even know how to begin to explain this to you."

She sat on the bed and wrapped her free arm around her middle.

"Start at the beginning. It's usually the best place."

Oh, God, he was soothing her. He probably thought it was a work thing that had upset her. "You know how I really didn't like Cameron Crane all that much when I first met him?" Her voice was wobbling even worse now.

"That bastard. What's he done? You get on the next plane home. We don't need his business that bad—"

"No. No! That's not it. You don't understand. I . . . Oh, Mark, I'm so sorry. I've done something awful to you."

There was silence on the other end.

"Mark?"

"What is this awful thing?" His tone changed, and now she heard wariness.

"It's Cameron Crane."

"My God. You're having an affair." He said it simply, the way he'd read out a newspaper headline he thought might interest her.

But the word "affair" struck her as blatantly untrue and had nothing to do with the way she felt. "No. I'm not having an affair. Well, I guess I am, but it's not like an affair. I love him, Mark. I really love him. I'm so sorry."

"I see."

Another silence. Tears were running down her face. One dripped onto the bed and she watched as it spread into a damp patch. "I see? That's all you have to say?"

"I don't know what I'm supposed to say. I'm thousands of miles away. I suggest we talk about it when you get home."

"Mark, I can't marry you. I'm in love with someone else."

"I did grasp that fact. Yes."

"Are you okay?"

"No. I'm not okay. I'm shocked and right now I don't think we can come to any kind of meaningful resolution. When you get home, we'll talk about things sensibly."

Suddenly, she wanted to scream. *Sensible?* What was sensible about love? If she were sensible, she'd marry Mark who had the same citizenship as she, worked in the same business, made similar money, and planned for things. She wouldn't turn her life on its head because of a man who was different from her in every possible way.

That didn't mean she had a choice.

"I'm sorry," she said again. "I wish I didn't have to do this on the phone."

"Why are you doing it on the phone? You'll be home in less than a week." She doubted any man had ever been so cordial about being dumped. If she weren't such an emotional wreck, she'd be half smiling.

Mark's question was a good one. Why had she been in such a hurry to tell him that she would have this conversation over the phone?

If Mark deserved anything, he deserved the truth. She sniffed and wiped her eyes. "I only have a few days left with him. I wanted them to be unhampered by guilt. I'm sorry I had to hurt you, and do it over the phone, but now I can be open and honest about my feelings."

"You don't seriously think a man with his reputation is going to marry you, do you?"

"No," she sniffed. "This isn't for him. It's for me."

There was a long sigh, and for the first time she heard pain. "I'll talk to you when you get home."

"I'm sorry, Mark," she said again, but it was too late. He'd hung up. Her former fiancé had hung up on her.

Cam couldn't sleep. Jen had refused to share his bed tonight on some hastily muttered excuse, and he hated being in the great stupid thing alone knowing she was in the house somewhere. He'd thought at first she was getting her period, but when he asked her all he got was a snooty glare down the nose.

He stared up at the dark ceiling, wanting that woman with every pore of his body. Not just for sex, which was surprising in itself, but simply to feel her there beside him in the dark. He sort of wanted to talk to her. Not about anything much, simply chatter nonsense back and forth. He wanted to hear her voice in the darkness. Feel her living and breathing beside him.

Was she pissed off with him about something? Maybe that's why she wasn't beside him.

Never one to put off until tomorrow what he could do right this second, he rolled out of bed. He was at the door before he thought Jen might not want him barging in on her in the nuddy if she was pissed off at him. He walked into his closet looking for a robe, remembered he didn't own one, and shoved himself into footie shorts and a T-shirt before heading off in search of his woman.

His bare feet made no sound on the carpet as he approached Jen's room and tried to work out how he should approach her. It would help if he knew why she was angry with him, but he was buggered if he could work out what he'd done. Of course, that was nothing new. He made women angry with him all the time and often had no clue why.

He was about to knock softly on her closed door when he heard her voice. In the quiet house, he could hear her words as plain as day. "You know how I really didn't like Cameron Crane all that much when I first met him?" he heard her say. What on earth had he done that she was on the phone in the middle of the night moaning about him? And if she was calling at this time of night, she must be telling people on the other side of the world what a shit he was. Without telling him first?

He was about to barge in and demand an explanation when he heard her say, "Oh, Mark," and he realized she sounded weepy. Having the guilts that she was having it off while the better half stayed home?

Bitterness crawled up his throat and he started to turn away, only to hear her say, "No. I'm not having an affair.

Well, I guess I am, but it's not like an affair. I love him, Mark. I'm so sorry."

Cam felt as though he'd taken a full body tackle. For a moment his head felt funny, and his knees threatened to give out. She loved him?

Shamelessly, he stayed where he was and listened to the rest of the conversation and heard her break off her engagement.

Because she loved him, Cameron Crane.

Through the numbness stole a feeling of warmth. And then the prickling sweat of panic because Jennifer Talbot was a forever kind of woman.

It wasn't a very long conversation going on behind Jen's bedroom door and when it was done he was amazed at this Mark who could let her go with so little fuss. If Jen was dumping him for another bloke, he'd leave his rival in a heap of broken bones before he'd let her go.

His first instinct was to throw open the door and take the noisily weeping woman into his arms. For once, he stopped for a moment to think.

She loved him.

Silently, he took his hand away from her door and headed downstairs to his office, knowing he'd never sleep now.

Had he planned for her to fall in love with him?

He didn't recall giving the matter much thought. Certainly he'd planned on getting her into his bed, though he was certain she'd known all along of his plan and come to him on her agenda, not his.

Still, if anyone had asked him a few weeks ago whether he wanted a smart, sassy, uptight Yank powerhouse falling in love with him, he'd have grinned and said, "Bloody oath."

Now she had. His smart, sexy powerhouse had fallen in love with him and he didn't feel the thrill of victory. He thought what he felt was a pang of fear.

He slipped into his office, closed the door, and flipped on his desk lamp. When he was unsettled, there was always work. He understood himself enough to accept that his business success was what gave him most of his self-esteem. It grounded him and was a reliable place to hide from anything he didn't want to face. Like the sounds coming from behind the bedroom door, and the phone conversation he'd overheard.

He'd work a few hours. Make more money. Ensure even greater success, putting yet more distance between the Cameron Crane whose name appeared frequently in the financial pages of the *Sydney Morning Herald* and the boy who'd left school at sixteen with nothing but a burning ambition. He focused on goals, he achieved them, he moved on.

He'd always done the same with women. He chose them, pursued them, enjoyed them, moved on.

They didn't fall in love with him. It wasn't part of the game.

He reached absently for the door handle of the small fridge on which his computer printer sat, opened it, and grabbed himself a beer.

The good old amber nectar felt good going down as he seated himself and with his free hand reached automatically for the closest folder on his desk.

He almost spewed his ale at the sight that greeted him when he flipped open the cover on the manila folder. Blown up glossies of the pretty boy Jen had salivated over in his office stared up at him. The bloke she wanted for their U.S. spokesman.

Once more his stomach churned, but this time he realized that he wanted to plow pretty boy's nose down his throat, and not out of any personal vendetta—the man looked as though he knew how to fight back, always an asset in Cam's opinion. No. His trouble stemmed from Jen's enthusiasm.

Flipping through the photos didn't help. In his mind's

eye he could see her face, hear her voice as she'd gushed over her perfect choice.

"Jealousy, mate. That's what this is," he said to himself, finally labeling an emotion as unwelcome as it was unfamiliar.

Jealous. He was jealous.

Jennifer Talbot would be flying home soon to her life on the other side of the world where the coffee was decaf, the footballers wore padding, and he'd heard even the men were getting facials.

If he signed off on this final part of the proposal, she'd go ahead with focus groups and some other nonsense to shape this man who'd come to Crane after a packing job into California's idea of an Aussie surfie.

The cold beer couldn't douse the uncomfortable heat in his belly anymore. He didn't want Jen going home next week as planned. Damn it, he wasn't nearly finished with her yet.

But how could he stop her from going back?

He tapped the file folder in front of him as though it were a treasure chest. He could make her stay. She was terrific at her job. He'd talk her into taking over the marketing right here in Oz.

He smacked his hands together as the idea struck him, blinding in its brilliance. Somebody else could groom pretty boy. Jennifer was needed for more important work right here.

What more important work? Hmm. Bit of a flaw in his plan there. His company already had the giant's portion of the domestic market, and a complete marketing and advertising schedule for the next twelve months—which Jennifer knew because he'd shared it with her.

No way she'd believe he needed her for work here. Besides, she likely had other clients in need of her services back at home.

Rubbing the back of his neck, he decided he'd simply have to dream something up for her. He'd leaped higher hurdles in his life—plenty of them—and never fallen flat on his face. One sexy woman with a funny accent and a posh wardrobe wasn't going to stop him.

Well, she loved him, didn't she? She'd said so, so she'd be looking for any excuse to stay with him, just as he was looking for excuses to keep her around. At least until they got fed up with each other.

Feeling a lot calmer now that he had a way to keep Jen around a little longer, he grew sleepy and anxious to feel her body naked against his. Not for sex, simply for the pleasure of having her there. He'd not mention the business of her broken engagement, but find an excuse for them to stay together longer, which he was certain she'd agree to. Then, when their passion had worn itself out, as it would in due course, they'd go their separate—as in half a world apart—ways.

Creeping up the stairs, he headed once more for her room, unsure as yet what he'd do if she was still crying. He dreaded tears as much as every other man he knew, but he also found he couldn't leave her to sob all night. But when he got there, he found her door ajar and no sounds of woe coming from inside Jen's room. Cautious, in case she should be asleep, he pushed the door open farther.

Even before he crept in for a closer look he was certain she wasn't in the room. Her scent didn't greet him, nor did the comforting feel of her presence. Sure enough, when he padded to the bed he found it empty.

She wasn't in the adjoining bathroom, either. The door was wide open and it was empty.

Puzzled now, he headed for his own room, and the instant he entered it he felt her there. Smelled the warm, sweet woman smell of her skin. When he held his breath he could hear her tiny huffing sounds of sleep. He smiled as he shucked his clothes and crawled into bed. She slept on her side, facing away from him, so he wrapped an arm around her waist and tucked her into the curve of his own body. Some kind of short silky thing stood between her and nakedness but he reached up until he felt the warm curve of breast and, with his nose just touching the splash of hair fanning onto her pillow, he fell into deep and dreamless sleep.

Sometime in the night she sighed and shifted. The flimsy bit of silk had ridden up so the rub of her bare bottom against his cock woke him instantly. She shifted again, and he wondered if she were really as innocently asleep as she seemed. He rubbed back, his body rapidly rising to the challenge.

Without a word, she tilted her hips, inviting him into her body. He slipped in just as quietly, with no fanfare, just a sliding sense of rightness. Right fit, right feel.

Right woman.

As he stroked, rhythmically and half sleepily into her, he ran a hand up her side, up the arm that was above her on the pillow, until they could link fingers.

Only then did it hit him—old Cam Crane, usually so quick off the mark, so sly to catch a hint—that her ring finger was bare. She hadn't yanked that diamond off her finger last night. It must have been before she broke off with her bloke back home.

He felt her fingers clutch him tight, as tight as her slick heat clutched his cock. Somehow, it was all related. She was wrapped around him everywhere, even, he suspected, around his heart.

"Your ring's gone," he said softly, his voice gravelly with sleep.

She nodded, her hair tickling his face as she did so.

"When did you take it off?" Okay, so he wasn't being brilliant about this, but somehow it was terribly important that he find out.

She stopped moving against him, and he wondered if she were going to answer him at all. Finally she said, her voice just as soft, just as sleep-fogged, "The first time."

The first time? First time what? First time she'd seen him? First time she'd kissed him? First time she'd—

"On the boat." She seemed to be mumbling the words into her pillow, but he caught them easily enough.

The first night they'd made love.

A wash of tenderness flowed over him, stronger in all the places their skin touched, strongest of all in the most intimate togetherness of the part of his body buried deep inside hers. The tenderness seemed to rise through his belly, against the smooth skin of her back. It radiated from his chest against her shoulder blades. He pressed his lips to the skin between them and felt her shiver. It was one of her sweet spots, he knew, since he'd searched and experimented on her whole body looking for those extra-sensitive areas. He kissed his way up to the nape of her neck, feeling the shiver spread, and then he did something that surprised him.

"I love you," he said.

Chapter Twelve

Cam blinked, stunned by his own revelation. How could he have been so bloody stupid? He loved this woman.

Since there was an apparently stunned silence coming from his companion, he hurried on.

"I overheard you on the phone tonight. I heard you break off your engagement and tell that Forsythe bloke that you love me."

"You were eavesdropping on a private conversation?"

"Well, I didn't mean to. I went to see why the hell you weren't in my bed, or I wasn't in yours, and I heard the voices. I heard what you said."

A beat passed. "Why didn't you come in when I was off the phone?"

She pulled away, knocking him out of her body and turning onto her back.

His scalp prickled with heat. "You were crying your eyes out, sweetheart. I didn't want to intrude—no, that's crap. I didn't know what the hell to do, or how I felt about what you'd said, so I hid out in my office for a bit. Had a beer. Thought things through."

"And what did you decide?" She was so rational. He really, really liked that about her. She wasn't throwing herself all over his neck, already phoning a florist and caterer for the wedding, which he'd half-feared. She was treating love the way she treated business. With calm detachment. Excellent.

Wasn't it?

He wished he could see better in the dark. Her face was pale as mist, her body rising from the sheets like clouds at dawn.

Unable to gauge her emotions in the darkness, but feeling pretty certain from her tone that she was still up to being calm and reasonable—businesslike—about this whole thing, he decided to go with the truth. "I decided not to say anything about what I'd overheard. I thought I'd find a way to talk you into staying and working on a new project."

"What project?"

"Don't know. Haven't thought it up yet."

"I see." A quiver of something, humor he suspected, danced in her tone.

"Yeah, well, anyway, so there I was, knocking back a Tooheys and wondering why I felt so damn peculiar and I decided it was because I really wanted you to stay. So I'd get you to stay awhile."

"And then how did you feel?"

How to describe the sense of calmness and the rightness of it all? "I felt beaut."

"Beaut."

"Too right."

"And then?"

"And then I climbed the stairs, went to your room and—"

"Weren't you afraid I might still be crying in there?"

"I'd rather face a sackful of snakes than a woman in tears," he admitted.

"But you went anyway?"

"Well, yeah. I couldn't let you cry all night now, could I?" Honesty compelled him to add, "And I was sort of hoping you'd be finished the crying and wanting to show me how much you loved me."

"And you were going to present your proposal then?"

"Proposal? Who said anything about a proposal?" He

scratched his chest as an itch seemed to develop above his heart.

"You did. A business proposal to keep me tied to your side until, I assume, you got tired of me."

"Or you got tired of me," he countered. Fair was fair. Although it hurt even to imagine Jen leaving him before he was good and ready.

Except that now he realized it would hurt indescribably if she ever left him at all.

"Too right. But then tonight, it hit me. We're right together. I bloody love you."

A low chuckle that sort of wobbled at the corners came from Jen's general direction. "You are such a romantic."

He rolled so fast she was squashed beneath him before she'd had time to do more than utter a muffled shriek. "You want romance? I'll show you romance," and he began to devour her with as little romance or finesse as he'd ever shown in his life.

It didn't matter. He couldn't stop himself from kissing, licking, nuzzling, nipping every bit of her he could reach.

"Ow," she squealed. "I'll be covered in whisker burn."

"Good." The urge to mark her as his was as strong as the impatient desire thrumming in his veins and bringing his body to ardent, aching life.

"What are you doing?" This a cross between a giggle and a moan.

"Don't know, really." He wasn't sure he could explain his position. His nose was in her belly button—well, as much of his conk as would fit. And he had a nose of manly proportion. And from this peculiar position, he was kissing the outlying surrounds of her belly. As he'd already discovered about her, Jen was inclined to be ticklish.

If she could talk, he wasn't being romantic enough. So he cupped his lips against her skin and blew, making a horrendous racket and making her squirm and giggle, her body trying to roll in on itself like an echidna rolling up into a ball when attacked.

She wasn't questioning what he was doing now, she wasn't being the cool professional either. She was rolling and giggling like a lunatic, banging him on the head and pushing at his shoulders. He was having trouble getting any suction going since he kept laughing himself.

"Stop it!" she managed.

"Only if you'll marry me." He practically had to shout to be heard.

Sudden silence descended. Her belly stopped wriggling beneath his lips and went rather rigid. Great abs. A natural surfer. Instead of giggling now, he heard only rapid soft panting.

"What did you say?"

"Marry me. I told you I could be romantic."

"Proposing while tickling me is romantic?"

"I'm an Aussie, love. That's about as romantic as I get."

There was a long pause, and even though this entire evening had knocked him for a six, he knew he was doing the right thing. His body had known first and it had taken him a minute to catch up, but marrying Jennifer was suddenly the answer to the problem that had baffled him. How not to let her go.

"What about your other proposal? The business one?"

"It was a crap idea. I knew it the minute I came up here."

Since she seemed to be pondering the idea, he went back to kissing her skin. It tasted like something he'd never grow tired of. Felt as soft as the silk undies she liked to wear.

"Now what are you doing?" she sighed.

"Buttering you up, so you'll say yes. Do you think you could say it soon? I'm in suspense here."

"I just broke one engagement . . ." Her muscles tensed again, and he felt her rise up to see over his head to the glowing numbers on his bedside clock. "Two hours ago. And you want me to get engaged again?"

"No. I don't trust you around engagements. I only want to marry you."

"Oh. When?"

He thought about it while he licked her belly, taking his time now that he was pretty sure he had all the time in the world since they'd be spending the rest of their natural lives together. "Tomorrow," he said.

"I can't marry you tomorrow."

"Why not?"

"Because I—I have things to do. I've got to go home and get this campaign started. I need to . . ."

"What?"

"I need to think things through."

"What's there to think about? You know you love me. I heard you tell the other bloke that."

She slapped her hand over her mouth, so it made a soft popping sound. "Mark. How could I forget Mark?"

By thinking about Cameron Crane and the sooner the better, if anyone wanted his opinion.

"I need to let some time go. I've got to at least talk to him in person. He deserves that much."

"What about me, then?" He was feeling aggrieved and let it out in his tone. "Don't I deserve an answer?"

"Oh, Cam." She maneuvered until she was on top of him, as much of her as possible touching as much of him as possible. "I love you. Thank you for asking me to marry you."

"You're welcome."

"And I need time to think about it."

"What?" he exploded. He'd made his decision and he liked to move quickly to implementation. That was his way. He couldn't bear dithering. "I love you. You love me. What's the holdup?"

"The holdup is there's more to marriage than love."

"Well, fair enough. But the sex is bloody marvelous, too."

She chuckled. "True. But there's the question of my job, my apartment, my season tickets to the ballet, my friends. My . . . my country."

"Who says we have to stay here all the time? Now that

we're launching Crane into the States, I'll be spending a fair bit of time over there. We'll keep your place. Or buy another one. I don't care. Whatever you like."

She groaned and flopped back. Fed up with all this fumbling in the dark, he reached over and turned on the bedside lamp. And as he turned back he wondered how he could ever have thought a simple affair would be enough.

The lamplight made coffee and cream of her skin. Dark where shadows fell and rich white where the light struck. He was prevented from reading her expression since she had an arm thrown across her eyes. It could be from the sudden light in the room, but he suspected she'd had her arm there before he'd flicked the switch.

Not good.

He was offering to live half his life on the other side of the world for her, what more did she want?

"Why couldn't you be poor?" she wailed.

Sometimes women simply didn't make any sense at all. "Why would I want to be poor? I've been poor. It's not all that crash hot."

"Well," she said, removing her arm off her face and finally looking right at him, "couldn't you be less rich?"

He thought about that for a second. "No."

She propped on one elbow and turned to face him. It took all of his concentration not to shift his focus to the breasts now dancing like sugarplums just at the periphery of his vision.

"This is going to look bad. It's going to seem as though I dumped Mark for a rich man."

"What do you care what a bunch of dickheads think? You know it's not true."

She nibbled her bottom lip. "Maybe it's because I'm in the image business. I always care what people think."

"I love you, that's what I think. It's all that really matters." And he found the more often he said those magic words, the more he liked the sound of them. He wouldn't mind hearing them back now and again, either.

As though she'd read his mind, she leaned over and wrapped her arms around him, pressing her breasts to his chest. "I love you so much," she said softly. "I don't want any ugly rumors to get in the way."

"Here's what we'll do," he said, stroking her hair and finding that this kind of intimacy had almost as much going for it as the thrusting inside her body kind. "We'll go on out there. I'll do some business. You'll do some business. You'll have your talk with the ex. Then we get married."

She sighed, ruffling his chest hair. "You make it sound so simple."

"It is simple. Some things are," he said, deciding the time had come to show her just how easy and uncomplicated they could be together. He kissed her, and using a technique learned young, managed to have her flat on her back in one smooth move, without breaking lip contact, bashing teeth, or any awkwardness.

He parted her knees gently, reached for her hands and linked fingers, and then, keeping his eyes steady on hers, he entered her body. "Slow," he murmured, "simple." He thrust into her just the way she liked, reaching that spot deep inside that always made her breath hitch. "Easy."

Her eyes filmed with tears but she didn't turn away or even blink, simply stayed with him, moving with grace and power.

"I love you," he said.

"I love you," she said.

He kissed her again and then slow became fast, simple became complex, as he loved her with all the skill and experience of a man who's spent time and effort learning to please a woman.

But in the end it was still easy. Easy to be with her, easy to slide in and out of her slick, grasping body, easy to imagine doing this every night for the rest of his life.

When she cried out his name he was right there with her, and her climax set off his own so that finally, he achieved satisfaction. More than that, he realized. Peace.

"So you'll wait for me?" she asked him later as they lay snuggled and wide awake as dawn crept into the room.

"I'll wait."

"Thanks for your patience."

"I haven't got any. I said I'll wait, but I'll be at you every day until you marry me. It's my way, see. That's how I get what I want."

"And do you always get what you want?"

He thought about it, feeling her hair tickle his throat, her breasts rise and fall with her breathing, thinking how far he'd come in his life and how he'd needed Jennifer to show him it was okay to slow down and enjoy his life. Did he always get what he wanted?

"Abso-bloody-lutely."

SURFER BOY

Chapter One

Lise Atwater grabbed the back of her neck as though it were a dog's scruff and tried to give herself a shake. The tendons beneath her squeezing fingers were like iron stakes, and she was on day four of a tension headache that showed no signs of taking a break. Even her shoulder-length brown hair felt heavy.

"What's up?" her assistant Sonia asked.

"My hair feels heavy."

"Lighten it. Try going blonde, hon."

Lise groaned. "That is so bad I should—"

"Think about it. Lighten your hair, lighten your load, lighten up! You are killing yourself. Repeat after me. We are not feeding starving children, curing cancer, or saving the environment. We are selling products people don't really want and convincing them there's a need."

"Do you think you're being helpful?"

"I see my role more as a thorn in your side. Cassandra, St. Paul, and Mother Theresa all rolled into one." Sonia was a vivacious Argentinian with just enough of a Spanish accent to sound adorable, dark sparkling eyes, and skin that always looked sun-kissed. She made Lise feel preternaturally pale, even as Sonia's fun-in-the-sun wardrobe—all of which seemed to highlight an impressively sexy cleavage—only made Lise feel dowdier. Not to mention more flat-chested.

Some people could make a navy suit appear chic, but Lise turned even expensive suits dowdy. She wasn't quite sure how she did it. Partly it was her shoes. Grandmother shoes, Sonia called them. But high heels gave her corns and she preferred comfort to fashion.

"Who's the hunk?"

Just looking at the photos spread over her desk made Lise feel even more dull. The tension wires in her neck creaked tighter. "Jennifer Talbot's sending him to me for training. She sees him as the spokesmodel for Crane Surf and Boogie Boards when they launch here in the States."

"Mmm, very nice. You should be doing the salsa on your desk, not holding your head like you are in pain."

Lise dragged off her glasses and rubbed her eyes, trying to remember how many hours it had been since her last dose of pain relievers. She couldn't remember and decided analgesic poisoning was preferable to the headache anyway. She opened her desk drawer for the bottle. Might as well kill two birds, she decided and washed the pain relievers down with a swig of Maalox for her stressed stomach. "He's all wrong," she said, after grimacing and wiping her mouth with a tissue.

"Are you crazy? Tell me one thing that is wrong with this man?"

She stared at the four glossy eight-by-tens tacked to her corkboard and at the rest spread over her desk, and took another swig of the antacid. "He's all wrong," she repeated, unable to articulate exactly why. "I feel it in my gut."

"Is that why you're giving yourself ulcers?"

"Ulcers are caused by bacteria. This is just stress stomach."

"I get a feeling in my belly, too, when I look at him. And it's not stress."

"His smile's too wide. His shoulders are too broad. His eyes are too big. His hair is too wavy. He's too tall, his skin's too clear, his nose is too straight." She snapped her fingers as she realized what was bothering her. "He's too damned perfect. No one will believe he's real."

Sonia plucked one of the photos and held it between copper-painted fingernails. "He's not perfect," she said in triumph. "Look at that. Right there." She pointed to the left side of his grinning mouth.

Lise squinted, then remembered she didn't have her glasses on. She shoved them onto her nose and tried again. "All I see is a dimple."

"Exactly. And look on the other side of his mouth. He doesn't have one. Only one dimple. He's not perfect at all."

She gazed at that gorgeous—too gorgeous for his own good or any woman's—face and felt twitchy. "I don't understand it," she finally said in frustration. "Jen's got the best instincts of anyone I know. She didn't have a second's hesitation about this guy. How could she not see he was all wrong?"

"What exactly is wrong with him?"

"Nothing. That's what I keep telling you. People don't buy product from perfect-looking people. They don't trust them. They want advice from the woman next door, the guy who could be their doctor. Sure, a man they find attractive—but this . . . this is way beyond attractive. He's in a whole new league. And, worst of all, he isn't even American. We might, by the skin of our teeth, be able to use an unbelievably handsome American to sell product, but it's like we're saying, if you want perfect, you have to go to the other side of the world. You'll be lucky to find anything passable on this continent."

"Honey, I'd go to the other side of the world for this one."

"For sex, maybe, but would you buy a surfboard because he told you to?"

Sonia stared thoughtfully at the print. "Maybe he's not so perfect when you see him in person."

Just thinking about picking him up at the airport later

today had Lise chugging more Maalox. "I seriously think Jen's judgment is impaired since she dumped Mark Forsythe for Cameron Crane."

Sonia blew her bangs off her forehead. "Well, I guess it's up to us to save Jen's butt. What are we going to do? Could we ugly your perfect man up some?"

Lise laughed. "Airbrush *in* some blemishes? There's a switch." But her friend's words had given her an idea. She squinted and tipped her head to one side.

"Let's try this . . ." She grabbed a black felt pen and dotted in a five o'clock shadow, dulling that far too-perfect complexion.

She tilted her head to the side. "Better."

But the hair. No one had hair that looked so naturally sun-streaked. She had no idea who his hairdresser was, but the guy must cost a fortune. And the result was too perfect. She shook her head. "The streaks have to go," she said, attacking the hair with a brown marker.

"Stop, I can't bear to watch," Sonia said, shielding her eyes. "I'm going back to my desk. You take a beautiful man and make him ugly? It's like rubbing dirt into a diamond ring. You are one crazy woman."

By the time she'd finished with the markers, Lise was feeling more hopeful. The man in the picture was still striking, but he looked more like a real man than a gift from the gods.

Speaking of which, she was going to have to pick up Jen's gift to the surfing world at the airport.

"Aaaah," she cried when she looked at her watch.

At the same moment, Sonia came into Lise's office. "You've got to be going or you'll be late picking him up."

"I know, I was hoping I'd get time to do a couple more things today."

"Do you want me—" Sonia started hopefully.

"No. I need to see him in person and get a feel for how Steve Jackson is going to be to work with. If he's a prima donna type, I need to know it right away. Did you check that his suite's ready? I don't want to start out with any temper tantrums." They grimaced at each other. They'd dealt with some colorful characters in their time.

"It's ready," Sonia assured her. "And I checked the flight; it's on time."

"Great. I'll make it if I hurry. Knowing models, he'll have so much baggage he'll take an extra half-hour anyway."

In one move she shoved her arms into her suit jacket and reached over to close the file on her computer screen. It wasn't one of the most coordinated moves of her life—and since her life was fairly chock-full of uncoordinated moves, that was saying something. There was a small and insignificant sound of plastic hitting a solid surface, then Sonia's cry of "watch out."

Startled by the cry, she glanced down and saw she'd knocked the Maalox bottle over and it was spilling thick, white, stomach-acid-quelling, ulcer-coating gunk down her suit jacket, her skirt, and pooling in a globby puddle in her lap.

Sonia righted the bottle, but the damage was already done.

"I guess I forgot to tighten the cap," she said. "Stupid, stupid." She rose, grabbing a tissue and dabbing at the gooey mess.

"You can't go out looking like that. I'm not even going to tell you what that looks like."

"I have to. No time to change."

"Honey, no male model is going to be seen with you looking like somebody barfed their vanilla milkshake all over you."

"I thought you weren't going to tell me what that looks like," Lise reminded her assistant.

Sonia sent her a knowing smirk. "I was being polite. What that really looks like is worse."

Another glance down and she got the general idea. "Eeew, gross," she cried and pulled out another wad of tissue, though what she thought it was going to do she had no idea. Now she was leaving behind bits of tissue on her suit fabric along with the chalky white stuff.

Sonia, meanwhile, reached for Lise's phone and pushed a couple of buttons. "Eddie? Can you bring Lise's car around to the front door in five minutes? I'll leave the keys out on my desk for you." She snapped her fingers and Lise, realizing she was going to do whatever Sonia told her to because she was tired, her head ached, and she had officially lost it, obligingly scrabbled in her purse and passed them over.

"Now strip," Sonia said.

"I'm meeting our model in my underwear?"

"We're switching clothes," Sonia said, wrinkling her nose. "And believe me, I am expecting a gigantic Christmas bonus."

"I can't—" But there was no point continuing, since Sonia was already running out of her office, the keys jingling in her hand.

Lise took one more look down at herself and slipped out of her jacket.

When Sonia returned, she shut the door to Lise's office and reached behind her for her zipper. Lise was already down to her underwear.

"The bra and camisole have to come off."

One look at the strappy sundress and Lise could see the woman's point. Okay, so she'd look like Gwyneth Paltrow at the academy awards, her small breasts swimming in a too-large bodice. It was better, she supposed, than her own soiled suit.

"Come on, off."

It was only for an hour, Lise reminded herself. She had to chauffeur a guy who, for sure, was going to be a lot more interested in his own looks than hers. Wearing a wardrobe that was a little on the wild side and skimping on underwear was not going to ruin her life.

But being late to pick up an international model, one

whom Jennifer Talbot considered critical to the campaign she was running, could ruin her life.

She yanked off her camisole, unsnapped her bra, and, as the much less modest Sonia, wearing nothing but a thong that looked anorexic even for a thong, wafted the bright colored dress over her head, she pulled the bra off.

"You're bigger than I am," she complained as the straps settled on her shoulders, leaving her modest cleavage immodestly on display.

"Attitude, babe. Stick your chest out and no one will notice."

She tried sticking her chest out and the dress did sit a little better, though she still felt like a little girl playing dress-up in her big sister's gown.

Still more naked than not, Sonia bent and pulled off one of her high heels. "And here, take the shoes."

"My shoes are fine."

"Fine to be buried in. You are not wearing those shoes with my dress."

Feeling as though a clock were imbedded in her esophagus, ticking away the seconds, she kicked off her shoes and stepped into the orange strappy things Sonia passed her. They were slingback and didn't fit too badly if she didn't actually try to walk.

"Great, thanks." She wobbled for the door, only to feel her hair practically dragged out of her scalp. "Ow. What are you doing?"

"Brushing."

"Gotta go."

"Lipstick," Sonia begged.

"No time." But even as she closed her lips on "time," a gold cylinder was aimed at her lips and—*swipe-swipe*—she was lipsticked. She really hoped it wasn't the same shade as the shoes.

"Now, go," Sonia said, giving her a sharp pat on the behind. Lise was not a woman who got swats on the butt, but somehow, she felt a woman in a dress like this was going to be vulnerable to butt-swatting. She'd have to be vigilant.

Although, she suspected her chances of breaking her leg—or neck—in the shoes was going to be a greater danger than itinerant airport gangs of bottom-slappers.

"Don't forget the sign," Sonia reminded her. Lise nodded. As she passed Sonia's desk she picked up the placard with STEVE JACKSON emblazoned on it, then slapped her prescription sunglasses on her face and rushed out into the sunshine.

By the time she made it to the arrivals lounge, out of breath and with cramped Achilles tendons from running in those stupid, damn, ice-pick-heeled shoes, the flight, of course, had hit some kind of delay.

She sat down to wait. Not a problem, she told herself. She'd practice those relaxation exercises her doctor had given her. Except she'd never felt less relaxed. The air conditioning was goosebumping bits of her that weren't normally exposed, and her mind began cataloguing everything she had to do.

Somehow, this was all Mr. Too Handsome's fault.

Chapter Two

Steve Jackson gazed out of the airplane window at the sparkling city below.

He couldn't stop the thrill of excitement when he saw the Golden Gate Bridge arch below him like a leaping dancer's spine. He'd worked on a good few bridges, hefting steel and welding sections that were never elegant, but which somehow became so once the whole was put together. But few bridges, and he'd seen his fair share, were as beaut as this one.

As much as he enjoyed his first sight of San Francisco, he reckoned he'd be a lot happier working at home with the ring of metal on metal in his ears and the smell of soldering lead in his nose, strapped high over the world doing an honest hard day's work for an honest day's pay.

Shifting uncomfortably, he wished for a pair of grubby jeans, an old shirt stained with the sweat of a full day's work, and that he was heading to the pub with his mates.

Instead he was in clothes that made him feel like one of those plastic fashion dolls his little sister loved to dress up. And instead of a decent job a man could do and still hold up his head, he was going to be prancing around like a bloody shirt lifter in a pair of bathing trunks to sell bloody surfboards to bloody Yanks.

He grew hot just thinking about it.

Think of the money, he reminded himself.

He was sitting here in first class, on his way to a few months of ridiculously well-paid work, and he consoled himself that he was so far from home none of his mates would ever know. He'd been right cagey about where he was going, saying only he was having a bit of a holiday.

He glanced back at the *People* magazine open in his lap. He'd taken to leafing through such publications in hopes of working out how they acted in America. If it was like on telly and in the glossy magazines, he was going to have a half-decent time. He wasn't here only for the money; he quite liked the look of those California girls. As far as he could make out, all they did was party.

Maybe he could do a bit of partying himself while he was here. Why not? He'd have a bit of extra money, and there was something about those girls with their long blond hair and perfect white teeth, their convertibles and light beers. Steve Jackson was determined to enjoy this crazy job that had landed in his lap. When he wasn't prancing around half-naked for this silly job, he was going to have the time of his life.

The plane banked and showed him more of the city. There was Golden Gate Park and a rocky island out in the harbor that had to be Alcatraz. Down there somewhere were cable cars and steep hills and—and a woman who was going to "groom him," according to Jennifer Talbot. Turn him into some git with bleached blond hair and oil on his muscles doing a body-builder pose, he reckoned.

His stomach turned over queasily, which could have been at the thought of what awaited him, or from the sudden movement of the plane. In truth, he was a lot more used to buses than planes.

For all the money they were offering—and he had to admit that would come in handy—he still might have refused the job if it hadn't been for Cameron Crane.

When he met the man himself, he instantly saw a blighter

he recognized. A rugged bloke who likes a beer and can play a round of footie without crying.

They'd met and shaken hands, and Cam had looked at him with eyes that understood and said, "Well? What do you reckon?"

He'd shrugged. "Dunno."

Crane had understood everything he needed to from that one word. "Don't you let those Yanks make him too pretty," the big boss of the operation had warned Jennifer Talbot, and at that moment Steve had believed it might just work. "He's a man, he surfs like a man, he looks like a man, right?"

"Of course. He's perfect. I don't want him to change," Jennifer Talbot had said in the exasperated tone of someone who'd said the same thing a million times. Still, he was glad to hear they weren't planning to turn him into something he wasn't.

Now as he headed for foreign soil in a brand new suit that felt like a posh stranger's, he wondered if taking the job had been the right thing to do.

"Only one way to find out," he mumbled as the plane bumped to the ground.

He rose to retrieve his swish new carry-on bag, careful not to let his head bump the ceiling. It didn't, but it was a close-run thing. Beside his bag was a tartan affair that he recognized as belonging to the older woman across the aisle. He passed it to her and she thanked him.

"Oh, would you mind getting my bag as well?" A younger woman who'd been eyeing him throughout the flight batted her eyes at him.

"Sure. Which one?"

"The green one."

He reached for the bag and almost recoiled when he touched it. Crocodile skin. And if the poor croc hadn't had enough to put up with, being hunted and turned into a lady's bag, he'd been further humiliated after death by being dyed to match the inside of a kiwi fruit.

He passed the bag over briskly, trying to rebuff the woman's efforts to chatter at him as they left the plane.

Thank goodness he was being met—and by a woman, he thought—as the crocodile bag and its owner tagged along by his side. They'd already been through immigration in Hawaii, so all he had to do was grab his bags and go.

The crocodile woman was clearly disappointed when his single bag came off the carousel and her fourth still hadn't appeared. Having hefted the first three off for her, he was amazed the plane had remained airborne.

As he emerged into the meeting lounge, he glanced around for Jennifer Talbot, although he hadn't really expected her to be here. There were a few people with signs but none had his name on it.

Lots of people were hugging, a few crying, as families and friends reunited. A few tired souls were gathering in a bedraggled crowd under a tour company's logo, and a few breezed out clearly knowing where they were going.

Steve felt utterly and completely alone.

Well, he reckoned someone would show up sooner or later, so he decided to find a cup of coffee and sit in the lounge and wait.

As he made his way through a seating area he saw his first party girl. Or, more accurately, his first morning-after-the-party girl.

In fact, what caught his attention was the soft mound of a smallish breast perilously close to committing indecent exposure in an already eye-catching dress.

The owner of both the dress and the breast was asleep, her bright, red-painted mouth open slightly on a gentle snore. Her bag was open on her lap and he guessed she'd had quite the party based on the large bottle of headache tablets and the economy size bottle of antacid. Her thick brown hair was a sexy tumble and her dark glasses were skewed across a face that was unremarkable but for the full red lips.

She must have quite a hangover, he thought to himself. Even her lip stuff was a bit sketchily applied.

He shook his head. Eight hours or so ago and he'd have liked to make this lady's acquaintance.

He thought about waking her to let her know her purse was wide open and her dress all but, then decided she'd be better off for her sleep.

He made to walk on past and stepped on something that snapped like a dry twig in the bush. The sharp sound had him glancing down to see his name staring up at him. He looked back, puzzled, at the woman who'd jumped at the sound.

Her eyes were wide open but with the blank expression of a rudely woken hangover victim.

That final jiggle as she'd jerked awake was all it had taken. Her left breast, about the size and shape of a mango, lay on top of the bright dress. Her skin was so white, he thought, and her nipple the exact shade of caramel toffee.

Following his gaze, the woman made an indeterminate sound between a squeak and a moan. She clapped both hands over the escaping mammary, her face filling with embarrassed color. Even her chest seemed to be blushing. "What are you doing?" she whispered in outrage.

The humor of the situation was fast gaining on him. He bent down and picked up the now broken dowel with the sign attached. "I'm Steve Jackson," he said.

There was a moment when he seriously thought she might disclaim all knowledge of him or the sign. But, after a moment, she pulled herself together.

"Oh. Well. I'm Lise Atwater. Welcome to San Francisco," she said and keeping her left hand clamped over her breast, offered her right to shake. Her voice was soft and clear and her eyes were a rich chocolate brown. At least, he assumed they were both brown. The wonky sunglasses covered one eye and left one peering at him with a mixture of mortification and censure.

His aunt Gwen would clip him a good one if she could see him standing here trying not to laugh while the girl sat there frozen, one hand clamped over her chest and the color in her cheeks fluctuating between deathly pale and fevered.

Maybe it was the thought of Aunt Gwen, but he suddenly remembered his manners. He pulled off his suit jacket and popped it right over the woman's top half so it blanketed her from shoulders to thigh.

"Thank you," she said stiffly.

He turned, partly to act the gentleman and partly to release a grin worthy of the green bag in its former life.

Chapter Three

"All right," Lise said, determined to be all business. She glanced up into that meltingly gorgeous face and stifled a sigh of longing.

On the negative side, she'd made a complete fool of herself, flashed her less-than-impressive assets all over San Francisco International Airport, and snoozed when she should have been meeting the man who was going to be her most important project to date.

On the plus side, she knew Crane's U.S. spokesmodel wasn't gay.

It wasn't simply that he'd stared at her breast—anyone would stare at a woman whose breast fell out of her dress at the airport; it was the frankly carnal way he looked at her. This guy had more testosterone than ought to be legal in one man.

No wonder Jen had been so enthusiastic. On TV he was going to be amazing. Still pictures showed his way-too-perfect-to-be-real looks. But in the flesh, his animal magnetism and blatant manliness somehow imbued his face with ruggedness.

She was going to suggest to Jen they do as much as they could with TV. Once people recognized him from the tube, she'd be willing to bet they'd never look at a still photo of him in a magazine, newspaper, or grinning down at them from a billboard without adding in for themselves the strong personality behind the face that they'd already seen on television. And movie trailers, she mentally added.

"All right," she repeated, realizing that she was staring and that he was gazing back at her with barely banked amusement.

Great. She was supposed to be his guide and mentor, the woman who would transform him into the perfect face, voice, and body of Crane Surf and Boogie Boards, and he thought she was a joke.

Since she was pretty sure all her body parts were tucked back where they should be, she held out his coat to him. Feeling at a disadvantage to be sitting here staring up at a man so very much taller than she'd imagined he'd be, she hoisted herself to her feet, trying to keep the wobbling of her ankles to a minimum.

"You must be tired," she said primly as she tottered along beside him, knowing he was half-crippling himself to keep to her pace. Couldn't Sonia at least have let her keep her own shoes?

"No. I'm right, thanks. I slept on the plane."

"Oh." She felt at a bit of a standstill. She'd assumed he'd want to head to the hotel and go straight to sleep. "We should check you in first anyway."

"All right. Then I'm ready to go to work."

"I really hadn't planned to start until tomorrow."

"That's fine. I'll look around a bit."

She nodded. "I can arrange a car and driver."

He looked at her as though she'd just tossed her breasts out in the open again. "I've got legs. I'll walk."

"Don't get lost." He was expensive property. Already plans had been made, campaigns toyed with around his image. If he wandered into the wrong area and got murdered, she'd lose her job.

"Don't worry about me. I can take care of myself," he said, and she realized that he was probably six foot three and had the muscles of a bodybuilder. Still, she ought to go with him, but not in these shoes.

"Where are the rest of your bags?" she asked when she realized he had only one modest carry-on piece, which looked expensive and new, and a well-used backpack.

"This is it."

"Oh," she said faintly. So he was both manly and traveled light. Two surprises. She hoped there wouldn't be any more today. She was pretty sure she'd reached her quota.

"Nice place," he said when they pulled up in front of the hotel.

"I'm glad you like it. It will be home for a while."

She checked him in and he stood meekly behind her. They rode the elevator in silence up to the executive level, and she led him to his suite. He didn't say "nice place" when he saw it. He didn't say anything at all, merely walked through twice, then opened the sliding door and peered out at the view.

"Is everything all right?"

"This whole place is for me?"

She nodded.

"It's enormous," he said.

Steve watched Lisa roll her head around on her neck as though it were too heavy to hold up. The gesture caused her hair to dance and her dress front to shift about. Since he'd already had a tantalizing glimpse of exactly what was under that dress, he was hard-pressed not to stare.

Sexy, she was, but then you'd expect that of a hard-partying California girl.

She closed her eyes briefly, then dug into her purse for the headache tablets he'd spied earlier. "Do you mind if I get some water?" she asked.

He shook his head. "You want to take it easy."

Those sexy brown eyes blinked at him slowly. "That's what everyone tells me. But you've only known me an hour."

"I'm very perceptive."

A knock sounded on the door and before he could move, she was opening it and ushering in the bellhop with his single bag. A bag he was well able to carry himself without help, but he'd felt so oafish and out of his element in the swish hotel that he hadn't protested when a uniformed bellhop picked up the bag he'd dropped at his feet.

"Can you put that in the bedroom?" she asked and fished out a bill. It was hard to tell with all the American bills looking the same, but he thought it was a fiver.

"Did you tip that bloke five dollars?" he asked her once the boy had gone.

"Yes." She seemed surprised at the question, then nodded briskly. "Right. I forgot. You don't tip much in Australia. It's very important to do so here. Especially at the hotel or anywhere where anyone might associate you with Crane Enterprises."

"Well, Crane's from Oz, too. I doubt he tips."

"When he's in the States he does. Image is everything. Believe me, you don't want it showing up in *People* magazine that you stiffed the waiter at Le Cirque."

Since that sounded both French and expensive, he doubted the waiters there had anything to fear from him.

"*People* magazine?" He'd taken a peek at that one in the airplane. He couldn't imagine them having any interest in Steve Jackson and his tipping habits.

"Steve, once the campaign gets underway, you can't be too careful, so it's better to practice now." She pulled out an electronic notebook and scribbled something on the screen. "I'll get Sonia to put together a tipping guide for you."

"Ta," he said, wondering what he'd stumbled into.

"Oh, and here's some cash for incidentals," she said, handing him a fat white envelope.

He felt strangely as though he'd flown, not to another continent, but to a parallel universe.

Once Lise Atwater had gone, Steve stripped out of his fancy suit and into jeans and a white T-shirt, and felt much more like his old self. His real self, and he'd better remember that.

He slipped into his boots, stuffed some of the American bills into his wallet and the rest carefully into the safe the hotel provided inside the closet, and headed out.

"Taxi, sir?" asked a deferential guy in uniform who held open the door for him.

"No, thanks."

And he was free to set foot as he pleased on American soil.

The hotel was on a hill, so he followed the slope down toward the sea. Then, working from the tourist map he'd found on his hotel desk, he headed for the busier area. Fisherman's Wharf and so on.

He let it all flow over him. The voices, with their different accents, the endless cell phones, the atmosphere of Europe mixed with the drive of America.

He bought a newspaper and sat at an outdoor café drinking frothy cappuccino while he tried to work out the who's-who of California politics. Maybe he was jet-lagged after all, for the politics here seemed too complicated for words. He was in a state where a bodybuilder could become state governor; no wonder he felt more like an extra at Disneyland than a man with a job to do.

People-watching was more rewarding anyway. So he sat idly in the sunshine and watched the beggars and hustlers, the business people and shoppers, the tourists and students and masses of people who could be anyone out doing anything.

After a while he got up, bought a few postcards, and wandered on down the street, where he bought two slices of pizza. After he'd devoured those he discovered he was still hungry, so he went into a likely looking pub and ordered a beer and a hamburger with chips. The waitress came back with a mound of potato chips on the plate beside the burger. "I asked for chips," he reminded her politely.

"That's what those are, honey. Potato chips."

He was a friendly man by nature, and the busty woman seemed nice in a harried way, so he decided to ask her for his first lesson in American. "Where I come from we'd call these crisps."

"Hunh," she said, wiping his table clean of beer rings.

"What do you call the long, deep-fried potato sticks?"

"French fries, honey."

"Right, thanks a lot."

"You want me to change these for you?"

"No, that's all right."

Since he didn't have his tipping guide yet, and for all he knew, the fellows in baseball caps at the next table could be spies for *People* magazine, he tipped the waitress five dollars. She seemed happy, giving him not only a big smile, but her home phone number, "In case you need somebody to show you around, honey."

He thanked her politely. He'd been receiving similar requests since he'd left his teens, and he was always polite about it. He wouldn't toss the scrap of paper with her name and number on it until he was out of sight.

Steve wolfed down his first American hamburger while half watching a golf game on the telly mounted behind the bar. Not so very different from a Saturday afternoon at home, he decided, as he finished his beer and made his way back to his hotel.

He settled back with a second beer, this one from his own personal mini-bar, and wondered what his family would make of this. They all seemed so impossibly far away just now. He calculated the time and figured he'd just catch them at home.

His uncle picked up the phone and was as delighted to hear from him as though he'd been gone a month.

"How are they treating you over there, son?"

"Great. I've got a nice room in a decent hotel. All the comforts."

"How are the birds?"

Since Steve didn't think his uncle had taken up ornithology, he said, "Not bad so far." Though in truth he'd only met one American woman who'd whetted his appetite for more.

"A pretty girl in a sundress met me at the airport," he informed his uncle.

"Pretty, eh?"

"Nice tits. Well, I only fully saw one, but it was very nice."

"Young dog," his uncle chuckled. "I know you're only teasing, but you watch out for those girls. They're terrible, with their cosmetic surgery and take-no-prisoners divorces."

Steve rolled his gaze. "You been watching those *Dallas* reruns again, haven't you?"

"All right, all right," his uncle muttered. "Your aunt wants to talk to you."

Steve grinned into the phone. He hadn't lived with them for years now but he could picture the scene because it hadn't changed in longer than he could remember: the working-class row house, rising astonishingly in price now that Sydney real estate values had climbed to such absurd heights, but that didn't make a damn bit of difference to his aunt and uncle. They'd never move.

After his mum got sick and his dad left, his aunt and uncle had stepped in. When she died, they took the younger children to live with them while seventeen-year-old Steve went to work on his first steel rig.

It was the only real fight he ever had with Gwen and Sid. "You're smart, you could get a scholarship to the uni, boy. Don't be a fool."

But what kind of man didn't stand up and do what was right? What kind of man didn't support his family?

A man like his dad, and that's the kind of man he'd never be.

After talking to Aunt Gwen for a few minutes, and having a quick chat with Sara, his younger sister, who was studying for an exam, he felt better. Sometimes you made sacrifices for the people you loved. Sara was going to get the chance to use her brains and go on to university next year, and this job was going to get her there.

Not that staying in a swank hotel and getting paid to have your picture taken was exactly a hardship, but if it ever got out back home, his life wouldn't be worth living.

When he hung up, he noted the message light was flashing. Someone had called when he was on the phone. But who had his number?

Lise Atwater, that's who. He heard her breathy voice sounding half-panicked that he wasn't answering at—he glanced at the clock on the desk—eight o'clock at night. "Please call me as soon as you get in," she pleaded and left two numbers.

Since he didn't believe in torturing women—and besides, he quite liked the sound of her voice—he gave her a ring back right away.

"Oh, thank goodness you're safe," she gushed.

He was amused, but also mildly irritated. He wasn't the sort of person to run into foul play in broad daylight in a tourist area. "Yeah," he said. "It's a good thing you called. Bloody dangerous city this. I was nearly run down by a tram."

"Cable car," she corrected, then laughed dutifully. "This is an important job for me. I can't let anything go wrong."

"Well, I'm safe tucked in for the night," he said. "You can go off to your parties without a thought."

She laughed a second time, a lot more genuinely, he thought, and he found he liked the sound. He wondered what it would have been like if he'd met her at a party. And damn, he wished he could get the image of that single, tantalizing breast out of his mind.

"I'm putting together your schedule for tomorrow. How about I come and pick you up at nine in the morning? We'll do a script run-through back at the office."

He made a face at the phone. But it's what they were paying him for, so he'd be there. "Sure. Fine."

"Listen," she said after a short pause, "I'm really sorry about earlier today—when I picked you up. I can't believe I fell asleep."

"No worries," he said in utter sincerity, thinking again how a glimpse of unexpectedly intimate flesh could be amazingly erotic. "That was the nicest thing that happened to me all day."

There was a kind of choking sound coming from the phone. "I—I have to go."

"Enjoy your party."

Lise put down the phone slowly, as though it were a baby she'd just rocked to sleep and it might start to wail if she wasn't very, very gentle.

"He thinks I'm a party girl," she said.

Sonia snorted with laughter, pretty much as she would have expected. "It's eight o'clock and we're still in the office. When does the man think you party?"

"It was your dress," Lise said, "that's what gave him the idea."

"And the way you spilled the goods, so to speak," Sonia agreed.

"Don't remind me," Lise dropped her head in her hands on a groan. "And you know the worst part of all?"

"There's something worse?"

"He said it was the best part of his day."

"You know, I like the sound of this guy. I think he likes you. He's gorgeous and he likes you."

"He thinks I'm a total flake, underwear-challenged, and a party girl."

"You see? It's what I keep telling you. Men really go for that stuff."

And she could really go for Steve, Lise realized. She didn't think her stomach had yet recovered from the impact of first staring into those mesmerizing green eyes. It was totally like being Sleeping Beauty and waking up to look into the eyes of the handsome prince.

Except, of course, in fairy tales princesses tended to have a stricter dress code.

Her poor stomach. Between the stress and the lack of sleep, she didn't think her gastrointestinal tract could survive unrequited lust for a man so good-looking he'd never give a woman like her a second glance.

"He likes women like that because they're the kind he usually hangs out with. He's either a professional model or a surfer boy they picked up off the beach somewhere. He's into partying, girls, no responsibility—" She gasped as a dreadful thought occurred to her. "I'd better tell him that drugs are absolutely forbidden while he's working with us. Can you imagine what would happen if—"

"You know, you worry too much?"

"Thank you. Yes. I know. But someone has to take life seriously."

Sonia shrugged. "Not me. I finished proofing all that ad copy. I'm going home. You should, too."

"In a minute," Lise said, already getting back to her computer.

"I still think he likes you."

"Well, he'll see the real me tomorrow," Lise said, feeling a momentary pang for the loss of Steve's mistaken version of her.

"What if he didn't?" Sonia said in a totally different tone.

"Pardon?" She glanced up to find her assistant and friend, back in her own dress, since Lise had stopped by her apartment to change on her way back from the airport, leaning against the credenza and staring at her.

"Simple. You need to keep his attention so you can train him. He likes the party-girl type. He thinks you are one. So why not keep dressing that way? It's not difficult and frankly, it would do you a lot of good to dress like a woman in her twenties instead of a matron of a correctional institute."

"I'm not that bad!"

"A middle-aged matron."

Lise gasped. "I can't think about this right now. I have to get our schedule arranged for tomorrow. Here are the scripts for the TV spots. Can you make sure there are enough copies before you go?"

"Sure."

"Thanks." She sighed. "He may be a great surfer, but I sure hope he can act."

"You should do some acting, too," Sonia said as she picked up the script. "Start acting like a woman in the prime of her life."

Chapter Four

"There are three things a man likes Down Under," Steve said into the camera, "a warm woman, a cold beer, and a Crane Board flying over the ocean. And a real man likes them at the same time."

"Okay. And now you wink at the camera," Lise said, in as carefree a tone as she could manage.

What she really wanted to do was throw her head down on the boardroom table and wail. Right after that she was going to have to send her resume out, because based on this reading, her career was over.

There was a pause that had so much weight to it she could feel her shoulders slump.

"You want me to wink at the camera?"

"Yes," she said through gritted teeth. "It's in the script." Steve Jackson had been pretty easygoing at first, but instead of improving, his delivery was growing more wooden. In the last four takes in front of their in-house video set-up, he hadn't winked once.

He glared at her, clearly trying to get some message across that she wasn't receiving.

She glared right back, wondering why she couldn't have gone into medicine like her parents wanted. Surely blood and gore and broken bones couldn't be any more difficult to deal with than temperamental models who couldn't act worth a damn.

Well, he was messing this up so badly, there was no way they could call today a success, and she didn't have the energy to go through it again. She rose, stiffly.

"Why don't we take a break." She smiled at the camera crew, at the script writer, at Sonia, and even at Steve. "Steve, let's you and I rehearse this a bit more before we put it on film."

He didn't even answer, merely nodded in a curt manner she found both rude and high-handed.

He was gold, she reminded herself, as her stomach threatened to burn right through the front of her clothes. Jen adored him. Jen believed in him. It was Lise's job to get him up to speed.

Once everyone but she and Steve had left, she closed the door.

She grabbed the back of her neck and squeezed, almost yelping in pain. "Okay," she said, "let's try it again."

"What's the matter with your neck?" he asked in that voice that seemed to resonate from the floor beneath her feet and travel through her bones. Why the hell couldn't he talk with that intimate timbre when the camera was turned on?

"I'm a little tense," she said with a tight smile. In fact, she was so tense she wasn't sure she'd ever turn her head again.

"I'm a bit tense myself," he admitted.

All right. This was good. He was admitting he wasn't doing a great job. Excellent. Yelling at him would be counterproductive. She remembered all this from her communications course at Berkeley. She just hadn't realized when learning all those theoretical notions of communications that she might be intellectually pleased that a spokesperson admitted he was performing badly at the same time she might want to stuff his stubborn head up his ass.

Breathe, she reminded herself, but she felt as though her lungs were welded shut.

"Is there anything I could do to make you a little less tense?" she asked sweetly, thinking that if the reply was hookers with whips she'd do her best to comply. She felt like her job, her whole future, was riding on this one.

"Yeah, you can take off your jacket."

Her head snapped up as she glared at him. "I beg your pardon?"

"I don't know what it is." He shrugged but she felt he was almost as tense as she was. "I'm not good with suits. Everyone in the room except for me is wearing a suit."

He gestured to his body in a sweeping motion and she nodded. He wasn't wearing a suit. He wore jeans so well-worn they'd molded to his body, kick-ass boots, and a shirt advertising some rugby team she'd obviously never heard of.

He looked elemental, dangerous, and good enough to eat. And he was worried he wasn't wearing a suit?

"Nobody cares what you wear, Steve. This is just a practice session. I thought you knew that?"

"Yeah. I know. But look at this from my perspective. I'm up here in a T-shirt and everybody else looks like they came out of a fashion catalogue. Even you. It puts a bloke off."

She blinked. "You're telling me you flubbed your lines because you didn't like what the people in the room were wearing?"

"Yeah." Pause. "Well, and the lines are crap."

"Of course the lines are crap, Steve. This is advertising. For Beat poetry readings, head down to Union and Filmore."

Immediately she wanted to bite out her tongue. He wouldn't know what she was talking about, and her sarcasm wouldn't help anyone.

To her immeasurable surprise, he laughed. "I'm not sure how many surfboards you'd sell reciting "Howl," but it would certainly catch their attention when it came on the telly, eh?"

"Right." She agreed weakly. He must have read his *San Francisco Now* and come across something about Ginsberg. Still, he'd thrown her for a second.

He threw her even more when he said, "I s'pose this is hard on you, too. All right. Let's give it another go."

"Are you sure?"

"Yeah."

"Great. I'll call the others back."

She walked to the boardroom door and he blocked her exit, his body so big and rangy she felt absurdly small and feminine. "No. I only want you."

The words echoed around and around in her head and she wished so much they were true. This man, she realized, was going to sell a hell of a lot of surfboards if she could find the way in to get him pronouncing all his lines the way he'd just said, "I only want you."

His shirt was soft with many washings and smelled faintly of soap and sexy man and something foreign and exotic that she assumed was Australia. She had to look up to catch his gaze.

"You'll read the lines as written if I practice with you alone?"

"Yeah."

"Including the wink?"

He rubbed his jaw and she saw a hint of the humor she'd noticed the day before. "The wink's negotiable."

She could yell at him and tell him his contract specified winking and he was damn well going to wink, but the twinkle in his eyes intrigued her and besides, she wanted to prolong standing here in his personal space where it was all sex and heat and possibility.

"You want to negotiate the wink?" she asked, trying to keep her voice firm but reasonable.

"Yes."

"I see. What are your terms?"

"Take your jacket off."

She blinked. Even a simple *Huh?* seemed beyond her.

"You looked more . . . I don't know, approachable yesterday. I thought I knew who you were and I liked what I saw. Now, today, you're all done up in this suit and your hair's . . ." he pointed to the bun at the back of her head, "different. I liked you better before."

Well, she could tell him that she'd been in another woman's clothes yesterday. And she could explain that her hair was in a bun because she'd been at the office until midnight last night making sure everything was ready for today's read-through (which he'd blown), so she hadn't had time to style her hair this morning and had therefore bundled it up wet from the shower.

Or she could play along.

She didn't think they'd ever covered this contingency in her communications course at Berkeley, but was pretty sure this was an unorthodox way to run a commercial taping.

"So," she said, ignoring the flutter of awareness that danced across her chest, "if I take off my jacket, you'll wink."

"Nah. If you take off your jacket, I'll read those crap words properly. I told you, the wink's negotiable."

"You haven't told me the terms."

He didn't grin. His lips never moved, but there was some seriously evil grinning going on in the green eyes. "I'm making this up as I go along."

"Well," she snapped, "I'll only go so far."

Her own words seemed to echo in the air around them, adding to the charge of sexuality that seemed to hum whenever he was around. Never taking his eyes from hers, he murmured, "What if I want you to go all the way?"

She couldn't resist the urge to give in to the skittering sensations tripping over her skin and play a game she'd never been much good at.

Because, unless she was very much mistaken, the most amazing-looking man she'd ever seen was flirting with her.

And she really liked it.

The challenge was there, in the barely banked green fires of his eyes.

Instead of answering directly, she slipped the jacket off, feeling the slide of soft wool down the skin of her arms and hung it on the back of a chair. Beneath it she wore a sleeveless white silk tank top. She'd never before thought of it as a remotely sexy garment, but when Steve's eyes dropped to her chest she felt as though she were the sexiest woman alive.

All of a sudden she was reminded of the moment when he'd looked at her naked breast spilling out of Sonia's dress yesterday and she'd wanted this total stranger, and his eyes seemed to telegraph the same message back at her.

She swallowed and moved out of seduction range to reset the video camera. She felt his eyes follow her every step of the way and her body had never felt so fluid or alluring.

He walked to the front of the room where he'd stood before and repeated the spiel.

"Well," she said carefully. "That was better." Better like frozen soup was better than canned, but nowhere near the fresh homemade taste she'd been promised.

"You didn't give me much incentive," he explained.

"I took off my jacket," she reminded him curtly.

"I need more."

He stepped closer and she decided to clobber him if he tried to take off any more of her clothes. But he only reached behind her and unfastened her hair.

With a tiny gasp, she felt the thick, soft slide of her hair around her face and falling to her shoulders. She put a hand to her head, knowing it must be a mass of kinks since she'd shoved it in the bun while it was still wet.

"Leave it," he said, stilling her hand. "I like it like that."

He went back to the front once more; this time, he leaned forward so his hands rested on the edge of the board room table, reminding her of his strength. He stared at her as though she were the only person in the universe and said, "There are three things a man likes Down Under." He paused as though he were letting her in on a great secret. "A warm woman, a cold beer, and a Crane Board flying over the ocean." She was mesmerized. In her wildest dreams she hadn't imagined him capable of this. He paused again, then moved slightly closer as though instinctively reaching for a close-up.

"A real man likes them at the same time."

She knew exactly what he said, but what she heard was, *You are the most beautiful woman in the world and I want you.* She felt each word as though he were saying it solely to her. In fact, when he stopped speaking and silence fell, she longed to run out and buy a Crane Board.

"That was so much better," she gushed.

He cocked an eyebrow and she reviewed the take in her mind. "There was just one thing missing," she said, enjoying herself so much her stomach forgot to hurt, realizing they were playing some kind of game here where she had no idea of the rules. But she didn't care, she was making it up as she went along, too. "You forgot to wink."

"Ah, for a wink I'd have to feel that I was really winking at someone, and for a reason. I'm not a trained actor, you know."

"I can understand that," she agreed. "What kind of incentive would you be looking for?"

"Well, let's say I'd just kissed a beautiful woman. I might wink at her."

Her throat felt so dry, and at the same time her lips felt so moist and dewy, she could barely believe they were both attached to her body.

"Yes," she said huskily, "I can see how you might wink at a woman you'd just kissed."

"A beautiful woman," he reminded her, stepping closer and closing his hand on the back of her head. She felt his fingers moving in her hair and her oh, so heavy head tipped back of its own accord.

The pounding ache that had lived with her for days began to subside. Her eyes slipped shut and her lips parted.

And Steve Jackson, the most gorgeous man in the world, kissed her. It was a simple kiss, just his lips warm and sure against hers. No tongues, no body bumping, just a kiss.

So why the hell did her toes curl and her temperature climb? Why did she have to school her own tongue to stay in her mouth and her own body to hold itself back from rubbing against him with suggestive abandon?

He walked back and she returned to the video camera, hoping her hands weren't shaking.

Steve stared right at her and said the words. And then he winked and she felt that wink right down to her toes. Sure, it was corny. But it didn't matter. When Steve Jackson winked at a woman, she felt winked at. More, she felt important, sexy, cherished.

The room was so silent she heard the whir of the videotape and the sound of the traffic down on Market Street, and even the quiet hum of the air conditioning system.

"That was great, Steve. I think we've got enough for today."

"Will you go out with me tonight?" Steve asked, the lips that had just kissed her moving to form the words.

And reality snapped back.

He thought she was a party girl. What on earth was she going to do with him? She wasn't a casual woman who partied with anyone she felt like, who was winked at by gorgeous men on a regular basis.

She was a twenty-four-year-old professional who had far too much in common with a spinster twice her age for her own peace of mind.

Sonia's borrowed feathers couldn't have given a more false impression of the kind of bird she really was.

On the other hand, Steve didn't know that. And he wasn't going to be around long enough for it to matter. She might not be the most experienced girl on the block, but she knew there was sex in the air. A man like Steve Jackson didn't normally look at a woman like her twice, but he'd gotten it into his head that she was his kind of girl, and for a couple of weeks, she'd like to see what that might be like.

So she blinked, took a deep breath and a big fat gamble that she could be the bird Sonia's feathers proclaimed her—at least for a few weeks.

"Yes," she said, with an assumed casualness that impressed her. "I'd like that."

"Great." His smile was so warm you could roast marshmallows.

"I've got, um, some things to do first."

"No worries. I'll look around a bit. I was pretty tired yesterday, so I didn't see as much as I wanted."

"Right. Of course. How's the jet lag today?" He'd looked so good she hadn't thought to ask.

"Oh, right as rain. What time do you want me to come and fetch you?"

Oh, no. The last thing she wanted was him coming to her apartment. It was as far from party girl central as you could find. In fact, if she was honest with herself, it looked more like an office than a home, with her computer set up in the living room and the vast numbers of books and videos stacked on Ikea shelves pretty much giving away the truth about her social life.

"I'll come to you. It's easier."

"Right. I'll leave it to you where we go, shall I? I don't know the nightlife here yet."

And he thought she did?

"Absolutely. Leave it all to me."

Chapter Five

The minute she'd seen him inside the elevator and the doors had shut she dropped her I-know-what-I'm-doing act, turned, and sprinted for Sonia.

"Help!" she cried when she arrived panting at her friend's desk.

"Is the building on fire?" Sonia looked slightly alarmed and was already reaching for the desk drawer in which she kept her bag.

"What? No. The building's fine. Something much more important happened." She paused to catch her breath. "Steve Jackson asked me out."

"But this is good news. Why are you looking all in a panic?"

"Because I *am* all in a panic. I don't know what to wear, where to take him." She looked at the indefinably sexy air Sonia emitted along with a whiff of spicy perfume. "I don't know how to be you."

"Well, chica, it's not me he's asking for a date, and believe me, I batted my eyes every time he went by." She shrugged her bare shoulders and the straps of today's Latin sexpot dress rode up, hoisting her impressive cleavage along with them. "He likes you."

For some reason, this made Lise feel worse instead of better. If Steve Jackson chose her over someone as sexy and voluptuous as Sonia, he must think she was even wilder. She was never going to be able to pull this date thing off.

She grabbed her stomach. "Maalox. Must have Maalox."

"Would you just chill? You're a bag of nerves. If you ask me, an affair with a sexy hunk is the best thing for you."

"But I don't know where to take him. I hate clubs and parties. They're too noisy. I don't know how to be wild and free. I've been serious and focused my whole life," she wailed.

"And look where it's got you. Pain relievers and antacids are your two major food groups. You have way too much stress in your life. And sex," Sonia reminded her in a sexy Latino teacher's voice, "is the best stress reliever I know."

"If I'm not too stressed to actually have sex."

"There is that." Sonia sank back into her chair, deep in thought. "Okay," she said. "Here's what you do. We go shopping, we buy you something you wouldn't wear to the office, we get hair and nails and makeup done."

Lise glanced at her watch. "I hope you don't mean today. I couldn't possibly go today. I have a ton of work."

"Name me a day when you don't have a ton of work." She waved a hand toward Lise's office, where she could swear she heard the hum of her computer scolding her. "It will still be here tomorrow."

Sonia was right. Intellectually, Lise knew it. She was too focused on work, too stressed about making sure everything went perfectly on each campaign. And when she'd finished the campaign, she only continued to stress about the sales of each product she'd helped advertise and market: Had their branding worked? Was the media reflecting good or bad news?

If the product did well, she worried it was a fluke and sales would soon drop, and if it didn't do well—then she had to move up from the over-the-counter stomach stuff to something her doctor prescribed. And even her doctor had taken to lecturing her about her stress level.

Fair enough, she could try casually dating a handsome

surfer and see if it did anything for her stress level. And if it meant a few hours of preparation on her appearance, then she'd take them. After all, she told herself, it wasn't like she was cheating the company of her time. Steve Jackson was a critical part of one of the most exciting and ambitious campaigns she'd ever worked on. The hours she took off this afternoon she could make up by using their dinnertime to talk about his role in promoting Crane. "Okay. Then what?"

"You take him for dinner. You do those business dinners all the time. It's familiar territory."

Already she was feeling calmer. Of course she could do dinner; she wined and dined clients with reasonable frequency. "Okay. Dinner. Then what?"

"Then you suggest a nightcap back at his hotel. There's a nice bar on the top floor. Lots of fun people go there."

"Really? Do you?"

"Sure. Then you decide if you want to take it down a few floors to his place. Easy as pie."

"I make terrible pie." Lise was fairly certain that was deeply symbolic of how easy a time she was going to have with this dating-possibly-leading-to-an-affair business.

Still, it wasn't like she was a recluse or a nun. She'd just been on a temporary hiatus from men, fun, and sex for a few months or so. Around twelve months, in fact. Which brought to mind another problem.

"I'm not sure I remember how to have sex."

"It will come back to you," Sonia said with all the confidence of someone who's never gone without longer than a week. "You remember about safe sex?"

Lise rolled her eyes. "Yes."

"You take your own condoms and you use them."

Great. In between shopping for clothes for the woman she wished she was, getting her hair, makeup, and nails done, she had to squeeze in a trip to the Condom Shack.

Surely dinner with one man wasn't worth so much effort.

Then she viewed the final footage of Steve's commercial

run-through and her kneecaps melted. Oh, yeah. He was worth it.

So Lise found herself several hours later standing outside Steve's suite in the only dress she and Sonia had been able to compromise on. One that was sexy enough for Sonia and acceptable to her: a soft, pink-rose wrap dress with geometric flowers on it. The neck was a vee, but not too big of a vee. However, the silky material clung to her shape and, as Sonia had helpfully pointed out, one pull of the tie at her waist and she was out of there.

The shoes were pink and strappy, with a heel that had her almost pitching forward. A ridiculous little bag, not even big enough for her palm pilot or cell phone, held her wallet, lipstick, breath mints, her house keys, and, tucked at the bottom, three brand new condoms.

She took a deep breath, reminded herself this was her chance to live life to its fullest for a few weeks—nothing terrible could go wrong in such a short time. Even if he dumped her tomorrow—which she personally considered a pretty sure bet—she'd have had the experience of hopefully sleeping with the sexiest man she'd ever met.

She tapped on the door, wished she'd stuck at least a roll of Tums in her bag when Sonia wasn't looking, and waited. It seemed like a long time went by and nothing happened.

Maybe he hadn't heard her. She rapped again a little louder.

The door opened, and there was Steve in a hotel robe.

She blinked.

After taking in the glimpse of a chest so perfectly muscled that she almost whimpered, and musing that one tug on his robe would have him naked in exactly the same amount of time it would take her dress to come off, she realized that she might be a temporary party girl but she wasn't a call girl.

Had she misunderstood his request so completely?

Had he misjudged her so totally?

"What . . . ?" she began, still standing in the hallway feeling her anticipation of the evening drain away.

He blushed. The sexiest man she'd ever seen in her life blushed and looked uncertain. "I don't know what to wear," he said. "Can you give me a hand?"

Suddenly she felt better than she'd felt in a couple of hours. Steve unsure made her feel a little steadier on her feet. Of course it hadn't occurred to her that a man who spent most of his life on a surfboard would have a tough time knowing how to dress for dinner. "Sure," she said. *Ha*—like she had a clue.

She followed him in and could see through the open bedroom door that there were clothes all over. It looked like he'd had a tantrum and tossed them around the place.

"What do you usually wear at home when you go out?" she asked. Sydney couldn't be that different from San Francisco, could it?

"My jeans, my boots, and a T-shirt."

She felt happier by the second. "Then wear that."

"But I want to look good for you."

No worries there, as he might say. "You'll be fine. It's better to be comfortable."

He snorted. "Are you comfy in those shoes?"

"No." Emphatically, no. She was certain she could already feel a nascent corn on her baby toe, which was being squished hideously into the triangular toepiece of the shoes.

"Well, then. I can't wear jeans when you're all spiffy."

An idea that Sonia would absolutely hate occurred to her. The hell with Sonia. Part of Lise Atwater's job was to keep Steve happy and satisfied. If he wanted to wear jeans out to dinner, she'd have to accommodate him. Sonia might think her idea was terrible, but her toes were loving it. "I've got some workout stuff in the car. Shorts and T-shirt and sneakers." And thank goodness everything was actually clean since it had been so long since she'd had time to work out.

He looked so relieved it was her turn to laugh. "I'll run down and grab them. Be right back."

So she found herself shucking the new dress within an

hour of putting it on—and not for the reason she'd envisioned.

Oh, well. Her hair and makeup still looked good, she decided as she emerged from the opulent main bathroom of the suite.

He eyed her from top to bottom and she could have sworn his eyes warmed more than they had when she was wearing the fancy dress.

Steve wore those jeans he loved so much and a T-shirt advertising something with a lot of Xs that appeared to be a beer.

"If you're going to advertise a product, you should be wearing Crane casuals," she said.

He turned to her with an expression as though he'd just eaten something moldy. "Have you seen those things? If I want to look like a tropical fruit, I'll put a pineapple on my head."

She tried not to smirk. "They aren't all that bright. And the focus groups suggest they'll be amazingly popular when we launch," she wheedled.

"Do you mind if we don't talk about business tonight? I know it seems like we ought to, but I'd quite like a night off."

"I'm sorry." When had this happened to her that she'd become so obsessed with a job? "I get a little carried away sometimes. Wear your beer shirt."

"Right. Fancy a drink before we go?"

Well, she did and she didn't. It was so nice to be here alone with him and so scary to be here alone with him. Besides, he'd never been to the States before; he was probably dying for some nightlife. She had to think *party people* or she was going to blow this affair before it got off the ground.

"No thanks. Maybe when we come back later." Realizing what she'd said, she blushed scarlet. "I meant . . ."

He chuckled and, walking toward her, looped an arm around her shoulders that was friendly and yet . . . not. She had a strong feeling he had the same ideas about later as she did. "Let's go get some food."

As they headed for the door, she was looking anywhere except into the open bedroom door at the huge bed he'd miraculously emptied of clothes. A man didn't bother cleaning his bedroom unless . . .

A book caught her attention on the coffee table. She recognized the cover. Blinked, and blinked again. What was Plato's *Republic* doing on Steve Jackson's coffee table? Even stranger, what was it doing with a San Francisco tourist leaflet sticking out as a bookmark?

Was it possible her surfer boy read philosophy?

Chapter Six

Lise was acting really weird. Almost like she was new at this. Was it possible his party girl didn't party?

Whatever it was, he liked Lise a lot better in some decent walking shoes than those tippy-tappy things that all but hobbled her. Since he'd already had more than a fair glimpse of her upper body, he was pleased that her shorts were on the short side and showed off a pair of nice legs. They were long, and a bit on the slim side, but then so was Lise, and pale as though she either slathered on sunscreen or didn't get out much.

He was beginning to wonder which it might be.

They rode the elevator, and Lise seemed as preoccupied as he was so they didn't talk, but he couldn't help but notice the faint glow on her cheeks or the way her small breasts rose and fell under a T-shirt that interestingly enough didn't sport a single logo. They exited the elevator and strode across the lobby, her stride not so very much shorter than his now she was wearing proper shoes.

"Taxi, Mr. Jackson?"

He glanced at Lise, but she shook her head.

"No thanks, Ralph," he said.

"You know the doorman?" she asked when they were out of range.

"Well, not intimately. I know his name and he knows

mine, though I tell you I wish he'd stop calling me Mister. It gives me a funny feeling. Still, he's a nice bloke. Helps me with directions and places to go."

"Oh. You've probably already been to the Wharf."

"Well, yeah. Lots of good spots to eat, though."

They settled on an unimposing little place that served fantastic hot pot. It was the sort of place she went with a friend on a weeknight for good food and a comfortable atmosphere, but it wasn't the sort of place she'd take a client. Or a date she wanted to impress with her good taste and trendiness.

She was so screwed. Unless he believed that the trendy people of San Francisco wore a lot of tweed and denim, her rep as a trendsetter was done for.

Steve didn't seem to care who else was in the restaurant. He glanced around and nodded, visibly relaxing. "I like this place," he said. "It's comfortable. I won't spend all night worrying about which fork to use."

"And the food's great."

Once they'd ordered and he had a beer and she a glass of red wine, there was a pause.

In his well-washed T-shirt, she was reminded of his incredible torso. His arms were tanned and bulged in a mouth-watering way. Cynically, she knew he probably paid a fortune in personal training, owned his own tanning bed, and had his hair retouched every couple of weeks, but just for the moment she was falling for the fantasy that nature had actually endowed one man with so much. Some of the sun-smooched hair and muscles had to be from surfing. At least she hoped so.

"So, have you been surfing all your life?" she asked him.

"Well, I know how, but no. I'm not a big surfer."

"Oh." She tried not to let her disappointment show. She wasn't marrying the guy, she just maybe wanted to have some hot sex with him. What did she care if his hair was done my Monsieur Claude and his bronzed bod came via UV tubes?

Actually, she cared a lot. In her experience—and in her job and her personal life she'd had some—men who spent more time in front of the mirror than she did and paid more to get their hair styled tended to be a little self-absorbed.

The kind of guy who thought clitoris was a new, anti-aging skin serum was probably not going to be a big thrill in bed.

Oh, well, he looked good. She could sit here all evening, watch his incredible face while he talked, inevitably, about himself, and pretend she was watching him on TV and turn the sound down. Then she'd fill in the dialogue with what she wished he'd said.

"Can you surf well enough to fake it for a commercial?"

He shook his head and her heart sank, but he said, "Remember, we're not going to talk business."

Okay, she was going to assume the head shake was to indicate that he was admonishing her for bringing up work, not that he couldn't surf.

Please, let him know how to surf. No way she could find a pro to teach him in the short time available.

There was another pause. If they didn't talk about business, there was only one topic left that could possibly interest this man.

Giving in to the inevitable, she said, "Tell me about yourself," and turned the sound down, ready to watch his lips—those wonderful, half-smiling, excellent kisser lips—while he prepared to indulge in his favorite subject.

She had the sound properly adjusted and her first dubbed statement ready.

In her fantasy, he'd say, "There's really not much to tell. I'm modeling to put myself through medical college. Of course, I'll spend a couple of years with Doctors Without Borders before settling down to my own practice. All that's missing is the right woman to share my life with."

His lips started to move and the first couple of words shocked her so much she forgot to turn down the sound and listened to every word the man across from her said.

"Not much to tell, really," he said with an uncomfortable shrug. "I go to work, come home, mess about with me mates." He paused to think deeply. "Watch a lot of footie."

She blinked. "You watch people playing footsie?" She thought her own hobbies were on the sad side, but that was pathetic.

He laughed, not in a loud way, but enough to get his chest moving and his eyes dancing. "Not footsie, footie. Football to you, love."

"Oh." She'd heard vaguely about some barbaric sport where they banged heads a lot and bloodletting was normal. "Is that Aussie Rules?"

"Yeah, that's right."

"I hear it's brutal and that there are no rules."

"We-ell." He appeared to give the matter some thought. "It's not as formal as your American football, but there are rules."

And he could explain every game and every rule within that game if he looked at her with those amazing eyes and called her "love." Sure, she knew it was a casual endearment, but she didn't care.

"Do you like modeling?"

He looked at her and stopped mid-chew as though something he'd eaten didn't agree with him.

"I'm not a model!"

Right. Of course not. They all called themselves actors these days. He had three lines in a commercial, and he was an actor.

She helped herself to more of the hot pot, surprised at how her stomach was behaving itself. "How did you get into the business?"

"What? You mean Crane?"

She nodded. She meant modeling/acting, but at this point she wasn't going to argue definitions.

"Didn't Jennifer Talbot tell you about me?"

"Tell me what?" Jen had been beside herself with excitement over her find and sent him over. That was about all she knew. Oh, great. He'd probably won some Australian version of the Academy Awards and she'd just brutally insulted him by never having "seen his work." Damn it, when she'd found nothing about him on the Internet, she should have looked harder. Made Jen send her a bio to go along with his pictures.

"I was after a job in the shipping department at Crane. Jennifer spotted me standing at the reception desk and talked me into doing this."

Lise swallowed too fast and an entire fiery pepper went down the wrong way. She grabbed her water glass and gulped, blinking tears out of her eyes. She coughed and spluttered, feeling an unfamiliar burn, but even having her whole esophagus on fire couldn't prevent her squeaking, "You're a shipper?"

"Naah. I'm a steelworker, but there's not much work about at the moment. I'm on a temporary layoff."

"A steelworker?" she echoed faintly, her voice emerging kind of breathy and raspy. Her windpipe felt like a fire-breathing dragon that's breathed its last.

He seemed to be enjoying her shock. "That's right."

"Do you model on the side?"

He shook his head.

"Done any acting at all?"

Even before he shook his head his face twisted in a grimace, and she had her answer.

"I don't think I can act," he said. "That's why I needed you there today. I could say those words and pretend they were about me wanting to kiss you, and then it was all right."

"I wonder what you'll have to fantasize about before you can pretend to surf for the camera," she snapped, reverting to her suspicion that Jen had completely lost it.

His eyes darkened and her insides went hot in a way that had nothing to do with the misdirected pepper. "That's easy," he said in a tone that made her wish for silk lingerie and a queen-sized bed.

"So you're a steelworker," she said primly, not sure how to answer his obvious innuendo.

"That's right."

"What do you build?"

"Lots of things. Buildings, ships. I worked on a bridge for the better part of a year." He grimaced. "Hot work. Outside all the time, but I like being part of something permanent. You know? People will drive or walk or bicycle over that bridge for generations, and I helped build it."

She nodded, but really she couldn't relate. Her business was the opposite, style not substance, the advertisement not the product.

Wait a minute. If he'd worked outside—"Did the sun do that to your hair?"

He stuck a hand through his hair as though he'd forgotten he had any on his head. "Made it a bit lighter, I suppose."

"You'd pay a few hundred to get that look in a top salon."

He snorted. "*You* might."

And she didn't even have to ask about the tanning bed. She bet he had tan lines at mid-thigh, if he wore shorts to work, and at the sock mark because he'd wear work boots on the job.

Her heart began to pound so hard she felt dizzy.

It was real. It was all real. The muscles weren't gym-designed but literally forged by steel. The hair, the tan—they were natural.

He was real.

She was so used to dealing with people who, while they may have been given a very nice package in which to hold their bones and blood, liked to help nature along a little. But this guy was the real thing, in a world where even the phrase *the real thing* was an advertising slogan.

"That's me. Nothing very exciting. What about you then?"

"Me?" She almost fell off her chair as she received her

second powerful shock of the evening. When was the last time a man she was out with had asked about her?

When had she been out with a man on a real honest-to-goodness date, come to that? It had to have been six months ago at least, and so forgettable she hadn't repeated the experience until now. She'd been so immersed in work she'd forgotten—or maybe, a small voice whispered, she'd been using work to avoid the whole messy man/woman thing.

"I work too much," she admitted. And the pitiful truth was that work was becoming her life. Since she didn't seem to have anything more pressing to take its place, her job was growing like some science fiction blob, oozing into more and more of her waking hours and taking over.

"So you're a workaholic?"

She grimaced, hating the sound of that word and everything it implied, but feeling the need to be honest. "Yes."

He nodded and seemed to ponder something. How he was going to get out of here gracefully—and fast, perhaps. Then she saw his lips curve ever so slightly as though he were enjoying a private joke. *Great. Just great.* No wonder she rarely dated. Provoking barely contained laughter in an attractive man wasn't a big inducement to get back out there.

"Tell me something," he said, his mouth serious again but amusement lurking deep in his eyes. "Have you got stomach trouble?"

She rubbed her middle, which was surprisingly calm considering she was out on a date and eating spicy food. "I get stress stomach now and again."

He nodded and the single dimple creased. It would be devastatingly attractive if she didn't suspect it was caused by him laughing at how pathetic she was.

"Headaches?"

She blinked so hard it hurt. "What, are you a steelworker by day and a doctor by night?"

"There were headache tablets and some sort of antacid hanging out of your bag the first time I saw you."

"That's not all that was hanging out," she replied as the whole humiliating incident rose before her like Marley's ghost clinking and clanging, an endless round of mortification.

"Right." He didn't laugh. The dimple didn't even deepen, but she could tell it was an effort. "I thought you were a bit of a party girl."

Well, obviously now he knew her better he'd figured out that wasn't the case.

She shook her head, letting go of the brief fantasy. "That wasn't even my dress. Or my shoes."

"I like the shoes you've got on better."

"You do?"

"Sure. You can get about in those without tottering along like you've got bunions."

"Well . . ." She was so delighted she was almost speechless.

He leaned a little closer. "I did like that dress, though."

The atmosphere between them seemed suddenly too warm and she recalled that moment just before he'd kissed her back at the office, when she'd wanted him to, felt him think about it, hesitate, and then quietly move in.

She wanted him to kiss her again, so much she could hardly stop herself from making the first move.

"So," he said, suddenly seeming to reconsider and draw back out of imminent kissing range, "are you disappointed?"

"Disappointed?" She was disappointed he hadn't taken her up on her obvious invitation and kissed her. At the moment her mind couldn't hold a lot more.

"I'm a working man. I'm not sure what you were expecting, but—"

"A surfer boy. That's what I was expecting. A party-hard, life's-a-beach, model-on-the-side-for-some-extra-cash surfer boy."

"That's not me."

She started to smile. It began somewhere down in the region of her normally tortured belly and worked its way up. By the time it got to her face, it was a full-blown sunflower of a smile. "No," she said. "It's not."

He reached across the table for her hand. "Is that a good thing?"

She felt as though something in her love life might be about to go right. "Oh, yes," she said, the smile still stuck on her face. "That's a good thing."

For another moment they stayed like that. She felt the warm current running back and forth between their hands, felt the calluses she should have noticed before, felt his eyes on her face, and a quick glance up told her what was going on behind them was as hot as what was going on in her mind.

He pulled out his wallet and yanked out some of the cash she'd given him, threw it to the table. "Let's get out of here."

His urgency fed hers, but still she hesitated. "We should get a receipt. This is a deductible expense."

He raised their joined hands and kissed her knuckles.

"Oh, the hell with it," she said cheerfully, confident that they'd grossly overpaid for dinner, would deduct not a cent, and that she didn't care in the slightest.

Chapter Seven

It had seemed as though they'd walked quickly to get to the wharf, but that was a snail with a limp compared to the way they sprinted to get back to the hotel.

Sprinted uphill.

She gasped along, knowing the exercise was good for her, thinking maybe all her cellulite would turn to hard, trim muscle in the time it took to get back to his place, before her lungs gave out. As happy as she was that he was in such a hurry to be alone with her, she really needed to breathe.

But not to slow the pace. There was only one solution. "Taxi," she managed to gasp.

Luckily it was Friday and the place crawled with cabs. Soon they were bundled in one and sliding smoothly uphill. Still she felt the tension in the man beside her, was certain she heard him mumble, "Come on, come on," under his breath.

She knew exactly how he felt. She half-expected him to grab her in the taxi, but whether from shyness or manners or maybe men just didn't do that sort of thing in Australia, she was unmauled and anxiously wanting when they got to the hotel.

This time she was ready with her company credit card, which meant an instant receipt and no wasted time or money. She started to pass the card forward, caught the urgent expression in Steve's eyes, and thought, What am I doing? It was her turn to grab a twenty dollar bill for a seven dollar cab ride and toss it into the front, with a hurried thanks.

"Evening, Mr. Jackson."

"Hi, Ralph."

The doorman nodded to Lise. "There's a good crowd up on top tonight," he said. Steve stopped and stared at the doorman.

"He means in the bar on top of your hotel," she explained. "It's usually busy on Fridays."

"That's right, miss. Wonderful view of the city from up there."

"Thank you," she said. "Good night."

"There's only one view I want tonight," Steve said in an urgent undertone.

"Shh," she said as they broke Olympic speed records racing to the elevator.

Once the silver doors shut them in and they were fortunately alone, she wondered if he'd lunge for her the way she'd half-suspected he might in the cab.

He didn't. But the way he looked at her had the clothes damn near melting off her body. Maybe his hands didn't touch her, or his lips, but his gaze touched her everywhere, igniting tiny flames across her skin.

Anticipation, she decided, was the most potent aphrodisiac of all. He was staring at her body blatantly, and she felt all her womanly bits do their best to flirt with him. Her nipples fluttered to coy attention, her pulse thrummed to some ancient jungle beat, and her belly was growing heavy and warm with excitement.

"I've wanted you since the minute I saw your breast pop out of your dress," he said softly. And darned if both of her breasts didn't do their level best to toss themselves out for him a second time.

She heard a soft sigh and realized that it was hers.

"It's been driving me crazy that I saw only one. I want to see them both." He stopped to drag in a hungry breath. "I want to touch them."

"Mmm."

"And taste them."

Oh, this was more foreplay than she'd had in her entire last relationship. She was so hot it was all going to be over before they hit his suite.

She should have booked him on a lower floor.

"I wanted you before we even met, when I first saw your picture," she admitted, finally recognizing that had been the source of her dissatisfaction at first seeing the eight-by-tens. She'd felt not so much like Cinderella looking into the face of Prince Charming, but like one of the ugly stepsisters knowing that her foot would never fit the dainty glass slipper and that there could never be a chance for her.

But even as she'd wanted him so much, she'd felt twitchy and restless.

"Then I saw you in person."

"And?"

"And I only wanted you more."

"That's good."

"I guess."

"I've never had sex with anyone who wasn't Australian before," he said, looking momentarily shocked.

"I've never had sex with anyone who wasn't American," she realized.

"Christ, I hope I get it right."

They'd hit his floor, but the *ding* of the arriving elevator didn't come close to blocking out her snort of laughter. She'd been petrified of disappointing him, and even his half-joking admission of his own fears had her relaxing.

Maybe it was the way he'd kissed her earlier. Maybe it was the way he'd talked so sensibly at dinner, but somehow, she knew this was going to be okay.

They left the elevator together but the hurry had dispersed. It was as though something momentous were about to happen and they wanted to savor every minute. Or the anticipation was so strong they wanted to draw it out.

Or they were so scared they'd mess it up that they were in no hurry to dive between the sheets.

He pulled out his key card and they entered the room. He flipped on a lamp and in the pool of golden light he appeared mysterious, his eyes dark and serious but oh, how they pulled her to him.

"Do you want a drink?" he asked.

"No. I just want to get the first time over with."

She gasped when she realized she'd said those words aloud, feeling herself blush scarlet. "I mean—" Oh, he might as well know the truth. He was going to find out soon enough. "I'm just so awkward at this."

"What, sex? Of course you're not."

"Excuse me, but I think I'd know better than you."

Steve shook his head at her. "It's all those flipping magazines you women read. I went through a load of them on the flight over, and I've never seen so much rubbish."

"What are you talking about?" She did a lot of advertising in those magazines.

"Those articles," he rolled his gaze. "How to look better naked, what men really mean when they say I love you, thirty-seven-and-a-half tricks to drive him wild in bed." He dropped his voice back to its normal register. "No wonder everyone in America thinks they need an analyst. How can a magazine article tell them how to have better sex or more orgasms?"

Oh, she wished he hadn't mentioned orgasms. Her stomach gave its first twinge of the evening. What if she didn't have one? She was so nervous she wasn't sure she had it in her. In fact, this whole thing was a terrible idea.

"I think maybe—"

"I'll tell you what I think; if people spent less time worrying about what they look like naked and keeping score-cards on how many tricks they pulled in bed, they might actually enjoy sex more."

"Do we have to talk about this right now?" Never mind the antacid, she was heading into Valium territory. And frankly, she wished she could have a time-out and read up on how to look slimmer when naked, have more orgasms, and hell, if there were thirty-seven-and-a-half sex tricks, she was short about thirty-five.

But he was grinning at her in a totally appealing way, and despite the fact that she was feeling insecure, she was also feeling that if she walked away from this now, she'd always regret it.

"I don't know thirty-seven-and-a-half tricks," she said. "I don't think I know any."

He took a step closer. "Darlin', tricks are for magic shows." He reached forward and touched her face, skimming the leathery working-man pads of his fingers down her cheek and over the ledge of her jaw, and down the soft, sensitive skin of her throat.

It felt so good she let her head fall back, offering him the full length of her throat. She felt the increasing warmth as he neared, and then the soft brush of his lips against the hollow beneath her jaw.

"That's a trick," she murmured.

"What is?" His words rumbled against her skin in a way that made her shiver.

"You kiss my throat and it makes my heart pound."

"Does it?" A lazy note of amusement curled through his words and she felt herself smile along with him as his hand traveled down the left side of her chest, settling just above her breast where her heart was knocking itself out.

"It's happening to me, too," he told her and, running a hand down her arm, picked up her wrist and placed her palm against his own chest. And he was right. His heart was beating out a nice tattoo of its own.

"I think you're beautiful," he said, his lips cruising slowly back up her throat to her mouth.

"I'm not." She always thought she was sort of funny-looking. Her chin was too square, her nose a little more defined than was seemly, her eyes were pretty, but they belonged in a softer face.

"That's part of your charm. You don't even see how pretty you are."

She'd have to find that magazine. He seemed to be pulling out the whole bag of tricks and dropping them at her feet. Not that she really cared; she liked flattery. God knows she got little enough of it.

Then his mouth closed over hers and the running commentary in her head seemed to shut down.

Zap. Like her brain had been shocked into a coma. This was all about feeling. The warmth of his lips against hers, the feel of his strong, bridge-building arms around her, the way he eased her up against him so smoothly she was pressed chest to groin before she noticed they'd moved closer.

And everywhere they touched something was happening. Little jolts and surges of electricity zapping back and forth, his body hardening, hers softening, his continuing to harden until she felt the bulge of him so far up her belly she wondered if men were built different in Australia. Maybe all that sun and football and beer did something to their development.

And maybe an entire year without sex had closed her up like a squeezed-out tube of toothpaste.

With a tiny groan, she wondered if it was too late to back out of this.

"Hey, what's going on?" he asked, raising his head to look down at her."

"Nothing."

"I could have sworn you were right with me and then you went somewhere. What's going on in that busy brain of yours? What were you just thinking about?"

"Toothpaste."

"Toothpaste?" He pulled back to stare down his nose at her. "Is this some California sex thing I've never heard of?"

"No. It's just me being an idiot."

"Well, stop it. You stay with me, got it?" He squeezed her shoulders. "No thinking."

"I can't help it," she wailed. "I warned you. I'm hopeless at sex. I can't turn my mind off."

"Well, don't turn it off then. But channel it into a better direction than oral hygiene, or you'll put me off."

"I don't know how," she admitted miserably.

He sighed. "I can see I'm going to have to get brutal with you."

She gulped. "You are?"

"Yes. Very brutal." He sounded fierce, but those crazy lights were dancing in his eyes again, the kind that turned her blood to fizzy soda. While she was focusing on those eyes, she felt his hands at her chest and realized with a spurt of shock liberally mixed with excitement that he'd bared her right breast. Without any finesse or buildup, he'd simply pulled up her T-shirt and popped the thing out of her bra cup.

Now that it was free, she felt the air against her nipple and the warm, rough heaviness of his hand where she was so sensitive.

"Now what are you thinking about?" he asked her.

She swallowed. "Not toothpaste."

"Come on." He feathered his fingertips over her nipple and her whole body responded. "What are you thinking about when I do this?"

"Not thinking," she murmured. "Feeling."

"Good," he whispered. "That's very good. Now, every time you want to go off on another toothpaste tangent, bring yourself back and concentrate on what your body is feeling at that very moment."

"Where did you learn—? Hunh," she gasped as a thumb and finger pinched her nipple.

"What does that feel like?"

"A pinch of fire." She stopped to pant in a breath. "Spreading heat."

"Good. Stop thinking. Stay focused."

"Don't do that again."

"Don't make me."

He kept playing with that one breast, driving her semi-crazy, and making the other one feel frustrated and left out. "I haven't been able to stop thinking about the sight of this one breast at the airport that day. There was something about just the glimpse of that one that's kept me wondering what the rest of you looks like."

"Nothing special, believe m—" Her word ended on a tiny squeak as he squeezed her nipple again.

"Would you stop that?" she ordered, but her protest was wimpy at best. She found she liked the radiating warmth that followed the quick pinch.

"When you stop putting yourself down."

Chapter Eight

He kept touching and toying with that one breast, but she didn't think he was doing it any longer to keep her mind on the proceedings; he was doing it because he was enjoying himself. She didn't need any more reminders to stay in the moment. She was so far in the moment she might never get out.

"I can't tell you how much I've thought about this one breast. I've wanted to touch it, and taste it."

"I have two breasts, you know," she informed him, since the other one was starting to act like a jealous sibling and demand attention.

"Do you?" he said, half-laughing, and dropping his hands to the hem of her T-shirt, pulled it slowly up and over her head. When she'd dressed in her sexy dress she'd imagined a seduction scene of whispering silk and perhaps a little champagne, not that she'd be stripping out of T-shirt, shorts, and running shoes. Still, at least her underwear was as sexy as she knew how. With her arms raised above her head for the T-shirt to slide off, her breasts were going to look their best. Perky and uplifted. Of course, since he'd left the left one exposed and the right still covered by her coffee-colored silk bra cup, she was going to look a little odd, but she was in the moment and beyond caring.

And the little growling sound he made when he glanced

down at her had her feeling pretty damn good about her less-than-perfect body.

He tossed the T-shirt aside and stood looking at her, then with one quick move, he scooped the second cup beneath her right breast and smiled as though one of the universe's great secrets had been revealed.

Her breasts felt cantilevered and thrust forward against the underwire that provided most of her cleavage, but it made her feel wanton and daring.

Deciding that fair was fair, she went to work on his shirt, pulling it up and over his head.

Oh, she thought when she saw him naked from the waist up, no personal trainer in the world was that good. He had a long torso, wide at the chest and narrow at the waist, a nice triangle of reddish brown hair at his chest, and just a sprinkle of freckles on his shoulders.

Unable to stop herself, so very in the moment that the idea of holding back was impossible, she put her arms around him, pulled forward, and buried her face in his chest. The hair tickled but the skin beneath was silken leather. He smelled of warmth and sun and maybe a bit like steel.

She put her tongue out and tasted him and just as she was thinking about a nibble or two, she felt big hands cup her butt and she rose into the air. Instinctively she wrapped her legs around his waist and her arms around his neck as he carried her into the bedroom and then tossed her backwards onto the bed.

He leaned down and untied each of her shoes and pulled them and the tennis socks off. Then, grasping the waist of her shorts and panties together slid them down and off.

He put his hands to the snap of his jeans and she watched, mesmerized. He slid them and his underwear down with no ceremony and she decided there was definitely something to her theory about the Australian sunshine. Never had she seen a more spectacular male body.

She wasn't going to think about squeezed-out tubes of

toothpaste; she was going to stay in the moment and trust her body. Which was sending urgent messages letting her know it was up for the challenge.

"You're staring at me like you've never seen a naked man before," he said, half-laughing but she thought a little embarrassed, too.

"I've never seen one as gorgeous as you before," she told him.

"I like the look of you, too."

He eased down beside her on the bed and kissed her as though he had all the time in the world and there was nothing he'd rather do for all eternity than kiss her.

His fingers traced patterns on her chest and belly, inching slightly lower on each pass. "Do you still want to get this first time over with?" he asked softly.

Had she said that? What had she been thinking? This wasn't something to be rushed, but to be savored and enjoyed.

"No," she said. "I don't want to rush." She sighed as his fingers brushed just below her belly button. "I don't have to be anywhere until Monday morning."

Although, admittedly, there were parts of her body that did want to move right along. Certain anxious parts, too-long denied, were ready to celebrate in full force.

But no. She wanted not only to stay in this moment, but to stretch it out and make it last.

"I don't have to be anywhere until Monday morning either," he said and began kissing her breasts. He gave them his full attention for a minute or so and then abruptly reared up to gaze down at her with mild irritation. "Now what?"

"Pardon?"

He held her gaze with eyes that seemed to see right into her. "You're thinking again."

Damn, this was getting spooky. "How do you know?"

"I make my living working with my hands. When you start thinking, I dunno, your skin changes, and your muscles start to tense up." He continued to gaze down at her and then smiled a little. "And you get a furrow right between your eyes," he said and leaned forward to kiss a spot midway between her eyebrows that she didn't think had ever been kissed before.

"Sorry."

"What were you thinking about that made you turn into a plank?"

She threw her arm across her eyes. Now she was a plank. *Great.* "I'm such an idiot. I wish I hadn't said I don't have to be anywhere until Monday. It makes me sound like I have no social life. And maybe you don't want me hanging around until Monday." There. He'd asked, and she'd told him the truth. So she was pathetic and had no social life. Now he knew.

"That's what you were thinking about?"

"Yes."

"That's all?"

Pause. "Ye-es . . . mostly."

From behind her arm she couldn't see anything, but she felt the shifting and then the lack of warmth and knew he'd moved away. She dropped her arm and found him getting right off the bed. She felt so miserable she wanted to curl into a ball and start wailing.

While she watched, he grabbed one of the matching upholstered armchairs, dragged it to the bedside, and sat down.

"All right," he said. "Let's have all of it. What else is going through that maddening head of yours?"

"Nothing. I—I . . ."

"You what?"

"I forgot to ask if you're married."

His brows flew up at that. "Do you think I'm the sort of bloke who'd be sitting here naked with you if I had a wife at home?"

She shook her head. "But my judgment isn't always the best."

"I'm not married."

She released the breath she'd been holding, and then wondered how he could possibly be single? A man who looked that incredible in nothing but a hotel armchair had no business being unattached. But then he hadn't actually said he was single. He'd said he wasn't married.

"Girlfriend?"

He shook his head. "Broke up three months ago when she started looking at wedding rings."

"Oh." So he wasn't a commitment kind of guy. Fair enough. She wasn't looking to marry the man. So long as he wasn't committing adultery in sleeping with her, did she really care that wedding rings freaked him out?

No, she thought, giving him her best shot at a comeback-to-bed smile; wedding rings were the last thing on her mind.

He seemed to get the message pretty loud and clear, tipping forward and out of the chair until he was a heartbeat away, his lips so near to kissing her that her own tingled.

"No more thinking," he ordered.

"I'm all done." As she wrapped her arms around him she accepted that he was absolutely, exactly what she needed.

When he kissed her she opened her mouth to him, wanting to give him everything she had. But even with the heat of their fused mouths, she felt the soft touch of his skin against hers, and the sliding of their limbs as they eased against each other, testing and finding the best ways to fit.

She was aware of his strength, of the muscles that had so much in common with the metal he worked with, and beneath that the solid core of integrity she'd sensed. He was a simple working man; nothing fancy or contrived about him. For a woman who made her living creating illusions, it was amazing to find a man who was exactly what he seemed.

He was also frighteningly perceptive, and more sensitive to her body and its nuances than any man had ever been. He didn't need to worry about her getting carried away with thinking; she was here and this was now and his body felt so very good moving against hers that thinking became impossible. She focused instead on enjoying this amazing night that might never be repeated. His mouth whispered secrets to her when they were kissing that went deeper than words.

For once in her sex life, she didn't close off, or back off, or turn her mind on to shut her heart off. Instead she opened herself to everything. To the sensations of touch and smell and taste, and behind them the sneaky deeper feelings that filtered through her barriers. If, in the back of every- thing, she suspected there might be an inevitable hurt, she decided tomorrow's pain was well worth tonight's pleasure.

And that was the last thought she allowed herself.

With a sigh of acceptance that any Buddhist would be proud of, she let herself open to the moment and only the moment.

While he kissed her, his chest rubbed hers, sending warm waves of sensation eddying to every part of her. His belly crowding hers added to the warmth, and when his erection nudged at her softness, warmth spiked to heat.

Heat so hot her insides were melting. She found she was moving mindlessly with him and against him in a kind of dance where she seemed to know every move.

She discovered she was on her back with her legs wrapped around his waist and he was nudging her open, and she'd never felt so open or receptive. With lazy assur- ance, he reached past her head to a canvas zippered pouch she'd noticed on the bedside table. He flipped it open and removed a condom. While continuing to kiss her, he sheathed himself with so little fuss and such easy grace that the moves felt like part of his foreplay. Indeed, just knowing that he was that close to entering her upped her heat quo- tient.

He entered her with a long, smooth slide that felt so inti- mate she experienced a moment's panic, and might have backed off except that he held her gaze, his own open and locked on hers. And because she'd already opened herself up too far to close off now, she left her eyes open and watched his pupils darken, certain her own were doing the same.

He thrust up and back, sliding faster, and she met him thrust for thrust until not only were her eyes open but her mouth as she gasped for breath. Every part of her was open and receiving: her lungs, dragging in the air she needed, her heart, pounding to keep up with her excitement, her legs, widespread to wrap around him snugly, and her very core, open to receive all of him.

What she hadn't opened, he did, pushing up inside her where she'd never been stretched before, open and opening farther and wider until the center wouldn't hold and the circle burst upon her as every part of her—heart, lungs, eyes, mouth, vagina—seemed to blow apart. And yet he didn't stop, but drove still harder and higher, so she was hanging on for dear life, as a cascade of mini-explosions shook her and then with a great roar, she heard and felt his own explosion.

Even as he lay collapsed on top of her, his sweat dampening her body, she knew something momentous had happened.

He lay on top of her, heavy but not, and she traced the muscles of his back, still warm and heaving a little. His hair was damp when she touched it, and when she kissed his neck where it joined his shoulder, his smell was as potent as any aphrodisiac.

She felt him twitch inside her. This amazing, gorgeous, sexy man, come from the other side of the world to pleasure her, was hers until Monday. She smiled and kissed his neck again.

"You're not thinking are you?" a low voice rumbled into the pillow beside her head.

"Nope," she assured him. "I am completely in this moment."

"It's a bloody good moment."

She smiled all over her body. "Yes. It is."

Chapter Nine

"You know," she said, when her breath was back and she was in her body once more, "that really worked for me. It's not easy for me to shut off my mind and go with my feelings, but you really helped me do it."

He started to laugh. A quiet chuckle that built until he had to sit up in bed and bend over.

"My sexual performance renders you helpless with laughter?" she asked tartly, trying to push him away, which was a bit like trying to push a bus over with one hand.

"No. Stop or I'll go off again." She waited in annoyed silence until he'd got hold of himself. "You know where I got that from?"

"Some Australian woman named Bridget who's a champion diver and sex goddess and strips on the side?"

He shook his head, still shaken by silent chuckles. "That bloody stupid magazine I read on the plane. I think it was sex tip number three. Stay in the moment. It seemed so damned silly to me that anyone wouldn't be in the moment that the notion stuck."

Somewhat mollified, she made a mental note to start reading more women's magazine articles—usually she concentrated on the ads. "It's a pretty good tip," she admitted. It had certainly worked for her. "Maybe we should write a letter to the magazine."

"Does everything in your life have to revolve around the media?"

She thought about it, then slanted a look up at him through her lashes. "Well, it is my job. I always think in terms of exposure for my clients."

There was a more than usual ruddiness about his cheeks. "You may want to expose yourself for a silly women's magazine, but I'm not going to."

It was her turn to laugh. "Don't worry. This will stay our little secret." Besides, he'd be exposed enough in the ads they'd already booked for a national campaign.

But that was work, and work was banished until Monday. She leaned over and kissed him. "I think I should practice that again," she told him.

The sexy glint was back in his eyes. "Practice what?"

"Staying in the moment."

"You expect me to provide you with another 'moment'?"

She reached behind her to the canvas pouch, which she saw was well-stocked. She handed him a small square pouch. "Yep," she said.

He laughed. "I was thinking the same thing myself."

She was still smiling when she awoke the next morning and lazily replayed all the events of the night before. Her body felt pliant, satiated, and earthy. It might be a cliché, but she had to admit she'd never known sex could be like that, so intimate and tender and yet raunchy and fun.

Steve was the kind of man a woman could wait years for, the kind she'd stopped believing existed, the kind who . . . her fantasy dissolved as she recalled one particular detail from the night before.

"You've got the furrow back," said a sleepy voice beside her and she realized he'd woken sometime during her mental reverie and been watching her.

She glanced up at his sleepy, sexy face, the shadow of morning stubble only adding to his appeal. "You don't want to get married," she said, voicing the thought that had stopped her foolish fantasies cold.

Now it was his turn to furrow. "Not at the moment, no."

"Just haven't found the right girl?" It was strange, to say the least, to have this conversation while naked and still in the blissful morning-after state, but it seemed important to know. Not that she wanted to marry him or anything, but she felt she ought to understand a little more about the man who'd spent a good part of the night inside her body.

He scratched his head using both hands, which made his sun-kissed hair stick out in adorable tufts. "In order to answer that, I have to tell you a bit of my life story. Sure you want to hear it?"

"Yes. I'd love to." She sensed he was uncomfortable talking about himself, which made her all the more determined to hear the story.

He reached out and idly began to play with the ends of her hair, but she could tell he'd as good as left the room. He was looking inward and it was obvious he didn't like what he saw.

Even without knowing what he was about to say, she put her arms around him.

"When I was a teenager, my mum got sick." He paused for a moment. "Cancer."

"Oh, I'm so sorry."

"Yeah. Thanks. She died."

Not knowing what to say, she bit her lip and listened.

"I've got younger brothers and sisters that I had to help look after."

"What about your father?"

His eyes, usually so wonderfully expressive, were blank. "He couldn't handle it. He left when Mum's hair all fell out from the chemotherapy."

She wanted to cry for that poor boy who'd lost so much so young. "How old were you?"

"Sixteen. I was lucky enough to get taken on to apprentice as a steelworker. My uncle helped me get the job, and he and my aunt took us in, but it was a hard go for a bit."

He'd had to leave school early to help support his family. Now the philosophy book she'd seen on his table made sense. He must be on a path of self-education.

"Anyway. I'm in no hurry to settle down."

It wasn't much of an answer, and she found herself sorting through what he'd told her to find the answer to her question. "You mean you don't want to get married because you feel like you've already raised a family and now you want to live your own life?"

He shrugged and looked uncomfortable. "I s'pose."

Well, she hadn't let him pry into her head at uncomfortably intimate moments to let him get away with this kind of evasion. Obviously, it wasn't fear of family commitments that was stopping him. What then? He wouldn't meet her gaze, kept glancing off into the corner furtively, almost as if he were guilty of something.

Guilty. That's when it hit her.

"It's your father, isn't it?"

"What about him?" He said the words with a belligerent edge.

Bingo. "You're afraid you're like him, aren't you?"

"You don't know—"

"You're afraid you'll walk out on a woman when she needs you most. That you've got some deeply defective gene inside you that—"

"All right." She jumped at the force of his words. He threw off the covers, got out of bed, and stomped toward the door leading out of the bedroom. "That's your answer," he threw over his shoulder. "I don't ever want to get married in case I turn out to be a shit like my old man."

"But you've already proven you're not." He was standing, staring out of the open bedroom door into the outer room, and she had a good idea he was thinking about walking through it. Naked or not, she jumped out of bed and threw her arms around him from behind, pressing her breasts to his back and hugging all of him she could reach. She kissed him between his shoulder blades. "You're a good man."

"Just don't get any dreamy-eyed fantasies about me," he said gruffly.

Too late, she thought, but wisely kept that one to herself. "Okay, I won't. Now come back to bed."

He turned and she could see the bleakness still lurking at the back of his eyes, but he made a fair attempt at a return to his earlier mood. "You're all done now with thinking?"

She nodded. "All done."

He walked her backwards to the bed and as he did so, he kissed her long and hard, and she was pleased to note his erection returned to all its former glory—also long and hard.

But when they got back to bed somehow a deeper awareness had followed them. He made love to her as though he were desperate. And she gave him every bit of herself.

Including her heart.

"So," she said, as they lay sated and lazy in bed, her index finger idly tracing the muscles of his chest, "do you have an agent?"

His chest went up and down as a laugh/cough hybrid shook him. "What would I want with an agent?"

"An agent looks after your interests, so you get paid a fair rate."

"Have you seen how much I'm getting paid? Even with overtime that would be about a year's wages at home."

"Yes. I've seen your contract. And Jen's a good person, she wouldn't cheat you. What you're being paid is fair. But you should still have someone looking after your interests."

He scratched his chest where she'd been idly pulling at the hair there. She must have tickled him. Too bad, she was having fun.

"I'd have to pay an agent, right?"

"Yes, of course. They'd take a percentage of your earnings."

"So I'm going to pay some California shark a portion of my wages so he can tell me I'm getting good money? No, thank you. Let the agent parade around in his bathing cossy and wink at cameras if he wants the money."

He was so cute she had to stop and kiss him. Which, naturally, led to more kissing and soon kissing wasn't enough and after missing breakfast they were in serious danger of missing lunch.

"Let's order room service," she said.

"It's a terrible price," he informed her.

"I know." She grinned at him. "We'll eat in bed."

"Now you're talking."

They might be eating naked in bed, with hotel pillows piled behind them, but still she wasn't finished with a subject that could be to Steve's benefit.

"So, let's say your commercials and magazine ads are amazingly well-received and Crane's success in the States is due partly to you as the spokesman."

He grinned at her. "Let's."

"Now we want you for more commercials. In fact, we want to bind you to an exclusive contract. That means you can't work for anyone else."

"Thanks, I know what exclusive means."

Okay. Sore point there. Interesting.

"Right. I get a bit pedantic sometimes." She paused, but he didn't seem to have any trouble with pedantic, either, so she went on. "If Crane wants an arrangement like that, and I'm not saying it will happen but it could"—especially, she thought, if he steamed up the screen on every commercial the way he'd come across on the video recorder when he'd winked at her—"then what would you do?"

"I'd go home. I'm not staying here forever, you know. I've got my proper job to get back to. We should be called back in another month or so."

Her mouth dropped open at the notion that he might give up a seriously cushy deal right here to go back to hammering steel or whatever he did, until he got laid off again. "You have got to be kidding."

He shrugged. "This isn't a proper job. It's a holiday.

Good money, travel, staying in a swanky place," he glanced her way, "and spending time with a sexy California girl."

A small pang smote her heart, but she stifled it. Of course he was going home. Who was she kidding? She'd somehow managed to do an end run around the fairy tale and she, the ugly stepsister, had crammed her oversized clodhopper into a dainty slipper. Naturally, it couldn't last.

Handsome fairy-tale princes might play footsie with stepsisters, but it was Cinderella they married.

Some as yet unknown antipodean Cinderella was going to spend her life with Steve Jackson, and she'd be nothing but a memory. A shoe that never really fit.

Oh, well, she reminded herself, she had now. And he had called her sexy.

"Steve," she said, keeping her voice calm and business-casual with an effort, when she wanted to throw herself on his spectacular chest and beg him to love her, "do you have any idea of the kind of money we'd be talking? If you become a fresh face and you can move product, a lot of companies are going to want to talk to you. You should have an agent simply to protect your interests."

"I'm sure everything you're saying is real smart, and I appreciate what you're trying to do for me, but I'm not a fresh face. I'm a bloke who builds bridges."

"Okay," she said softly. "Pass the lox and cream cheese."

She knew a couple of reputable agents who would be a good fit with Steve. She wasn't giving up. For his own good.

Chapter Ten

"I can't do this," Steve said to Lise, knocking away the hands of the man currently attempting to rub baby oil into his biceps—and knocking them none too gently.

She smirked as though she thought this was all a great joke, him in boardies you'd need sunglasses to look at and with some Bruce putting his hands all over him. He'd had a better day the time a bit of scaffolding had fallen on his head and left him with a broken hard hat and a concussion. At least he'd kept his pants on and still felt like a man at the end of the day. He might not have known which man he was, but once the headache abated, all his wits had returned.

Two weeks of reading nauseating scripts for radio adverts, of practicing for TV, and the only reason he hadn't bolted for home was that at the end of every day, Lise was his. But today was the worst.

Today he was half-naked, his hair had something sprayed on it that smelled like his sister when she was going out, they were rubbing oil on his body to make him look wet, and there was a makeup woman eyeing him in a way that made him extremely uncomfortable.

They were in the dressing room of a studio where they were shooting ads for magazines. It turned out they weren't even going to snap the photos near the sea. They'd put the sea in later, with a computer, Lise had told him.

He was less than pleased. He might be able to pretend he was having a great day of sun and surf on one of Crane's boards if he was actually standing in the sun with the ocean at his back, but he was being asked to pretend. The whole thing was fake.

Big round lights and silver umbrellas to mimic the sun, a pile of sand trucked in from somewhere to create a beach, baby oil instead of ocean water, and an enormous fan that he suspected was going to be the sea breeze.

The fellow with the baby oil looked as exasperated as Steve felt. "Look," he said, waving his oily hands about, "I really need to—"

"Could we have a minute?" Lise asked in that calm way she had, as though this sort of thing happened every day. Maybe to her it did.

"We're shooting in fifteen minutes," baby oil boy said. "You know how Sebastian is about his schedule."

"Sebastian?" Steve was pretty sure he wouldn't trust anyone named Sebastian.

"The photographer," Lise explained.

"Great. Why couldn't they find a pretty girl to take photos? I've got to prance around in shorts in front of a guy named Sebastian?"

Lise looked at him for a long moment as though trying to work something out. How to get him off the job and on the next plane to Sydney, he hoped.

She was very much the working woman today, with a skirt that was longer than he liked, and a white top that looked like a man's shirt.

She glanced at her watch and took a step closer. "This shoot is important, Steve. I really need you to work with us."

"I know, but it's bloody hard when I've got to play pretend all the time."

She took another step closer and smiled, not the wonderful open smile she offered him in their intimate times, but the business, everything's-going-to-be-all-right-if-you-do-as-I-say smile he wasn't so keen on. "I don't want you to think about the photographer, or the makeup people."

"What about these damn shorts then?"

Her lips quivered, but she shook her head solemnly. "Not them, either. We've talked about this, and we've practiced," she reminded him. Well, they'd practiced mostly at his hotel or her apartment when she'd been a lot closer to naked and sex had always ended up a part of the session. "You need to imagine you're catching a wave and the feeling's exhilarating, the wind's whipping through your hair, and you're hanging onto the crest and ready to ride it right into the finish. Just like we practiced."

She picked up the bottle of baby oil and poured some into her hand. As she rubbed it into his shoulders he relaxed a little, but only a little. He said, "When we practiced, I didn't smell like babies and girls."

"Forget it. Concentrate on the surf scene I just described. You were fantastic when it was just the two of us."

He shifted a little and admitted, "When we were practicing, I wasn't thinking about surfing."

"You weren't?" Her hand stalled in mid-circle so he felt only her fingers—four delicate touches on his shoulder. "But you had the fiercest look of concentration on your face; I felt the ride you were taking."

"I wasn't thinking about riding a surfboard," he told her grumpily. "I was thinking about riding you."

She made a tiny sound behind him and it seemed as though she moved closer. "Riding me?"

"That's right. I thought about riding you, cresting the wave, taking it all the way into the beach. I can do it when I'm looking at you half-naked, and know we're going to end up all over each other, but I don't think it's going to work when I'm looking at a bloke named Sebastian."

He could see his words were having an effect on her, and in spite of his disgruntlement, he began to stir as he felt her fingers go back to rubbing the oil into his body.

"All right. Whatever works."

"You naked works."

"When you smell this baby oil," she said softly, "don't think about babies. Think about how it's going to feel when I rub oil all over you." Her movements changed from efficient to sensual. "When you finish here, we're heading straight for your hotel, with this oil, and I will rub it all over you."

He was glad the boarder shorts were so baggy because his focus was coming back as sharply as she could wish. But he didn't want her thinking he was a complete pushover. "Not enough," he said, turning.

Her eyes widened slightly as he looked down at her, so prim and proper, but for her glistening oil-drenched hands. "I need to be able to see you in order to keep my mind focused."

"All right." She nodded slowly. "I'll stand behind the photographer for the whole session so you can see me."

"Still not enough," he said, liking the way her eyes were starting to smolder. Her tits were probably jumping to attention too, but who could tell with that ridiculous shirt.

He stared at her chest, and smiled. No one could tell what was under there, no one but him. "I need more incentive."

Since his hands were perfectly oil-free he didn't so much as smudge the white cotton when he swiftly undid the buttons. With her greasy hands she couldn't stop him without covering herself with oil, so she flapped them about helplessly, saying, "What are you doing?" "Stop it!" and "Steeve," in increasing agitation until he had every button undone and the whole shirt flapping open.

Instead of the sexy lingerie she wore in the evenings, she now wore a sensible white cotton bra that was all about support and comfort he imagined since it certainly wasn't sexy. Well, it was to him, but he doubted that had been her intent.

He reached around her back and unsnapped the bra.

Now her eyes verged on alarm. "What do you think you're doing?"

"Hold your arms out very still so you don't get any grease on your shirt," he ordered her, enjoying himself more by the second.

"If you think I'm going out there naked, you're crazy," she whispered, startled and blushing, and checking over her shoulder every other second.

"Don't worry. You'll get your shirt back," he said. All he planned to keep was the bra. Since he was already sliding the shirt down her arms she had little choice but to hold her hands still. He was careful not to let the fabric touch her fingers. Then the shirt was in his hand and she stood before him in an undone white bra and a businesslike skirt, bare legs, and flat navy sandals.

He slipped the bra off her arms while she gasped and glanced over her shoulder yet again toward the door. "Hurry up, I hate this," she muttered, but her caramel-colored nipples told a different story. They were perky as hell, and just the sight of them had him feeling more and more confident.

He stooped to kiss each one in turn, sucking them swiftly into his mouth so she moaned and shivered. He anchored the bra into the waistband of his shorts temporarily and then politely held the shirt for her to slip her arms into.

"What about my bra?" she asked, not moving.

"I like knowing your breasts are naked under that shirt, and waiting for me."

"Oh," she said it matter-of-factly, but he could hear that she was turned on.

He slipped the buttons back in place, working from the bottom up so her breasts were on display as long as possible, while she kept glancing over her shoulder and telling him to hurry.

There was a knock on the door and she jumped. "Five minutes," the snotty oil applier yelled through the door.

"We'll be there," she called back in a loud, clear voice, then in an undertone gasped, "What are you doing now?"

"Your panties."

"No!"

But his hands were already under her skirt and he was grasping the waistband. Even through the cotton he could feel her heat. He laughed up into her blushing face. "It's to help me focus."

She might want to look stern, but he could see the smile trying to peep through. He hooked his thumbs and slid the cotton down her legs and waited while she stepped out of them. As he'd suspected, they were a match for the bra. Sensible, white, and cotton.

He took bra and panties and walked to where he'd left his rucksack in the corner of the room. He stuffed the garments in the outer pocket and zipped it.

"All right. I hope you're satisfied. Now let's go."

"Wait, you missed a bit with the oil," he said, reaching for the bottle and tilted it so oil coated the tip of his middle finger.

"Where?" She was looking him over critically, so she jumped when he raised her skirt with one hand and reached under it with the other. He slipped his hand between her thighs before she'd quite grasped his intent.

He knew her body so well that he found her sweet spot unerringly, touching the oil to her skin so she gasped, and then rubbing lightly. Her breathing changed in a way that meant she was starting to climb out of her skin. He kept up the motion until she became slick all over, and her intimate flesh plumped up.

"Just there," he said, and careful not to touch her clothing with his oil-coated torso, leaned down to kiss her. "When this is over," he mumbled against her lips, "we'll be taking turns with that oil."

"This is ridiculous," she gasped, when he withdrew his hand from under her skirt. "I can't go out there. I feel—"

"Half-naked, covered in oil, and horny? So do I. Just be glad no one's taking your picture."

She might not like it, but she did exactly what he needed her to do. Once they got out front, Sebastian turned out to be a middle-aged German who was as business-like and matter-of-fact as Steve could wish.

And it wasn't Sebastian that Steve watched, anyway; it was Lise, standing behind and to the right. When the photographer changed his pose, or told the makeup girl to push his hair behind his ear, Steve would glance at Lise and she'd shift her shoulders so he saw the quick play of her nipples against the shirt, or she'd shift her weight from side to side so he knew her naked thighs were rubbing together, where he'd lightly slicked them with the oil.

"Lean forward, into the wave," Sebastian ordered at one point. He maneuvered his feet on the surfboard, and glanced down to see it wedged into the sand, which would be computer-generated waves when this was done. The absurdity of it all struck him and he glanced helplessly at Lise.

She stared at him, licked her lips, and said, "Bend deeper into it, like this." As she bent her own torso, he watched the pull of fabric across her breasts, imagined the air wafting against her nakedness beneath the skirt and suddenly bending deep was not an option, it was his only hope to protect his modesty. He squinted into the fake sun in an effort to see her better and all he could think about was the moment he could plunge into her heat.

He felt her excitement building as they stared at each other, and wanted to walk right 'round behind her, lift her skirt, and plunge into her from behind. She must have picked up his silent message for her nostrils flared slightly and her lips parted.

He heard the camera shutter flash like a cascade of bullets. "Good, excellent," Sebastian said. And suddenly it was over.

He didn't even stop to say g'day, but grabbed Lise's hand and pulled her along to the dressing room.

"We've got another appointment," she explained over her shoulder.

"Ja, Ja. Go. I'll call you when the contact sheets are ready."

He didn't even bother to change out of the ridiculous shorts, he was in too much of a hurry. And she didn't even try to get her underwear back. Instead, they grabbed their stuff, ran for the car, and Lise, the most careful driver he'd ever seen, actually went a mile or two over the speed limit, such was her haste.

They left the car for a valet to park, and ran for the elevator. He wanted nothing more than to thrust his hand under her skirt and find that nicely oiled spot, but just as the elevator was about to close, a businessman got in, gave them a stiff nod, and then stared at the floor numbers.

Steve stared at Lise.

She stared back at him, her irises so wide and dark her eyes were full of secrets. All of which he wanted to discover.

The elevator stopped and with a jolt he realized it was his floor. They managed to exit at a walk, but no sooner did the doors slide shut behind them than they sprinted the rest of the way to his room.

Once inside, there was no possible way he could make it to the bedroom. With all the grace of a rutting bull, he turned her so her back was to him, pushed her against the nearest sofa, bent her over the arm, lifted her skirt.

She was already panting. She slipped her legs apart and when he touched her she gasped, so hot and wet he knew she was as desperate for fulfillment as he.

"Take me, take me now," she gasped, and he thought he'd never heard sweeter words.

He dropped the ridiculous shorts, sheathed himself in a second, and then, with a great groan of satisfaction, slid into her ready body.

The sound she made, when he was as deep as he could thrust, and his hips were pressed against her bottom, was somewhere between a sob and a cheer.

He knew exactly how she felt. His body was standing up and cheering while somewhere inside he felt like wailing. He wasn't a man given to crying, so it was odd to say the least, but somehow, when he moved inside this woman's body, he felt an emotional pull deep inside him.

She was bent over, her upper body sprawled on the couch, her blouse pulling out of the waistband of her skirt from the thrusting movements of her hips. Her hair tangled in disarray and her hands clutched and unclutched against the upholstery as she pushed herself back against him; but there was a space where her hair had parted away from the nape of her neck. The skin looked so white and silky against her dark hair and he could see the bump of a vertebrae.

Something about the sight of that patch of skin filled him with tenderness, even as his body rutted with animal need.

Her lower body was pushing and squirming against him, her mouth open and panting. He felt the walls of her vagina begin to close in on him, a hot squeeze with every thrust. He slipped a hand to the front of her body beneath her skirt and found her hot button, slick with oil and her own juices. The minute he touched it she started to shudder and the pleasant squeezing increased in intensity.

He was only human. He'd fantasized about this moment while he'd been propped and bent and photographed and ordered into some new and equally ridiculous position and photographed again. Now here she was, gyrating madly against him, her body hotly milking him, those crazy sounds coming from her throat and that sweet, vulnerable skin at the back of her neck shining up at him.

He felt the wave build somewhere beneath his feet, felt it pick him up, while he battled to stay on the crest, battled to hold her with him, until the wave seemed to break between them, tossing them out into the ocean before bringing them softly into shore.

Anyone who didn't believe surfing and sex were related was crazy.

Chapter Eleven

"What would you have done if you hadn't had to leave school when you were sixteen?" Lise asked Steve. They were in bed, having crawled from the living room straight to the shower and spent so long together under the pounding water that she felt cleaner than she ever had in her life, and more satiated.

There was nothing like good sex for making her loquacious, and while Steve wasn't a big post-coital chatterbox, at least he didn't go from orgasm to REM in under ten seconds like her last boyfriend.

His chest rose and fell with his steady breathing and under her hand she felt the regular beat of his heart as he pondered her question.

"I wanted to go to university," he said at last. "I was interested in engineering."

"You still could. You're young enough."

"Dunno. I've got my life now." He waved a hand around the elegant hotel suite. "It's not like this. This was just a bit of fun." He rolled over until he was heavily on top of her and stared down into her eyes, as serious as she'd ever seen him. "It doesn't feel like a bit of fun, though, does it?"

Unable to speak for the lump in her throat, she shook her head.

He kissed her softly. "Come home with me."

"Pardon me?"

"When I go home, come with me."

Her heart jerked and stuttered painfully in her chest. "What are you saying?"

He glanced off to a spot on the pillow. "You must be due for a holiday, you work hard enough. Take a few weeks off and come back to Oz with me. I'll show you 'round a bit. Take you for some proper surfing. I won't be going back to work for a few more weeks."

"And then what?" she asked, her voice as hollow as the feeling in her chest.

He shrugged, but she could see from the frown pulling his brows together that he was as confused as she.

She tried to smile, but it wasn't easy. "Or you could stay."

She could see he was going to refuse so she rushed on, heedless of the fact that she was probably making the hugest fool of herself ever. "There are wonderful universities here, and you could organize your schedule so you could still do some work for Crane."

Lise's instincts were pretty good, and when she'd seen the photo shoot, she'd known, just as she had from the commercial shoot, that they had a winner on their hands. When Steve found his focus, he had the most amazing ability to project both a rugged manliness and a mouth-watering sexiness. He was that rare man who could appeal to both the male and female consumer.

Sure, Jennifer Talbot had discovered him, but Lise knew she'd groomed and shaped him. She understood him well enough to help him through the inevitable awkwardness of changing from a steelworker to a product spokesman.

She could also help him realize his dreams. With her love and support, he could do anything.

Even as she accepted that she loved him, had fallen into love with him far quicker than was good for her, she also accepted that she might lose him. He had family, a completely different career, and another life on the other side of the world.

She'd even follow him there if he asked more of her than a few weeks' holiday. She'd give up her job and her life here in California to be a steelworker's wife in Australia. She knew she would. But for one problem.

He hadn't asked her.

His wedding ring phobia didn't seem to be any closer to being cured than when she'd first slept with him.

She tried to smile, but it went pretty crooked at the corners. "I don't think a holiday in Australia is a good idea for me right now," she said. "This campaign is really important to my career." And if a career was all she was going to have—*damn it*—she was going to have a stellar one.

"Once we finish all the nonsense that's in my contract next week, I'm going home," he told her softly, running a hand down her cheek as though memorizing its texture.

She nodded, unable to speak.

How had she let this happen? She was a sensible woman in control of her life; how on earth had she fallen so completely for this man in a matter of weeks? Why couldn't she be like Sonia and change men like she'd change a dress? Why did she have to fall so heavily for a man she couldn't have?

"I'm sorry," he said, pulling her to him almost fiercely.

"Me, too," she mumbled into his chest.

The rest of the week was a blur. It wasn't so bad during the day when they were working, but at night she could hardly bear it. They were together every second, making love like two people doomed to be eternally parted.

But the week passed, probably at about the same rate most weeks passed; it was only to Lise that time felt like a trick rug being pulled out from under her feet.

His plane was booked. She'd seen the ticket. Everything they needed him for here in California was done. The rest could be tweaked in Sydney. Of course she knew there would be calls for his services when those ads started running, but he'd be sweating on a bridge somewhere thousands of miles away, his hair gilded by the sun, his body bronzed by it. And she'd be nothing but a memory.

"I can't take you to the airport tomorrow," she said the last night they were together. She'd made enough of a fool of herself when she'd met him there when he arrived. She'd top her own record if she wailed and clung to his knees trying to stop him from leaving her. No, if she wanted to hang on to any scrap of pride, she was going to say goodbye in private.

He nodded, looking so sad and lost she wanted to cry.

"I wish you could come with me," he said.

She shook her head slowly. "I can't, I—"

"I know you're busy now, but later, when the campaign's all done, couldn't you—"

"No, Steve, I couldn't."

"I love you," he said, almost breaking her heart.

"I know. I love you, too. But I think I must be an old-fashioned girl at heart. I want all of you. Forever." Her voice sounded husky and old.

"I never wanted to hurt you."

"I know. You couldn't help it."

So he made love to her one last time, and she made love to him, and when she woke in the morning, he was gone.

She got to the office, determined to carry on with the rest of her life just as though half of her wasn't missing. And within a couple of hours of her return to the office she almost did feel like her old self.

Her head ached and her belly burned.

"I thought you'd kicked that habit," Sonia said, walking in as she was in the middle of chugging a couple of pain pills down with antacid.

She screwed the white plastic cap back on and shoved the stuff into its accustomed place in her top drawer. "Nope. Just took a holiday." She sighed deeply. "But the holiday's over now." She pulled up the ad layout that had put the burn in her stomach and the pain in her head. Of all the possible jobs for her to be stuck with, did it have to be the advertising campaign that featured all Steve all the time?

His wonderful, strong, decent face that she'd kissed so many times. His gorgeous green eyes that had twinkled at her so often, and looked at her so sadly at the end, the body that had brought hers so much pleasure. The man she loved in all his parts.

How was she going to get over the man when she had to work with his image and his voice for weeks yet?

She grit her teeth and got on with it, knowing that this was still one of the most important clients she'd ever worked for and that this campaign was going to be the best work she'd ever done.

A couple of hours went by, and she refused to acknowledge that his plane must have taken off by now. He was on his way home to his steel and his family and those "shielas" that would soon make him forget about her.

A knock sounded on her open door, and she turned to find Anton from the art department standing there. "I've got the mock-up of the Crane magazine ad," he said. Anton was the best she had—intense, focused, and hip to the max from his spiky hair to his shoes.

"Come on in," she said, feigning excitement. Until she looked at the mock-up and then the excitement turned real.

"Oh, Anton, this is fabulous," she said. There he was. Steve, her Steve, balanced on a Crane surfboard, his glorious body bent forward into the wind, his eyes squinting right at her, fiercely focused. Anton had put him into the curl of a wave the likes of which she'd never seen, but she knew better. That man had been thinking of her, not the ocean.

A small smile played over her lips as she recalled the aftermath of that photo shoot.

Her desk phone rang, and because she was wandering, blissed out, down memory lane and had forgotten she was in a meeting with Anton, she picked it up.

"Lise," he said. Just that one word.

"Steve?" Her heart banged painfully against her ribs.

She calculated rapidly, he must be halfway to Hawaii by now. Was he phoning her from the plane?

"I need someone to pick me up from the airport. I was wondering if you were free."

Her head was spinning. Airport? "Which airport?"

"San Francisco," he said with the ghost of a laugh.

"What happened? Was your plane cancelled? Delayed?"

"No. It took off all right, but I wasn't on it."

She swallowed hard. With a mutter of protest, Anton removed the mock-up from her hands before her clutching, sweating fingers could destroy it. "I'll come back later," he said and left, closing her office door behind him.

"Why weren't you on the plane?"

"You know, I'm not entirely sure. I'd like to take some time to work that out."

"How—how much time were you thinking of?"

"As long as it takes."

Forever. She was thinking a question like that could take at least a lifetime to work out. In that time, so much could happen. There was Crane, acting if he wanted it, university if he still dreamed of being an engineer. They could spend time here and time in Australia. If they loved each other enough, anything was possible.

"Are you still there?"

"Yes. Sorry. You took me by surprise."

Why could she only find one shoe? She'd slipped them off earlier and now her questing toes could only reach one.

"So, you'll come to the airport and pick me up?"

"Yes, if I can ever find my other shoe."

He chuckled. "Borrow Sonia's. And maybe you can borrow her dress again while you're at it."

"I can't believe you—"

But she was cut off by a chuckle. "I love you," he said.

And really, what else was there to say?

THE GREAT BARRIER

Chapter One

"Flat white, please," Bronwyn Spencer said to the young guy at the coffee stand at Sydney Airport. Trying to organize coffee and smother a yawn at the same time was using all the energy she possessed this early in the morning.

A Saturday morning, too, her prime laying-in time sacrificed for some stiff-arsed Yank she had to babysit.

Honestly, if it were anyone but Cam who'd asked her to give up a Saturday for a boring suit she'd have laughed right in his face. But Cameron Crane was her big half-brother and, in spite of the fact that he drove her crazy, bossed her about, lectured her about her extravagance and poor taste in men, and generally interfered in matters he should leave well enough alone, she adored him.

Nothing else would bring her here at this time of the morning. Not after the party last night.

Bron was young, healthy, and attractive, and she firmly believed that youth was a time to party. Which she'd done heartily until hunger drove her out for a pie at Harry's Café de Wheels in the wee hours, and then reluctantly she'd gone home, deciding on a few hours of sleep before her babysitting assignment.

She dragged out the photo of the man she'd be looking after for the next fortnight. Mark Forsythe. Even his name sounded wet. He was some sort of finance type, coming over to sort out Crane's financial system and explain how all the taxes worked in the American market. She knew this was important, but she couldn't imagine anything more boring.

She'd tried to balance her checkbook once and found it so futile she'd given up. She'd discovered instead a wonderful thing called overdraft protection.

And after that ran out, in extreme emergencies there was always Cam. Except that he wasn't here. Off with his new lovey dove right when she most needed him.

Why did her overdraft have to run out right when the week's rent was due? Oh, well. Luckily she was a resourceful woman and had allowed Cam to bail her out of a jam once more, even though he'd done it without his knowledge. Which wasn't her fault. He hadn't been around to ask.

She wasn't going to stand around like a dickhead holding a sign with Mark Forsythe's name on it, so she was going to have to recognize the man. She studied his corporate photo while she drank the coffee.

Mark Forsythe gazed back at her from a corporate head shot, earnest and dull. Black hair that would look better if it was a little longer and not so neat, serious blue eyes in a serious, narrow face. Firm lips that looked as though they never smiled at a joke, never mind told one.

Her lip curled. It was going to be a long two weeks. Already she was irritated with the man since she was on time and his flight wasn't. She could have snatched a bit more sleep. Her feet ached from all the dancing last night, and she stretched them out, noticing the coral polish on her nails was already chipped.

With a quiet chuckle she remembered that Fiona had outlasted her at the party, and seemed pretty keen on a blond surfie from Brisbane wearing a shirt of so hideous a green that it ought to be burned. She wondered how Fi was faring and pulled out her mobile. She hesitated, and then decided that if she had to be up and functioning at nine in the morning on a Saturday, her best mate ought to as well.

She punched in the number and after a few rings, Fiona answered. "This better be life or death."

"Did you go home with your surfie?"

A great groan met her ears. "What the bloody hell are you doing ringing me at this hour?"

"Well, did you?"

A few passengers began drifting out from the California flight. Idly she watched them blinking with tiredness, or stretching after more hours than she cared to contemplate stuffed in a tin can thirty thousand feet above earth. Bron shook her head; she firmly believed that if God had meant man to fly, he'd have given surfboards wings.

She glanced down at the black-haired, serious and controlled-looking man in the photo and kept her eyes open while Fiona yawned and groaned.

"No," her friend said, finally. "I didn't go home with him. Now would you piss off."

A man came through the glass doors alone. Right general age and he had black hair, but he was nothing like the photograph. His hair was a mess. He must have fallen asleep against something that had pushed his hair up one side. His face was shadowy with stubble, giving him a disreputable look. He wore a navy short-sleeved shirt that had wrinkled badly and tan chinos. He moved slowly, but she liked the way he walked, with a kind of rolling gait, as though he were getting off a boat rather than a plane. He stood as though he were about to fall asleep on his feet, his gaze searching out someone. Then their gazes connected and she felt her heart flop over.

No photograph could have captured the blue of his eyes. They were the dark, smoky blue of a wailing sax at some bar at three in the morning, with a half-drunk whiskey and a smoldering cigarette. They were so tired, and so lonely in a cynical way that she wanted to fix everything for him and kiss his hurts better. It was an odd reaction for her to have for a stranger, but he didn't even look like a stranger she thought with a spurt of recognition.

He held a briefcase in one hand and a black suitcase in the other. She glanced at the photo and back at him, every hormone in her body doing a victory dance.

"Oh, my God," she said into the phone. "He's gorgeous."

"I dunno," her friend said in her ear. "He was all right looking, I suppose, but that shirt! I thought he'd—"

"What are you going on about? You can't see him." She'd have to remember never to wake Fi early on a Saturday again. "I've got to go." And she ended the call, while Fiona was in the middle of saying something.

Mark Forsythe's gaze had paused only briefly on hers and kept going, but *whew*, what could happen to a person's pulse in a few seconds.

Slowly she rose and approached. Could she really be this lucky and find that she was being asked to look after just about the sweetest sexpot she'd ever seen? Taking a deep breath, she said, "Mark Forsythe?"

He looked at her for a moment, and a crease formed between his brows as though he weren't quite sure what his name was. She wanted to kiss the frown away.

"Yes, I'm Mark Forsythe. You must be Bronwyn . . . I'm sorry. I've forgotten your last name." His voice was nice. Soft but commanding, somehow, and the American accent of course, that she usually only heard on telly or at the pictures.

She smiled. "That's all right. It's Spencer. I work at Crane Enterprises. I was sent to fetch you."

"I was expecting someone older."

"You'll have to wait a while then," she said briskly, and he blinked before smiling weakly at her bit of humor.

"You look tired," she said, longing to smooth down the hair that stood straight up.

"I've never been so tired in my whole life," he admitted.

"Did you sleep at all on the plane?"

"I never sleep on planes."

"Oh, dear," she said, barely resisting the urge to pat his cheek. "Come on. My car's this way."

He seemed almost shell-shocked. He walked stiffly, which she assumed was from having his long frame cramped for all those hours. He was so unkempt, in comparison to the perfectly clothed and groomed man in the photo, that she felt an unwanted intimacy, like accidentally seeing a stranger naked.

They walked out of the airport into blinding sun, and the man beside her recoiled. "Welcome to Sydney," she said cheerfully, giving him a moment to find and slip on a pair of sunglasses.

"Thanks."

They didn't speak again until they'd reached her Ford hatchback. She opened the boot, shoving a chartreuse knee board and her black and red wet suit to one side so he could stow his gear.

"Sorry, it's a bit daggy in there."

He looked horrified at the idea of putting his pristine cases into a mess of sand, but finally shrugged and placed the black suitcase gingerly inside, and hung onto his briefcase as though it contained state secrets.

There could only be boring tax things in there; the poor man needed to loosen up. And, she thought, he couldn't have picked a better country in which to do it. Or a better woman to help him.

She unlocked the driver's side door and as she opened it she collided with Mark. He was more solid than he looked, and the current as their bodies jolted sent a thrill to her toes. She thought he felt it, too, before he stepped back quickly. "Planning to drive?" she said with a grin.

"I forgot. You drive on the left. Sorry," he said, and he went around to the other door.

"Is this your first time in Australia?" she asked him as they sped through the relative quiet of a Saturday morning.

"Yes." He stared out of the window, but didn't talk much.

She described a little of the areas they passed, but she didn't think he was taking in a lot of what she said.

"It's not too far," she said. "Have a nap if you like."

"No. The only way to prevent jet lag is to stay awake until it's nighttime in the new location."

"Suit yourself." It sounded like a crazy idea to Bron. If you were hungry, you ate. If you were tired, you slept. If you were drawn to a man—as strongly as she was to this one—you let nature take its course.

From cursing Cam for foisting the Yank onto her, she now silently thanked him.

Since her passenger didn't seem up for talking, she slipped a Kylie Minogue CD into her player and drove, entertaining herself by wondering what the man beside her would be like in bed.

Her fantasies were rich enough that she was well-primed when she pulled up in front of the Crane corporate guest house right across the road from Bronté Beach. "Here we are," she said brightly.

He blinked owlishly. "This isn't a hotel."

"No. It's a corporate guest house. Cameron hates hotels and owns more houses than he knows what to do with, so he likes to offer a proper home to our out-of-country guests," she parroted what she'd been told. "It's fully stocked and comes with a maid who does daily. There's a cook on call."

"Then it's got more comforts than my home," Mark said, glancing up at the pale cream stucco house as though he mistrusted it. She bit her lip, thinking his instincts were bang-on.

For all of Cam's big love of buying homes, he'd never bought his own sister one. He wanted her to be self-sufficient, he'd told her. He'd given her a job, she conceded, but she was damn good at it. And sure, he paid her a good wage, but her lifestyle was expensive, and somehow she always slipped into financial messes. Cam didn't seem to have much sympathy for that. He told her she was spoiled, but it wasn't only clothes and shoes that did her in. There were her friends. How could you not help a friend out from time to time?

Honestly. If she didn't keep getting lovely offers for new credit cards, she'd really be in the basket. Although, come to think of it, it had been a while since she'd been offered a new one.

Oh, well, Cameron was out of the country and therefore out of her mind, and in his absence, he was being more than usually generous.

She grabbed Mark Forsythe's case before he could get to it, and walked on ahead of him. "Come on. I'll show you around."

She led him up the path to the two-story modern house with big windows and a balcony overlooking the beach. It was a bit sterile for her taste, and not as close to the heart of the action as she liked but beggars, and in particular squatters, couldn't afford to be choosers.

"That's great. Thanks," he said, when she'd finished the tour. He reached into his pocket and then stopped. She was pretty sure he'd been about to hand her a tip as though she were a bellhop.

Because he looked so adorably confused, she grinned at him. "We're not big on tipping in Australia. Anyway, I work for Crane. I have to help out for nothing."

"Well, I appreciate the ride and the house tour," he said, and stood staring at her, obviously waiting for her to leave.

"So, what do you want to do on your first day?" she asked brightly.

"Unpack, shower, and set up my computer."

"Well, I'll make some coffee," she said, heading for the kitchen.

"I really don't want coffee," he said with a slight edge.

"It's for me," she said. "It's the only thing that gets me through an early morning."

"It's ten-fifteen, local time," he said glancing at his watch.

"Exactly." So he was one of those organized sorts who

set his watch to local time when he traveled. Somehow, she wasn't surprised.

He disappeared into the bathroom and she got the feeling he'd have been able to get rid of her a lot easier if he wasn't tired and jet-lagged. The trouble was, she couldn't leave quite yet. There was something she was going to have to explain.

She'd lead up to her news over coffee.

When Mark emerged from the bathroom, his eyes were a sharper blue and a shade of annoyance crept into his tone. "There are cosmetics in the bathroom."

Damn. This wasn't how she'd planned to ease into her news. "Like I said, all the comforts of home."

"Used cosmetics. And a drawer of underwear." He held up a glittery thong that she wore on special occasions.

"Right. I was going to tell you about that. Over coffee."

She turned away and he stepped forward, grasping her forearm with surprising strength. "Why don't you tell me now?" he said pleasantly, but with no loosening of his grip.

"Well, we're sort of sharing the premises."

"Are you the cook or the cleaner?"

"Neither. We're sharing."

"Sharing?" He blinked in stunned disbelief. "As in roommates?"

"I suppose," she said, tossing her hair back over her shoulder. "Yeah."

He started shaking his head before she'd finished speaking. "No. We're not. Drop me downtown and I'll check into a hotel."

"No! You can't do that. Cameron..." Cam would chuck a wobbly if he heard of her latest stunt. "Cam specially asked me to show you around and look after you. I can't fail on the first day." She tried to look appealing, and earnest and hopefully a little scared of her big brother and boss.

She couldn't tell if Mark was buying it. His face remained

impassive—and implacable—and his eyes gave away none of his thoughts.

"There's plenty of room," she continued. "Two bedrooms, three bathrooms, and your own in-house driver and sight-seeing guide. Can't we give it a bash?"

"Tell Crane thanks, but no thanks," he said shortly and reached for his bags, hefted them, and started for the door.

"Wait! Where are you going?"

"I'll get a cab."

"No. Don't do that. I'll drive you wherever you want to go." She felt awful now. The poor man was wobbling with tiredness and trying to escape. "Just have your coffee. Please."

He turned and gave her a wary look, then nodded.

"Sit in the lounge and enjoy the view. I won't be a tick."

She brewed coffee, poured it into the white china cups, used the matching milk and sugar, arranged a few biscuits on a plate, even remembered blue linen napkins. How could the man not want her around?

He didn't fall all over himself being impressed when she put the tray down in front of him, merely added a dash of milk and stirred the coffee.

When she'd picked up hers and sipped, he said, "Why don't you tell me what's really going on?"

She bit her lip and glanced up at him, wondering why she'd ever thought this would work. "You have to promise not to tell Cam."

"The man stole my fiancée. Believe me, I'm not inclined to tell him much of anything." He spoke in a cool, clipped way, but still she heard a hint of bitterness. Everybody at Crane knew the story, of course. Jen had ended her engagement to Mark Forsythe in order to shack up with Cam, and they'd all been a bit surprised when they found out her ex was coming over to do a job for the company.

Bron had assumed, since he was coming here to help Crane Surf and Boogie Boards, that he harbored no ill feelings about the man who was now with his former fiancée. Maybe that's what he wanted everyone to assume. It seemed they'd been wrong. Still, a man who held a grudge against Cam could be trusted to keep her secret. He had problems of his own; maybe he'd even have a little sympathy.

"I got chucked out of my flat."

Blue. His eyes were so blue. In that calm, serious face, they were intensely sexy, even when he was staring at her with that expressionless gaze. "Care to tell me why?"

"I had a few people over. It got a bit noisy and the neighbors complained so the landlord chucked me out."

"Seems a little harsh. I would have thought a warning was deserved."

"Well, I think he was glad of the excuse. I got behind in my rent."

"Ah." He said *Ah* with the calm confidence of a man who's never been chucked out of anything in his life.

He drank coffee. She felt him deliberating over her words. He'd seemed older in the picture, but in the flesh, even with the lines of tiredness, she didn't think he could be much more than thirty. So why did he, at only four years older than herself, seem unimaginably more mature?

She stared out the window for a minute, barely taking in the sparkling waves and a couple of sailboats bobbing.

"I promise you'll barely notice I'm here, except in good ways, like having fresh coffee in the morning," which she was going to have to get up extra early to brew, "and breakfast and I'll do dinners."

He seemed less impressed by the second, so she threw everything she had at him. "I'll even clean the place myself."

"No offense, Bronwyn, but the answer's still no."

"But I—"

"Listen, since you've been good enough to share your personal agenda with me, I'll be up-front with you about mine. I'm newly single ever since my fiancée dumped me for

Cameron Crane. Now, I wanted this trip for two reasons. One," he leaned forward slightly and tapped one forefinger with the other. With his hair all stuck up one side like a toddler after naptime, he was adorable. "I'm a professional and no one can do the job better. Two, I'm going to sow some wild oats. I've heard about Australian women, about their free and easy ways and partying mentality, and I decided it was the quickest and simplest way to get over my former girlfriend."

Wow. He couldn't even mention Jennifer Talbot by name. He was really bruised. "You came to Australia to get over her?" Seemed an odd plan, since he must know that Jen and Cam would be back in the country in a couple of weeks. They'd be bound to run into each other at work.

"That's right. I'll be sleeping with a different woman every night I'm here. I hope you can understand that having you in this house would be awkward, to say the least."

The quick stab of disappointment surprised her. He'd looked like a man who was fastidious in all things. Like the last of the good guys, but he was as much a hound on the prowl as most men.

Since she prided herself on her practicality, she stifled her disappointment. She wasn't particularly averse to prowling, as it happened. And if he was so anxious to bed an Aussie babe, what was wrong with her? If he wanted to experience an Aussie party girl, he couldn't do better. "Well, I—"

But she stopped herself. Somehow, she was certain he'd turn her down flat if she suggested her own sweet self as his first taste of Australia. He'd probably have some rule against fraternizing with people he worked with or something.

She was bound by no rules. But warning him ahead of time of her intentions was seeming like a bad idea right now when he was half a cup of coffee away from showing her the door.

She thought quickly. "Well, if you want to check out the party scene, I'm your girl. I know all the hot places and can introduce you to a lot of really fun people. I can show you around. Just one more service I'll provide as your house-mate."

He crossed his arms and regarded her. "And what, the three of us return here? I don't think so."

The only time she ever came home alone was if she wanted to. However, her amazing instinct about this man kicked in yet again before she said any such thing.

A plan was forming in her mind, even as she tried to look crestfallen, but understanding. "All right. I understand. But would you do me a big favor and let me stay tonight? In exchange, I'll cook you dinner and we'll plan a strategy for you."

"Strategy?"

"Ye-eah. You're here what, two weeks? We'll plan all the places you need to go." She deliberately looked him up and down. "What to wear, what to order, what . . . what Australian women like in bed."

Swift humor lit his eyes, and she thought a man who looked so gorgeous when he smiled ought to do it more often. "How about I work out that last one by trial and error."

Her own quick smile flashed back at him. "All right. So, is it a deal?"

"One night."

She nodded. A lot could happen in one night.

Chapter Two

Mark blinked. If only he didn't feel so fuzzy-headed, he was certain he'd see all the flaws in Bronwyn's idea.

If she'd been thrown out of her apartment, how great a roommate was she going to be even for one night? He was going to need his sleep, so if she was staying here hoping to turn this place into Sydney's party central, he was going to have to put his foot down.

He'd showered, shaved, and was telling himself he felt fine. He refused even to calculate how long it had been since he'd slept.

While his one night roommate shopped for dinner, he unpacked. Then he set up his laptop at the desk in the fully equipped office area of the big bedroom and checked his e-mail.

And suddenly, California seemed worlds away.

Well, he didn't trust Bronwyn for a second, but somehow he'd scored a beautiful, sexy woman cooking him dinner and sharing his place his first night in Sydney. A woman who owned a glittery thong. He chuckled. His intuition had been right. He was going to like this city.

After he'd forwarded most of the e-mails to people who could deal with them, he shut down and decided he'd been cooped up long enough. He pulled on running gear and headed out.

He reached for the door handle as the door opened and there was Bronwyn, loaded down with shopping bags and a little breathless from the outside stairs. Her blond hair floated loose around her shoulders, her denim-blue eyes widened in surprise at the near impact. This close, he could see a cluster of freckles beneath the light tan.

She wore a navy tank top with the small Crane logo, and brief white shorts that showed a lot of slim, tanned leg.

She smelled of healthy young woman, salt air, and pineapple.

While he'd checked her out, she'd done the same. "Going running?"

"Yes."

"Need a map?"

"No." He had a good sense of direction, and he'd keep his route simple.

She nodded. "Okay. I could give you a key now, but I'll be here when you get back."

"I'll take your set," he said, keeping his voice even. "Tomorrow."

Her cheeks grew rosier. "Yes, of course."

Feeling churlish, he said, "Need a hand with the bags?"

"No, thanks. I've got it. I hope you like fish."

"Love it."

He let himself out and the warmth hit him along with a salt-tinged ocean breeze, around ten degrees warmer at a guess than the weather he'd left in San Francisco.

Knowing he was probably dehydrated from flying, he stopped at a corner store and bought water, then he kept his pace easy. He nearly collided with three people and awkwardly apologized before he figured out that the same rules of the road apply on the running paths. Left-hand side.

"Sorry," he said after the last crash.

"No worries, mate," came the cheerful reply.

Everyone in Sydney seemed cheerful, from the staff at the airport to Bronwyn to the woman in the corner store.

Everyone but him.

It was more difficult than he'd imagined to come to this place, to the very company where so much had been stolen from him. It wasn't just his woman, but the future he'd so carefully mapped out, his sense of himself as a man certain of his place in the world and certain of the woman by his side.

Jen.

She'd come here a matter of months ago with his ring on her finger and a caterer already chosen for their wedding. Then she'd met Cameron Crane and next thing he knew, she was dumping him on his ass.

He'd acted like a man, of course, and pride had brought him through the first awkward meeting with her and the excruciating one with Cameron Crane himself. She'd stripped him of a lot, but at least she'd left him his professional pride. She'd asked him to come here because he was the best. He was here for the same reason, and to prove to her, Cameron Crane, and anyone else who cared, that he was unmoved enough by the breakup to come and do a job for his ex-fiancée's new boyfriend.

They hadn't been right for each other, Jen had told him, but Mark didn't see it that way. They were both decent, hard-working people. They liked the same restaurants, both loved theater. She didn't care for baseball, but since he was a fan she'd made an effort, and he'd done the same for her with ballet. Now, instead of a wedding and a life plan, he had nothing.

No. Not true, he reminded himself. He had freedom, and a new cynicism that showed him the error of his former ways. If he'd learned anything in the past few months it was that nice guys like him really did finish last.

Well, no more. No more mister nice guy, Mr. Responsible, Mr. Sensitive to a woman's needs. He'd been tossed over for a marginally evolved, hairy brute with a boxer's nose and a swagger.

If that's what women really wanted, Mark Forsythe was going to give it to them. And what better place to start than this land of rugged, fierce individualists. And the women! He'd heard about the women. Gorgeous, free-spirited gals who sunbathed topless and partied as hard as the men. He was going to get him some of that. Every night a new woman. Maybe a handful. And when he was through, Jen and his tame dreams would be as much a part of the past as his ambition to be a fireman when he was eight years old.

He'd outgrown that silly red plastic fireman's hat with the stick-on gold badge, and he'd outgrown the idea of marriage and settling down. Jennifer Talbot had done him a favor by dumping him. Yes, she had.

As he ran the kinks out of his body and the fuzziness from his mind, Mark began to see the humor in the current situation. A gorgeous woman wanted to spend some time with him, and he was doing his best to throw her out.

He wasn't a fool—most of the time—and since his recent breakup, he'd grown increasingly cynical about women and their motives, about love, and most especially, about marriage. He'd eat this woman's dinner, let her stay the night, and then tomorrow he'd start on an aggressive plan to turn himself into the hard-bitten playboy that women seemed to prefer.

He'd probably have a lot of fun along the way, too.

He ran three miles or so. He passed families with kids in strollers, and tried not to notice. He passed lovers, arm in arm, giggling softly about their private jokes, and scowled. And he passed a couple of guys like himself. Unencumbered, free to wander with a Saturday morning latte, or run, or do whatever the hell they felt like. His people.

He began to notice the heat, and that sweat was dribbling down his face. Probably it was time to head for home.

He glugged water. The heat was different here. It was November, early summer, and the temperature was climbing by the minute. By the time he'd retraced his steps and returned to the house, he'd gone through two liters of water and still felt thirsty.

He entered the relatively cool entranceway and tried not to drip on the slate tile. "Bronwyn?"

"Yeah?" Her voice floated from the back of the main floor.

"Could you bring me a towel?"

She emerged, slim and golden, her long hair fastened into a sloppy ponytail, sent him an amused glance, and disappeared into the bathroom.

When she emerged with a big white fluffy towel, he had his breathing under control.

"How was your run?" she asked him, her gaze traveling up and down his body in a manner that had sweat breaking out all over again.

"Fine. It was fine. Hotter than I thought, is all." He felt like an idiot, mopping his face and limbs while she stood watching him. Personal grooming in front of a woman seemed uncomfortably intimate, although she obviously didn't feel that way; she merely stood watching. He glanced up at her, deciding to play it cool and ask some lame question about what she was serving for dinner, but the words stuck in his throat.

There was a gleam of sexual interest in her eyes that pulled at him. Awareness danced around them, and for a moment he could think of nothing but what she'd taste like.

As though she'd read his mind, her lips parted, and he noticed how young she looked, how fresh and dewy. She wore no makeup that he could see. Her freckles weren't smoothed and hidden by cosmetics, her blue eyes were as clear and dreamy as the Caribbean, her lips plump and pale coral.

He wanted her.

The knowledge made him blink. For all his grand plans to cut a swath through the female society of Sydney, he hadn't counted on feeling plain, sharp desire for the first woman he met.

Seconds ticked by and neither said a word. Did she move infinitesimally closer? Did he?

A warm droplet of sweat licked at his temple and all at once he realized that he was hot, sweaty, and probably smelly. In no condition to kiss anyone.

He pulled back and got busy with the towel. "I'd better shower," he said.

"Mmm. Let me know if you need help washing your back." And with that she turned and headed back to the kitchen, the sway of her hips as provocative as her words.

He thought about it while he showered.

Why not? Why not begin his post-Jen womanizing with a sexy young woman who telegraphed her interest to him in entirely unsubtle terms?

There were two possible downsides. One, she worked for Crane Enterprises. Two. She'd moved her stuff into the place already. If he slept with her, he might need dynamite to get her out. Balancing his lust against practicality, he dried himself on another fluffy white towel and decided to wait. He'd get her out of the place first before he made a move on her.

It wasn't like she was going anywhere. She worked for the company he'd be consulting with for the next few weeks. He could get to know her a little and make sure she was the kind of woman who could handle a brief fling with a co-worker. That was the sensible plan. And Mark was nothing if not sensible.

Bron debated, for the third time, whether to put the fish on the barbecue or to wait another half-hour. It was eight o'clock and she was starving.

After turning down her offer for a personalized city tour, a picnic at the beach, or a few hours on a sailing boat in Sydney harbor, Mark had claimed work and disappeared upstairs. She suspected he wasn't working, but napping, and a good thing if he was after the long flight.

But should she rouse him? If she didn't, and he slept through dinner, he'd wake at some ungodly hour with his stomach rumbling—and he might blame her. Since she was extremely interested in staying in his good books for the next two weeks, she decided to creep upstairs and wake him slowly, then leave it to him if he wanted dinner. If not, she could always put his on a plate for later, though the idea of cold fish in the middle of the night didn't sound very appealing.

Her tread was soundless on the carpeted stairs and upper hallway, but she needn't have bothered creeping about. He wasn't sleeping. From the doorway of his bedroom, she saw him at the desk beside the window industriously tapping away at a laptop computer, an open file folder in front of him. From it spilled a sheaf of papers dense with columns of figures. She shuddered at the idea of anyone cooped up on a sunny Saturday afternoon choosing accounting over pleasure.

It occurred to her that this man needed her help. If there was one thing she knew how to do, it was to have fun.

"Ready for dinner?" she asked.

Across the bed, their gazes met. *Phew*, he could generate some steam with those eyes of his.

They widened when they took in her outfit, which made her happy she'd spent an unusual half-hour primping. The soft blue and green batik print skirt brushed at her ankles, so he could see the tiny rose tattooed there if he cared to look.

She wore wooden sandals with leather straps, and a blue-green tank top. She'd even bothered with jewelry, donning the opal beads and earrings her brother had given her for her birthday last year.

Her hair shone with brushing, and a light and sexy scent emanated from behind her ears and between her breasts.

If she couldn't snag Mark Forsythe's interest with full battle regalia, then she wasn't the woman she believed herself to be. And he wasn't the sexually interested man she'd glimpsed in the hallway earlier. The one who was staring back at her right this second.

"Thanks. I'll be down in five minutes," he said, blinking.

He rose and stretched, and she was conscious of the lean power of his body. Nice, she thought. Very nice.

He smothered a yawn. The bed between them was as crisp and neat as it had been this morning.

"Didn't you sleep at all?"

"No. I told you. It's better to stay awake. Prevents jet lag."

"Right." She wondered if he was always this rigid. Always so hard on himself. Seemed a shame. What he needed was a little fun. She smiled a tiny smile. "See you downstairs."

He was as good as his word. In five minutes he was downstairs and, perhaps he'd taken his cue from her, but he'd changed his clothes. Now he wore a gray short-sleeved cotton shirt over navy pants that looked as though they contained silk. And they were sharply seamed as though freshly pressed, when they had to have been crushed in a suitcase for hours and hours.

"Your timing's perfect," she said, sliding two brilliantly barbecued fillets onto plates that already contained a paw-paw/mango salsa and green salad. She'd even made a risotto. Sure, it had taken half an hour to clean up the mess she'd made in the kitchen, but the results were worth a bit of mess. "I thought we'd eat out here."

"Sure. Great."

He didn't seem overwhelmed by the romance of the setting, the purply-gray night sky, the soft breeze, the shushing sounds of the ocean. In fact, she wondered if he even noticed.

She set the plates on the table and he waited until she was seated before sitting down himself. Such manners.

There was crisp, chilled white wine from the Hunter Valley, bread, fresh from the bakery looking crusty and golden in the flickering candlelight. Her meal, and her table, looked straight out of an *Australian Women's Weekly* glossy magazine. Probably because it was.

She was trying so hard to be charming, attractive, and hospitable that she was getting on her own nerves. The trouble was, that for all her talk about moving in with a friend temporarily, she didn't have a friend left who'd take her in. It wasn't really her fault; it was just that there were always incidents when she was around.

She didn't blame her friends. If she'd been them, she wouldn't invite her to stay, either. If they didn't end up with some dickhead who'd fallen for Bron singing at the top of his lungs in the wee hours, they got hassled by credit people. Very annoying.

She poured wine before Mark had a chance to refuse, and raised her glass in a toast. "Welcome to Australia."

He grinned and clicked her glass with his own. "Thanks. And thank you for this meal. It looks great."

"It's barramundi, a whitefish you won't find in North America."

"Wonderful. I'm starved."

She tucked in, happy that the fish tasted as good as it was supposed to.

"Hey, what's that bird?" he asked, staring past her shoulder.

She glanced over to where he pointed and laughed. "That's not a bird. It's a flying fox. There must be a fruit tree around somewhere. They're fruit bats, really. They sleep all day and then go feeding at night." Even as she spoke several more of the dark-winged creatures flapped past.

"I read about them, but they're so much bigger than I thought." He sounded carefree in that moment, when he lost himself in the thrill of a new sight.

The breeze whispered by her cheek, warm and soft as a lover's caress. In the distance, she heard good-natured, back-and-forth joking coming from the beach. Closer in, she heard the steady hum of traffic below. The scent of barbecuing meat traveled over from next door; recognizing it, she laughed. "That's what you almost got. Lamb. You'll probably get that tomorrow."

He smiled, but a crease formed between his eyes. "I don't

want to be rude about this, but you won't be here tomorrow."

"I didn't say I'd cook it for you, did I?" she said, exasperated. "I'll shove off," she paused, leaned forward, and said slowly, enunciating each word, "if you don't want me." She knew damn well he did want her. As she wanted him.

Although she'd wanted him a lot more before she'd heard his plan to be a lad about town.

Mark drank a lot of the fancy bottled water she'd put on the table, but he drank his share of the wine, too, she was pleased to note, and he seemed to relax.

"So, what do you do at Crane?" he asked.

"I'm with the product marketing team. We've got the lion's share of the Oz and Kiwi markets, but we've been really busy since Jennifer Talbot arrived. She's come up with some great ideas for the American launch," she said with enthusiasm, then could have stabbed her tongue with the fish fork as Mark's interested gaze clouded over.

"Anyway," she babbled on, "I'm also the head designer for our women's clothing line, which mostly means I get to boss about the real designers."

"Do you like working for Crane?"

She wasn't certain whether he meant Cam or the company in general, but having stuffed up once, she played it safe and decided to assume he meant the company. "I love it. The people are mostly young and really fun. We all love surfing. That's a prerequisite of working there." She looked over. "Do you surf?"

"Not since I grew up."

"Right." She imagined that insult was leveled at Cam and not her. Still, it rankled. "You'd be surprised how many adults do love to surf. It's our biggest growth area."

"Forget the job, what about you personally?"

"I grew up right here in Sydney. Mum was from the country, but after her first husband was killed in a machinery accident, she moved here and worked in an office. That's where she met my father. He's an engineer."

"Brothers or sisters?"

"A half-brother." Cam was her half-brother, and she was surprised Jen hadn't mentioned that when she'd told Mark about the job. Although, since she'd dumped him, they probably didn't chatter a lot about office gossip.

The last thing Bron wanted was to bring Cam's name into the conversation. The less they talked about Jen or Cam, the better. "He's eight years older, so I grew up more like an only child." She shrugged. "I took clothing design at school and now I have a good job and some great mates. When I'm not working, I love to surf and party. That's my life."

"Is there a man in your life?" he asked.

This was more like it. Moody purple shadows darkened his eyes, and once more she felt that elemental and unexpected connection between them.

"No."

"I'm surprised."

She laughed lightly. "I've always believed there's a perfect person out there. I haven't met him yet."

"You're a romantic."

"Well, what's the alternative?"

"Intimacy with strangers."

She reached out and touched his hand, which had been idly toying with the stem of his wineglass, then she raised her eyes and captured his gaze just as deliberately, letting the waves of attraction build, feeling her heart speed up. "Well, until Mr. Right comes along, I can go along with that."

"Bronwyn . . ." He was going to turn her down when she knew how much he needed her. He was gorgeous and sweet and hurting, and she wanted to kiss everything better.

"My friends call me Bron," she said softly and rising, walked around the table, then she leaned over and kissed him.

He muttered a protest that got muffled by her mouth. For a moment she felt his struggle, wanting her and wishing he didn't, and then his arms went round her and he pulled her to his lap.

Now things were going better. She smiled into the kiss, liking the way they fit together. He tightened his hold and kissed her back with meaning. His protest had been so weak and easily overborne that she knew he wanted her as much as she wanted him.

Her pulse picked up as excitement skittered everywhere like a bag of dropped lollies.

He felt good—lean, but muscular—and she couldn't help but remember how he'd looked when he'd arrived home after his run, his lightly bronzed skin gleaming with sweat and pulsing with the warmth of a workout.

"Bronwyn," he mumbled against her lips, "we should talk about this."

"Absolutely," she purred, and nibbled his bottom lip until his tongue was hers once more.

It had been a very long time since a man had made her so hot so fast, and they were both still fully dressed. He had a way of kissing her that was more about giving than taking, and it gave her a lot of confidence that once they hit the bedroom, her pleasure rather than his, would be top on his mind.

Very nice.

He felt so good, so warm and strong and dependable somehow. And he smelled good, too—a little foreign, no cologne or aftershave or scented product that she could identify, just clean, excited male. Her favorite kind.

He pulled away briefly, dragged in a breath, and said, "Bron, we had an arrangement, I expect you to—" He groaned helplessly as she shifted her bottom against the ridge of an impressive erection. He grunted something incomprehensible and gave up on his attempts at conversation.

About time.

"I want to see you," he muttered thickly, reaching for the hem of her shirt. "Been thinking about it for hours."

"Oh, yes," she sighed, tipping her head back. She pictured him peeling off her tank top, her breasts free to the night air, making love out here where . . . Wait a minute! This is where things always started to go wrong for her. Next thing she knew, offended old people would be watching, police would be banging at the door, or a riot would start outside. She shuddered. No. She had to be sensible for a change. If she caused trouble at the company house, Cam would kill her.

So she slipped her hands down to cover Mark's. "Upstairs," she said gently, and slipped from his lap, never letting go of his hands so he followed her, his front to her back. They managed a respectable bit of rumba as they mounted the stairs still pressed together. They were both breathing heavily when they reached the top of the stairs, and she didn't think it was from the elevation.

They reached his bedroom and he turned her to face him, not lunging as she'd expected, but taking a moment to study her face as if he were about to go blind and had to memorize it forever.

Slowly, she warned herself. Maybe she should take this slowly. But even as the thought flitted across her consciousness, she knew somehow that for all his rash talk about bedding every straight woman in Sydney in the next fortnight, Mark was essentially a one-woman man. And that he'd never deliberately hurt her.

"You're so beautiful," he said softly.

For all that his eyes were red-rimmed with fatigue and his skin pale with tiredness, she thought he was beautiful, too.

His fingers skimmed her breasts, bringing them to tingling life. "Now can I see you?"

"Get on the bed," she said, deciding to make tonight so special he'd never forget his first night in her country. "I promised you some sightseeing didn't I?"

His eyes took on a wicked glint that matched her own reckless mood. Even for her, things were moving a little fast here, but he felt so safe somehow, so right.

She was going to make love to this man because her body gave her no choice. But she wasn't going to be stupid about it, either. She'd protect her body and her heart.

What could go wrong?

Knowing that once she'd stripped in front of him, there'd be no turning back, she said, "Make yourself comfortable, I'll be right back." She slipped out of the room and ran to her own to grab a handful of condoms.

She stopped in her bathroom long enough to clean her teeth and run a brush through her hair, then, with every part of her tingling with anticipation, she reentered his bedroom.

"And now, for one of the most highly prized sights in all of Sydney," she announced, grabbing the hem of her tank and preparing to bare her breasts.

A gentle snore answered her.

Mark Forsythe was stretched out on the bed, gloriously naked, and sound asleep.

Before her horrified gaze, even his proud erection put itself to sleep.

Torn between frustration and laughter, she approached the bed.

"Mark?"

She shook his shoulder. "Mark?"

He was so deeply asleep she doubted the crowd at a footie grand final would wake him.

She placed the bright foil packs on the bedside table and stood there, gnawing her lip as she watched him sleep.

His clothes were in an untidy heap on the floor, and even one day's acquaintance told her this was not his usual behavior. So she picked up his clothes, tossed jocks and socks in the hamper in the bathroom, and hung his pants and shirt in the closet, where a row of crisp pants and plain-colored, short-sleeved shirts hung in precise order.

She could go back to her room and finish the night in a bed far too big for one person, or she could crawl in with Mark and hope all he needed was a short nap.

Maybe if she snuggled her naked body against his, he'd wake.

So she shucked her own clothes with a lot less showmanship than she'd planned and crawled in. She flipped the fancy light cotton cover over both of them. There was a moment's rekindling of excitement when she pressed against him and he grunted, turned, and captured her breast in his hand. But the slow deep breathing of sleep wafted against the back of her neck, and she felt he was cuddling her the way he would his teddy bear.

Chapter Three

Mark woke with his heart pounding, wondering where the hell he was. Something didn't feel right. He took a moment to breathe, and let himself come to full consciousness.

Of course. He wasn't at home in his San Francisco townhouse. He was in Sydney, Australia. In a corporate house. All that fit with what he knew. What didn't fit was the naked woman sleeping beside him.

No wonder his heart was pounding. What the hell was that about? What had happened?

He raised onto his elbow and gazed down at the woman beside him. Everything fell into place as he recognized Bronwyn, her hair a sexy mess down her back, her skin smooth and fresh, her lips parted slightly in what looked like a smile.

A naked and beautiful woman beside him in bed with a smile on her face was a good thing.

What wasn't so good was that he had no memory of the night. None at all. He touched her hair and wondered what had happened between them in this bed.

It would have been nice if the earth had moved. It would be terrific if she'd cried out three or four times in ecstasy; it would be stellar if one of those times, preferably the last, he'd cried out with her.

And it would be goddam stupendous if he could remember any of it.

No wonder his heart was pounding.

He didn't expect to be Mark, the Wonder Stallion every time out, but he liked to think he never left a woman unsatisfied. Could his complete mental blackout of the night before mean he'd humiliated himself as a lover and a man?

Okay, he said to himself, get a grip. He ran his hand in a light exploratory fashion over her back. Nice back. Long and muscular. It didn't ring any bells.

But it did cause her to shift in sleep so her back pressed intimately against him.

Casually, he put an arm around her and ran his fingers lightly over her breasts and belly. *Ooh, nice, nice, nice.* She had full, firm breasts with pointy nipples, and her stomach had the tightness and tone of a professional swimmer.

Whatever sense impressions his brain was receiving came across as brand new ones. He felt as though he'd never touched those particular contours before—all the textures and angles that made up her body. Odd to be so clueless about a woman you'd made love with.

The only thing in his life he'd ever blocked out was having his wisdom teeth extracted. Having decided against general anesthetic, he'd gone gamely into the oral surgeon's chair and to this day didn't remember a thing about the experience. He knew the procedure had been completed, since he was sans wisdom teeth, but he had no memory. Like certain shock victims who blanked out intensely painful experiences.

Had last night been one of those?

His hand froze, claw-like, against her naked breast. *Oh, God.* Had he been so terrible in bed that he'd blocked the experience from his memory?

Would Bronwyn have all the women of her acquaintance squealing with laughter over his performance while he was forever in the dark about what happened?

He squinted at the clock on the bedside table. Nine. Sun streamed in the windows, suggesting it was morning.

He rolled to his back and blinked hard a few times. What day was it? Sunday, he thought. It must be Sunday.

Sneaking out of bed, he headed for the bathroom where a nice long morning pee relieved his mind somewhat as well as his bladder. While he brushed his teeth, then splashed cold water on his face, he tried to pull himself together. If she was still in his bed, the night couldn't have been a complete disaster, otherwise she'd have sneaked out of bed sometime in the night.

Wouldn't she?

He walked back into the bedroom and watched for a moment as she slept. She had the kind of natural beauty that's as potent first thing in the morning as it would be when she was all made up to go out somewhere. Her shoulders were lightly tanned against the white of the sheet, and he wished he could see the breasts he'd so recently touched.

She shifted and made what could be a waking-up noise. Panicked, he didn't want to be caught standing there naked staring at her, and his robe was hanging in the closet.

Her eyelashes fluttered.

He dove back under the covers beside her and rolled up behind her in his previous position.

A bit of sighing and then a kind of morning stretch that had her spine elongating itself against him from shoulders to ass in a way that made him want to bash his head until his memory returned.

"Morning," a sleepy and very female voice said beside him.

Oh, no. Reckoning time. And he wasn't ready.

"Morning."

"Sleep well?"

"Yes." He said politely. "You?"

"Fantastic." She leaned over and kissed him lightly on the lips. That had to be good, didn't it?

Mark glanced over at her with her sleepy morning skin, golden hair tossed over the pillow, a twinkle of humor in her eyes. It was the humor that did it. If he'd made an ass of himself last night he needed to know. Insane as it was, he'd torture himself forever if he didn't have the truth.

He cleared his throat. "I had a great time last night."

Her smile dazzled him. "Me, too."

Well, she looked happy.

His sigh had more to do with relief than satisfaction. "I wasn't sure how good a time you really had, last night being our first time together." He sucked in another breath for courage. Since he had no idea what had happened, he was going to have to finesse the details out of her.

"Our first time?"

"As lovers," he said. Surely he'd managed penetration. Never in his life had his body let him down that badly.

"Right," she said, shaking her head so her hair tossed about. He wanted to smooth it back off her face, but held himself in check until he knew more. "Sorry," she said. "I'm not much of a morning person."

He could let it go and forget about dragging the details of his performance out of her, but for some reason he really had to know. "I was just wondering, about last night, when we made love . . ." This was a lot tougher to talk about than he'd imagined. It had been a long time since he'd been with anyone but Jen, he realized; he had no idea how to go about this.

"Which part did you like best?" she cooed, that smug little smile annoying the hell out of him, as did the fact that she got the question in before he could. *Damn it.*

Panic flooded his brain. He had no idea since he couldn't remember a thing. Bluffing was his only option. "Oh, um. The part where you . . ." he made a vague gesture with his hands, "and the part where we," he made another equally meaningless hand motion.

"Mmmm," she sighed, clearly interpreting the gesture and imbuing it with meaning. "Me, too. We were something, all right. I never remember coming so many times in one night."

Relief washed over him like an unexpected summer rain. Pure, cleansing, cooling. His pounding heart slowed. His panic receded. It was a tragedy that he couldn't remember last night, but at least he'd satisfied this woman. More than satisfied her.

All right! This Australian plan was already working out better than he could have imagined.

"And you," she said dreamily, her fingertips trailing down his chest to his belly, "well, I never knew American men could be so . . . creative." When she got to the last word she did a pretty creative move herself and wrapped her fingers around his cock, which had already perked up nicely with all the flattering talk.

She said they'd been spectacular together. Damn, he wished he could remember it. Maybe if he stopped trying so hard, it would be easier, or maybe if he started the day in his favorite manner he could bring it all back.

He rolled her over until they were pressed together. "Think we can be just as good the second time?" he asked, kissing her. A tiny sound of pleasure escaped her lips as their mouths met.

He let his hands stroke her sleep-warmed skin. Her shoulders, down her arms, up her belly to her breasts. They fascinated him, those generous mounds with the proportionately large nipples. He was dying to see them, taste them.

So he did. Easing the sheet down her body caused a soft sigh that was a caress to his ears. They were gorgeous breasts. Tanned all over, the tips dark apricot. When he sucked a nipple into his mouth, unable to wait, her back arched and she reached her arms above her head like a cat stretching in the sun.

He ran his tongue around her nipple, then sucked lightly, delighted to feel the peak harden against his tongue. Amazing he hadn't remembered the touch and taste and responsiveness of her body. He must have been more tired than he thought.

Her skin tasted warm and a tiny bit salty as though all her time on surfboards and in the sea air had imprinted her with the flavor and scent of the sea.

"You taste like a mermaid," he mumbled and felt the taut muscles of her belly shift as she giggled softly.

She moved as sinuously as a mermaid, too, when he took his tongue down her belly and she groaned as his ultimate target grew closer. Her shallow breaths of excitement spurred him on and heated his blood so he thought of nothing but plunging into that wet, pulsing heat.

Moving down the bed until his head was between her legs, he noted that her tan was smooth and even all over. He pictured her naked in the sun, imagined how the light would glint dark gold on the curls he was currently nuzzling.

She was as plump and juicy and succulent as ripe fruit. When he licked her, he felt her quiver, felt her glory in her own body and her pleasure in her own sexuality. He toyed with her gently, building her up slowly, exploring her mysteries with lips and tongue and fingers.

Her intimate flesh grew plumper and firmer under his ministrations. He licked at her, teased her, eased the tip of his tongue inside her, and her body pulled it into her like a riptide pulling an unwary swimmer. He was aching with the urge to let her suck his cock into her body in the same way.

His own breathing grew harsh as he stoked her excitement. She was panting, moaning, her lower body making crazy figure eights as he swirled his tongue over and around her hot button.

"Now," she cried, grabbing his ears and pulling, "now!"

As much as he wanted to feel her come right in his mouth, he wanted more to be pumping inside her body when she came, so he slid back up, grabbed one of the condoms off the night table, sheathed himself in record time.

Considering he'd made love so recently, he felt as eager as he'd ever felt in his life.

He was about to plunge into her in animal frenzy when he stopped himself.

He never acted like an animal. What was wrong with him? Aching all over with the effort, he slowed down, kissed her softly and sweetly and eased himself into her like a lover rather than a madman.

That lasted about a minute, then she started doing that crazy figure-eight thing again and madness gripped him and wouldn't let go.

He plunged and bucked, driven half-mad by the scent of her, the sound of her, and the wild way she gripped him.

She stayed right with him. Under him, while her panting grew loud and sweat sheened her forehead, she wrapped around him and they flipped, changing the angle but not the crazy speed now that she was in control.

He felt the squeeze, watched her eyes blank, and doubted she was even aware that her fingers gripped his shoulders like claws, her short nails still managing to make respectable dents. He kissed her when she climaxed, taking her wild cries into his mouth.

He flipped her again, thrust deep, rode out the aftershocks. Then she flipped them. For a wild second they teetered on the edge of the bed, but it was a losing battle between passion and gravity. Mark hung on to just enough sense to grab her hips and hold her to him so that when they hit the floor they were still joined.

She fell on top of him with a laugh and even though the breath was knocked out of him, he laughed up at her. God, she was gorgeous.

She leaned back, giving him a view that would be imprinted on his mind forever. Her position also gave him easy access to her sweet spot. He played her with his fingers, bringing her up again.

As much as he wanted to drag the loving out, he couldn't.

When she came the second time, he was lost. Maybe his grunt wasn't as musical as her cries of release, but it was heartfelt. He came deep inside her, burying his face in her neck when she slumped on top of him.

In the five years he and Jennifer Talbot had been together, he'd never considered another woman. He'd imagined growing old, faithful and true to his wife through thick and thin, richer and poorer, sickness and health.

Now he'd slept with someone new. Not only that, but it had been incredible.

Even as he breathed in the wonderful fresh scent of the woman he'd met and bedded within twenty-four hours, he was conscious of a desire to get to know her better. To make love to her again and again.

She was sweet, a little goofy, too gorgeous for words, and there was something about her that made him relax and have fun. He'd turned down all her offers yesterday to get outside and enjoy life, and forced himself to work. He'd spent more time wishing he'd said yes, than actually working, and since his reason for saying no was to keep his hands off the woman, it hadn't worked anyhow. Today, he was going to make up for lost time. He and Bron were going to have some fun.

"Have you seen the enormous bathtub in your bathroom?" Bron whispered in his ear, ending the question with a nibble on his earlobe. "It's a good size for two people."

Oh, she was fun all right. And that creative mind of hers didn't stop at designing beach fashions.

He ran his hands up her back, still slightly damp with the sweat of their mutual morning workout, and said, "I am a big believer in conserving water. Let's go."

Chapter Four

"Welcome to King's Cross," said Bron with forced cheer. "Where anything can happen."

She'd kept Mark as busy as she could manage today. They'd walked for miles, through the Botanical Gardens, around the Rocks, where they'd visited the market and she'd bought him a ridiculous sun hat with enormous koalas all over it, and he'd bought her a pair of earrings that only a half-blind Las Vegas showgirl could love.

Then they'd taken the ferry across the harbor to the seaside suburb of Manly and lolled around on the sand, gone for a swim, and eaten fish and chips on the beach.

They returned home and made love again, and she cursed Jennifer Talbot for taking one of the sweetest men she'd ever met and turning him into a cynic.

He wasn't a hardened cynic, though, and that gave her hope; he was more of a sweet, hurt darling with a cynical crust she was determined to break through.

After all the shopping and sightseeing, and some pretty athletic sex, she was certain he'd crash and put his party plan out of his head. But he was both tenacious, she discovered, and tireless.

She was cuddled against him, all but drifting into a nice early evening nap, his hand toying lazily with her breasts, when his hand suddenly stiffened as though he'd got a cramp and he said, "Where's a good place to go tonight where the singles hang out?"

So she'd pulled herself awake.

She could tell him to get stuffed, and then he'd probably go off on his own, make a fool of himself, and drag home some dreadful tart who wouldn't make him happy. Empty sex was never going to make him happy, she knew that already about him.

She was going to make him happy. He was sweet, serious, decent, and she was already halfway in love with him. So, she'd chaperon him tonight and keep him out of trouble, and out of anyone's bed but hers.

When Cam had told her to babysit the Yank, he couldn't have known how much Mark needed looking after, or that she was exactly the woman for the job.

"I'll take you with me to a party tonight." A party she'd already decided to skip in favor of a night in with Mark. What else could she do? At least she'd kept him so busy that he hadn't mentioned anything about throwing her out of the house today.

"You'll never have a better tour guide to the singles scene," she promised him cheerfully as she dressed. "These are my people. I can even give you the inside scoop on the ones you want to avoid." That would be anyone with breasts, but she wasn't going to give her plan away.

So, instead of spending an evening in with a man she couldn't seem to get enough of, she dressed in a man-hunting red mini dress, heels that damn near crippled her, and the ridiculous earrings Mark had bought her. She'd probably be mistaken for one of the hookers who worked King's Cross, but at least Mark was going to notice her. He wanted a hot Aussie chick?

He'd never find a hotter one than the girl right under his nose.

And just to remind him that two could play the pick-up game, she shouted down the stairs to him, "Can you bring up my gold thong when you come upstairs?"

He muttered something that sounded very grumpy and she tossed her head. A little of his own medicine would do him good. "Oh, never mind, I'll get it myself," she shouted back and headed downstairs. He stood at the bottom and waited for her, the thong a glittery wisp of gold in his hand.

He did not look pleased.

She took her time coming down those stairs in her killer dress and do-me baby heels. If he didn't know she was pantiless under the ridiculous dress, it wasn't from lack of giving him a peep show.

His mouth did open and close a few times as he watched her descend in her best imitation of a runway model, doing that pushed-forward thing with her hips. His desire for her was pulsing from him, but he never got any words out. His fingers clamped on her thong.

Standing on the lowest stair put her eye to eye with him.

"Am I going to have to break your fingers to get my underwear?" she asked softly, tossing her hair back and then teasing him further by licking her glossy red lips.

"You're going out like that?" he asked, sounding like a cross between a strict fifties dad and a man choking on his own lust.

"Unless you have a better idea," she said, giving him another chance to prove to them both that she was the woman he really wanted.

"I just think you're being a little obvious."

"I don't waste my time on subtle. I take what I want, Mark." She reached out and took the glittery thong from his fingers, and, while he watched, she stepped into the thong and pulled it slowly up her legs.

As she wiggled it in place she thought he was either going to start shouting at her or throw her down on the stairs and take her there. She really hoped for the latter, but after a struggle that had him turning an interesting shade of red and gripping his hands into tight fists, he turned away.

Not only was she disappointed, but she'd forgotten that she'd sworn never to wear the gold thong again. It was horribly uncomfortable—the thong version of a hair shirt.

"Now, before we go . . ." Mark gestured to the room where she'd been sleeping.

"Oh, no worries. I've got that sorted."

"You have? But we've been together all day."

She smiled. Since he thought she was so disposable, she'd let him see she had plenty of options, too. "Like I said. I live the singles life. I've got friends I can stay with."

Mark's eyes narrowed fractionally and she watched a flash of possessiveness cross his face.

Yes! She hadn't missed her guess. He was no womanizer. He was essentially a one-woman man. Bron intended, at least in the short term, to be that woman. He might think he was in control, but he'd soon find he was wrong.

She did the ditching in relationships. She set the boundaries and decided when it was over. She and Mark were just beginning. She hadn't nearly finished with him yet.

Mark seemed to struggle for another minute.

"You're not jealous are you?" she asked him.

"No." He leaned against the wall and shoved his hands in the pockets of perfectly creased khakis. This time he'd gone all the way to the sartorial wild side with a striped shirt. Yep, there really were two tones of blue in his shirt. The man needed her desperately, how could he not see that?

"Look, Bronwyn. I'm going to tell you the truth. I'm having a hard time with this. I want you, and it's killing me to think of you with other men." He shrugged, and looked a bit lost. "It's been a long time since I was on my own. I'm relearning how to be a single wild man, I guess."

If he'd ever been a wild man, she'd been raised by dingoes.

"We slept together." He glanced at her and she saw the banked passion glow like blue flame. Everything inside her quivered.

"And it was fantastic."

"Yes." He stepped closer. "It was."

"We don't have to go out," she said, soft and sultry, feeling her body start to tingle with arousal.

He stopped mid-stride, like he'd been bashed in the middle by a cricket bat. "No. I want to go out. I feel jealous. I admit it, but I've got to get over my middle-class American morals. You sleep with other men. I sleep with other women. That's the way it is these days, right?"

"That depends on the man. And on the woman," she said tightly. She wouldn't feel hurt. She wouldn't allow herself that weakness. He was struggling, trying to be something that wasn't in his nature. She understood that just as she understood it was up to her to keep him true to the man he was. One day he'd thank her.

For herself, she took lovers when they appealed to her, and the relationships lasted until they were over. But she'd never been a one-night girl, or indiscriminate in her choices. She might have made a mistake with Mark, but she didn't think so.

They caught a cab to the Cross and walked around a bit. She got sly enjoyment out of Mark's reaction. "It's quite something, isn't it?" she said after one of the bouncers at a strip club had done his best to entice them inside for a "fantastic show, mate." The neon lights made the whole area feel like a stage. A prostitute gave them a friendly greeting, two drunks leaned on each other as they staggered down the street, and a crowd of boisterous young men ambled past— not at the staggering stage yet, but the night was young.

"Probably a buck's night," she said.

"Buck's night?"

"A party for a bloke getting married."

As they strolled past the bars and the peep shows, she tried to see it through his eyes. The area was cheesy and dilapidated, but in a cheerful sort of way.

"Here we are," she said as they reached the club where they were meeting some of her friends.

"What do you want to drink?" Mark asked as they entered the crowded club.

"A cosmopolitan, please."

He grinned at her. "Now that makes me feel right at home," he said and headed for the bar.

"Hey Ronnie, who's the hunk?" Keili asked. Keili wasn't usually one to run right up to her the minute she arrived. The woman was acquaintance rather than friend, more enemy than ally. She had a nose for weakness sharper than a shark scenting blood, and an unfailing appetite for men. Especially men that Bron liked.

Her handling of Keili would be critical in her campaign to keep Mark to herself. Not only for her own satisfaction, but for Mark's protection. He could so easily be fooled. Keili was like a bluebottle, an attractive jellyfish floating by, seeming decorative and benign. But let her get skin to skin, and a man would endure brief but almost unendurable agony that could leave him marked for life.

Keili was adjusting her push-up bra and tossing her hair around—the bluebottle getting ready to sting. Bron reached for the only weapon she could think of that would instantly annihilate Keili's interest.

"Isn't he cute?" She glanced over at Mark with what she hoped was a casual motherliness. "He's American. He's doing some boring accounting job for Crane. I'm babysitting him over the weekend."

"Lucky you." Keili licked her lips glossy.

"Not really." She groaned theatrically and leaned in to whisper, woman to woman. "Why is it always the best-looking ones?"

A sharp glance her way. "You don't mean he's . . . ?"

"Well-groomed," she said significantly. "He irons his jeans. And he's from *San Francisco.*"

"Well, that doesn't—"

"I know. I didn't want to believe it either," she said. "It's a tragedy for womankind."

Keili did not appear convinced, probably because lying about a man's sexual orientation in order to keep him to herself was exactly the sort of stunt she'd pull. Bron needed to convince her, and fast.

"I think I'll go over and introduce myself anyway," Keili said after a moment. "It's nice to be friendly."

"Sure. He's a super guy. Ask him about his tropical fish collection and he'll go on for hours."

"Tropical fish. Right."

"Oh, before you meet him, you might want to remove the greenery from between your teeth."

Keili shoved a hand in front of her mouth. "Why didn't you tell me before?" she squeaked and hustled off to the bathroom. Once there, she'd have a meaningful love affair with the mirror, so Bron had a good few minutes' grace. But she still had to move fast.

She wandered over to Bill Freemantle, who was also eyeing her date for the evening. "I'm jealous," he said.

"You should go and introduce yourself. You two have a lot in common."

"You don't mean?"

"He's not out yet, but . . . I'm getting the vibes, if you know what I mean."

"Bron, darling," Bill said, putting a friendly arm around her shoulders. "Every man who doesn't want to sleep with you isn't gay."

"He's from San Francisco. He irons his jeans."

Bill glanced over. "Not entirely proof-positive, love. Although he's certainly giving me the once-over."

"He is?" She followed Bill's gaze and sure enough, Mark was staring at them like a dog watching over a meaty bone. Although she sensed it was her he was interested in, not Bill.

"You're gorgeous," Bill said softly, kissing her lightly on the cheek, "but he's better. See you around." And he sauntered over to Mark. She watched them shake hands and then Bill sat down and next thing they were chatting like old friends. She made her way over to get her drink, and then left them to it.

She'd feel a lot guiltier if she didn't think they would have a lot in common. Except, of course, for their sexual preferences.

Keili emerged from the bathroom a few minutes later, looking like she'd redone her makeup based on a Cosmo "how to lure him into bed" makeover. Her face fell so ludicrously when she saw Mark and Bill laughing together that Bron felt she'd paid off a few old scores.

As she'd guessed, she didn't have to do another thing to ensure Mark ended the evening in the same single state he began it. Keili's middle name was not Discretion. Every one of their mutual friends knew within a half-hour that the hot guy from America batted for the other team.

Her plan was working. Mark was in no danger of going home with anyone else. An added benefit, which injected extra sweetness to her plan, was the way she felt his eyes on her whenever she was near another man.

He stared at her as a jealous lover, not as a casual acquaintance, and she did everything she could think of to let him know he wasn't the only man in the southern hemisphere who thought her a knockout.

So he thought she was a one-night stand, did he? Not bloody likely.

By midnight the usual pairing-up and going-home ritual was in full swing. Mark, as far as she could tell, had made a feeble effort at best to talk to anyone but Bill. He'd been polite to the women who'd come by, but his behavior of friendly disinterest only added to the impression she'd given that he was gay.

For which, she was egotistical enough to believe, she was responsible.

"Come on then," she said, walking over to where he and Bill sat, "we'd best get home. We've got work tomorrow morning."

When they arrived home together, Mark said, "I haven't struck out that badly in years. The women at that party were all great, really friendly, but as soon as I tried to get to know them a little better it was like they all had to be somewhere."

Suppressing her smirk was a true test of character.

"It's only your second day in town. You can't expect to get lucky every night."

"You were the most attractive woman at the party, anyway," he said with a shrug. "No one else appealed to me at all."

"Thanks." She felt the same about him. None of the guys there did anything for her compared to Mark.

"You have a lot of male friends." He said it with just a suggestion of a question mark.

There it was again, that streak of possessiveness that made a liar out of him and his big talk of casual relationships. Well, if he wanted to know more about her, he was going to have to ask. She shrugged and said, "I have lots of female friends, too."

"You and Bill seem pretty close."

No, she didn't have enough character in stock to stifle a smug, "Are you jealous?"

Mark sent her a pitying look. "Bill's gay."

Her eyes widened as guilt smote her for setting him up, and possibly putting both him and Bill in an awkward position. She shouldn't have done that to either of them. "Did he come on to you?"

"Of course not. He's a classy guy."

"Then how did you know?"

He rolled his gaze. "I'm from California."

"Well, he's a very nice man."

"I thought so, too. He's promised to take me fishing."

More guilt smacked at her as she recalled how she'd egged Bill on. Running a finger over the arm of the corporate-executive upholstered couch, she said, "You don't think he thinks you're . . . ?"

"No. I told him I got dumped by my girlfriend. He told me he got dumped by his boyfriend. He's a good guy, and we're going fishing."

She heaved a huge sigh of relief. "I'm glad you made a new friend. And sorry you struck out with the women. Maybe you'll do better tomorrow night."

He came across the room and took her face in his hands, gazing down at her with those serious/sexy smoky blue eyes that made her crazy when she looked into their depths. "I brought home the woman I wanted to," he said, soft and slow, each word licking over her with husky warmth.

He kissed her, and nerves jangled in places that shouldn't have nerves. He kissed her thoroughly, then lifted his head a fraction. "Let's go to bed," he murmured against her lips.

If she'd ever wanted any man more, she'd blocked the memory. Every part of her, from the soles of her feet to the follicles in her scalp, was shouting the same message: *Yes, yes, yes!*

But after a truly heroic struggle with her own hormones, she managed to shake her head.

"Here's how it's going to be," she said when she could force herself to pull away from the warm, solid feel of him and everything those eyes promised. "I'm not the consolation prize. The little plastic rabbit you get at the show when you miss winning the big stuffed bear. Right?"

"Hey, I'm not suggesting . . . I didn't mean . . ." He looked confused and guilty at the same time, and she realized he hadn't meant to insult her. Still. He had.

Her body was aching for him, but she'd be buggered if she'd be little-Miss-Available whenever he couldn't score with anyone else. "If you want me, you'll need to work at it a little harder, mate."

She reached up on her tiptoes and kissed him lightly. "Now get some sleep. You start work tomorrow."

Chapter Five

For the second morning Mark awoke wildly disoriented, but unlike yesterday, he was alone in bed.

He decided that waking up with Bronwyn had been a lot more interesting than cruising this banana boat of a bed alone. He frowned momentarily to think of her waking similarly solo in her own room.

He took a moment to contemplate the ceiling as he thought back on his night with Bron, but the smug grin abruptly faded when he realized that last night he hadn't remotely wanted any of the gorgeous sun-kissed women at that party—he'd wanted Bron.

In spite of the fact that he'd tried to hide it, she was the one his eyes followed as she flitted from friend to friend—mostly men, he'd noted—like a confident hummingbird from flower to flower. A sip of nectar here, an energetic stationary buzzing there.

No wonder the other women had been so aloof with him. They must have picked up on his infatuation with Bron.

Shit. Some wild man he was turning out to be. He slept with one woman and immediately developed warm feelings for her. What was wrong with him? This trip was supposed to be his chance to change. And he needed to change. He wouldn't be made a fool of a second time in his life.

Throwing off the covers, he rose from bed and stalked to the shower. He was here in Sydney because Jen, in a move of monumental tactlessness, had asked him to take on this project—because he was the best at what he did. Oh, how he'd wanted to tell her to take the entire inventory of Crane surfboards and stuff them up her ass—or, better still, the ass of Cameron Crane. But if he did that, Jen would know she'd torn his heart out of his chest and stomped on it.

No. He had his pride. Pride had held his emotions in control and his temper on a leash while Jennifer had explained, with a few tears, that she'd fallen in love with another man. He'd been pretty cool about the breakup. Manly. He hadn't railed or shouted, sobbed, or even thrown her unfaithfulness in her face. He wasn't that kind of man.

If any guy had ever let the woman he loved off the hook easier, that man was a saint.

Of course, when she'd returned his ring and asked for his key to her apartment, he'd finally realized she was serious.

That night he'd gone on a bender that had likely done permanent damage to his liver. But even in the depths of drunkenness, he hadn't slobbered his woes all over some poor bartender, or put anyone at risk by driving under the influence. Even as a drunk he was a rule-following do-gooder. And wouldn't you think a woman would want a man like that? he mused as water pounded his body. Wouldn't you think a woman—Jen for instance—would want to spend her life with a man who did his own ironing, supported feminism, and even wore a pink ribbon for breast cancer awareness?

A wave of bitterness hit him so hard he ended up getting shampoo in his eye and cursing. What had being a decent, caring man got him? Dumped for a guy with a corny accent badly in need of a shave.

Would Cameron Crane wear a pink ribbon for anything? He snorted to himself. Not hardly.

Well, the days of Saint Mark were over, he decided, as he dried off and dressed in crisp khakis and a freshly ironed

short-sleeved shirt. Jen had warned him the Crane operation was casual, so he'd packed only one summer-weight
suit, but nothing was going to make him dress like he'd
pulled clothes at random from a thrift shop and then slept
in them a few nights. He'd leave that sartorial elegance to
Cameron Crane. The bastard.

His former fiancée and her new man were going to be in
Sydney during the latter part of his trip. Maybe by the time
she got here and saw him in the same room with that bastard, she'd realize what she'd given up in exchange for
whisker burn, body odor, and a whole lot of cash.

His plan was so hazy he was barely aware he had one.
But he planned that when Jen got here, she'd see that her re-
jected fiancé was doing just fine and was living life to the
fullest. If she saw him enjoying women like they were ciga-
rettes and he was a chainsmoker, then she might pause one
nanosecond to think about what she'd so blithely tossed
away.

A few months with Cameron Crane might have made
her realize all she was missing. She might beg clean-shaven,
regularly showered, and crisply ironed Mark Forsythe and
his much slimmer wallet to take her back. He smiled slightly
as he packed up his laptop.

Naturally, he'd say no.

He'd enjoy that scene very much.

He opened his bedroom door and a slight hint of floral
and spice in the air told him that his sexy housemate had recently passed this way.

He paused, inhaling Bron's scent, helplessly recalling
how he'd felt driving deep inside her body. He could have
had her in his bed again last night if he hadn't acted like a
pig. Was he really going to make her move out today as
he'd planned? No. He didn't want the most exciting sex he
ever remembered to end so soon. And he didn't want to
think he'd hurt a very nice woman's feelings because his
own were so battered.

He tapped his fingertips reflexively against his computer

case as he tried to figure out what the rules were in this kind of situation. Then he realized the rules were whatever the hell he decided they would be. He had to quit thinking of rules, good behavior, politeness.

Rule-breaker, maverick, lone gunman. These were his new ideals. If he wanted to sleep with Bron again, he would. Simple as that. He'd show a little more class about it than he had last night, is all. And with that he strode downstairs and nearly fell over his feet.

The smell of coffee had his taste buds weeping for joy, as did the sight of Bron in a strappy sundress that showed off her tanned, muscular legs, arms and shoulders, and hinted at all the other parts—which he knew from personal experience were just as gorgeous.

He'd been callow and stupid last night to think he could bed her when they'd both arrived home unencumbered. He felt a twinge of embarrassment, but amazingly, when she turned his way, there was no trace of antagonism.

"Morning," she said with a friendly smile. "I wasn't sure if you liked eggs or whatever on a work day."

"I, uh . . ." he cleared his throat. "Just toast and coffee."

She tsked. "Not very healthy. You should eat fruit and protein at breakfast." She'd managed to make a godawful mess of the kitchen in a short time, but he kind of liked the disorder. It was so unusual in his life.

"What can I do to help?" The dishes, probably. He felt ridiculous being waited on by this woman who also had to go to work today. It wasn't like cooking for him was her job.

Again that sunshine smile flashed. "Handy 'round the place, are you?" Her hair was still damp on the ends and he had to fight an impulse to grab a handful and, holding her in place, give her a proper good morning.

But of course that wouldn't be—

Saint Mark was dead. Badass Mark was in control, and Badass Mark did whatever the hell he felt like.

He grabbed a handful of hair, scrunching the damp

strands into a wet rope and, taking advantage of her squeak of surprise, kissed her open mouth.

She'd obviously been snacking on the fruit she'd arranged on the plate, for she tasted like every exotic flavor he knew and some he didn't recognize. Papaya, mango, starfruit, and under it all the elusive salt-sweet scent of the ocean.

For a second she hesitated, then kissed him back with all the enthusiasm he could handle.

"I missed you when I woke up," he mumbled against her lips as his hands moved from her hair down her shoulders to rest briefly on the small, tight waist.

"You were a dickhead last night," she replied, nibbling his lips.

He smiled a little. "I was indeed a dickhead," he agreed, giving the word her pronunciation, which made her chuckle softly. "I'm sorry."

"I missed you last night, too," she admitted.

With a glance over her shoulder to the kitchen clock, he saw it was still early enough for what he had in mind.

"I'll show you a California breakfast tradition."

"If it's anything to do with waffles, I'm not interested."

He slid the zip down the back of her dress and slipped the straps to her waist. "No waffles. I promise."

Saint Mark resurfaced only briefly, but long enough to rescue her dress from probable disaster, by the simple expedient of letting go of the straps so it slid with no coy hesitation at all to the floor. He bent, retrieved the dress, and laid it neatly over a chair before turning back to where Bron stood, a half-sweet, half-challenging expression on her face, the sexiest smile he'd ever seen on her lips, and a "come and get me" lilt to her nipples.

He didn't need to be invited twice.

Naturally, she hadn't been wearing a bra, and her salmon pink panties were soon disposed of.

And there she was, dappled in morning sunlight in a bright, compact, efficient kitchen, looking more appetizing than any breakfast he could imagine.

He reached for a papaya slice—orange and wet—and slid it around her nipple. The fruit was cold from the fridge, and she gasped slightly as the cold flesh of the papaya met her warmer flesh. The fruit tracked cold wet juice and goose bumps in its wake.

When he'd finished toying with her he palmed the fruit and smushed it with no elegance but much satisfaction on the mound of her breast. She giggled and sighed at the same time and he bent and licked at the instant fruit smoothie he'd made.

"You said I needed to eat more fruit," he reminded her, lapping up the orange mush and thinking nothing had ever tasted so incredible. He experimented with mangoes until the yellow juice ran between her breasts and his tongue couldn't keep up, and so he let the juice dribble down her front, hoisting her up to sit on the granite counter.

"Hey," she protested, "that's cold."

"I'll warm you," he promised, bending before her and following the tracks of juice where he'd aimed them. Down her stomach, a dip into her belly button to suck at the small pool there, the fruit scent taking on musk overtones as her own excitement built.

Leaning back on her hands, she let her head fall back as he followed the trail of juice lower to where it mingled with her own juices. When he touched her with his tongue her body jerked against his mouth, kissing him back, and that wonderful humming started deep in her throat. The orchestra pit practicing up for the big crescendo.

When he put his mouth on her, she started to pant. Then moan a little, and she could barely stay on the countertop, never mind keep still. The different juices were all mingling on his tongue, driving him crazy with wanting more. More of her flavor, more of her sweetness, more of Bron.

Her cries grew urgent, her body plumper and slicker, and he swirled once, all the way around, and then thrust his tongue inside her body. And just like that, she exploded.

He didn't stop, couldn't, needing to suck every bit of sweetness out of her until she was sobbing with release.

"No more," she panted. "I can't take any more."

He didn't think he could take any more either without seriously embarrassing himself, so he kissed his way back up her body and lifted her down from the counter.

Wondering if Badass Mark had gone too far, he turned away to let her gather herself, when he found himself attacked from behind. His belt buckle was open before he'd quite realized she was after it, and his pants and boxers sliding south.

"What did you—" The sentence ended in a grunt as he felt the cold squish of fruit against his very hot, very hard cock.

"I'm a bit short of vitamin C myself," Bron explained as she slid to her knees before him. He glanced down and was mildly shocked to see his normally white flesh covered with an abstract arrangement of color and textures. Red, orange, green—all fruit, all squishy, and all cool. Against the fruit mask came the warm, firm swirl of Bron's tongue. Her eyes were half-closed, her mouth faintly curved in a smile like that of a chocoholic biting into her first Godiva's.

Her tongue curled around him, and she made these wonderful sounds of pleasure. Explosion was imminent.

"Condom," he grunted.

"Mmwhn?"

"Condom." More desperate, trying to think of the balance sheet of the last company he'd saved from bankruptcy. But all he could think about was the pungent smell of papaya, mango, and orange, and the feel of—no, can't think about that.

Her hands were on his butt now, squeezing, and her mouth was all over him, her tongue so sweet, so warm, so . . . oh, no, one hand slipped lower, between his legs. No, not the balls, please, not the balls.

Too late, gently she cupped and squeezed and it was too much.

A moment of such exquisite delight gripped him that he had to reach behind him for the countertop in order to remain upright.

When she had squeezed the last of his climax from him, he felt soft kisses as she made her way up his body much as he had up hers.

They held each other, wordless for a few minutes, until a muffled squeak brought him out of the state of bliss in which he'd been floating half-conscious.

"We've got to go."

"Shit," he yelled, glimpsing the clock. One glance at the pants crushed and papaya spattered around his ankles and he knew he'd have to change. "Give me five minutes."

He bolted for the stairs but at the bottom couldn't help but turn and enjoy the sight of Bron naked and sun-dappled, calmly stepping into her panties, and then slipping on the sundress.

"Thanks for breakfast," he said.

She glanced back at him with her sweet, sultry smile and he wished they didn't have to go to work today. "Any time."

He couldn't help the grin, or the urge to whistle as he raced up the stairs.

Chapter Six

"Oh, the man doesn't just work a spreadsheet, he makes love to it. He's so amazing he could balance *your* checkbook," said Fiona, the front-office receptionist and center of a gossip network the size and complexity of which amazed Bronwyn. It might have questionable authenticity, but was always good for a laugh.

Bron snorted. "For that he'd need supernatural powers."

Mark had worked here for three days and Bron hadn't missed the way the women in the office, Fiona especially, had been checking him out. Her only consolation was that so far he remained oblivious. Give the man a computer and a bunch of boring numbers, and he went to some completely different plane of existence. It was creepy.

"I bet he's amazing in bed." Fi gave her a, "come on it's just us girls, give" look.

Fiona was terrific. Fun and upbeat, almost as daring a surfer as Bron and she genuinely loved men. All sorts of men. Fiona was exactly the kind of woman Mark had come to Sydney to find, but Mark and she would be all wrong together. Bron knew that.

She was doing them both a favor, she rationalized with great virtuousness and a large dollop of self-interest, when she leaned in close and kept her voice low.

"If you're thinking of giving him a try, you might want to stock up on Viagra."

Fiona's eyes opened wide. "Viagra? You mean he has trouble . . . ?" she made vague motions in the direction of her lap.

Bron felt a moment's guilt. She might as well publish Mark's supposed impotence in the in-house e-mail system as tell Fiona. However, she couldn't go with the gay angle here, since everyone knew Jennifer Talbot and he had been engaged. They might find it suspicious that being dumped by a woman turned him gay within a matter of months. Probably such things happened, but her story wouldn't hold up under the faintest of investigations.

"I'm not saying that's why Jen gave him the flick. Maybe it was being dumped for another man that's given him some . . . um, confidence issues. All I'm saying is . . . well," she tried to look sad and confidential, "I shouldn't really tell at all. I don't want you to waste your time, that's all. Not after that surfie from Brisbane turned out to be such a letdown."

"Oh, don't bring that up. I finally brought him home and he got drunk and spewed all over the bathroom."

"Right. Who needs two disasters in a row?"

Fiona nodded sagely and took off her glasses to gnaw the earpiece, a habit that should have been revolting, but she somehow managed to make sexy. The slightly out-of-focus expression in her eyes appeared sensual but was really myopic. "Maybe he needs an understanding woman to help him through his bad patch."

Oh, no. That was exactly what Mark didn't need. "Sure," Bron said brightly. "Great idea. And, penis size is vastly over-rated, don't you think?"

The glasses clattered to the reception desk as Fi's mouth fell open. "He's only got a little willie?"

"Shhh." Bron glanced around the busy reception, but fortunately no one appeared to be listening. "Don't tell anyone. I only wanted to warn you."

"Oh, right. Yeah. Thanks." Fiona picked up her glasses

and put them back on. "No wonder he makes love to his calculator. Those buttons are so nice and tiny."

"I'll cook tonight," Mark said as they headed home.

"Why would you do that?" Bron asked. She was driving him home from the office as she'd been doing most days.

"Because you shouldn't have to do it every night. Besides, I'm a neater cook. Dishes won't be such a marathon."

They stopped to shop and she immediately wandered to the display of fruit, like a magpie to shiny beads.

"Bron, I made a list."

She turned and laughed. "Mr. Efficient. Of course you did."

It *was* efficient to have a list, and they could have been done in no time if she hadn't insisted on wandering around and making an adventure out of a chore, making him sample some kind of dip she liked enough to buy, and showing him all the kinds of foods he wouldn't find at home. He had to admit shopping, like everything else, was more fun with Bron around.

When they got home, he reached for the grocery bags and handed her the lightest one, thinking this was a ritual like married people might share, only he suspected rituals would never become dull or routine with Bron.

He was right. As they climbed the outside stairs, it seemed there was someone waiting for them. A man with an official-looking briefcase.

"Bronwyn Spencer?" the man asked in a snotty tone that irked Mark immediately.

"Oh, crikey, not again," she muttered behind him.

He made a motion to her with his hand, making a grocery sack swing. "Who wants to know?"

"Ms. Spencer is three months overdue paying for her new fridge," the man said in that same snooty tone. "And she seems to have changed addresses without informing her creditors."

Irritation surged through Mark. How dare this little pipsqueak talk to and about Bron this way? And how could she put herself in this position?

He put down a grocery bag and reached for his wallet. "I'm Ms. Spencer's accountant," he said with impressive terseness. "If there's been an oversight, we'll correct it." He pulled out a business card and his pen and carefully wrote his local number at Crane onto it. "You can reach me at this number, tomorrow."

The man opened his mouth to protest.

"During business hours," Mark said, and waited until the toad had scrambled back down the stairs before letting Bron and him into the house.

"Wow, thanks," Bron said when they were inside with the door shut. "I can't believe they tracked me down here."

She kept babbling as she hauled her one bag of groceries to the kitchen, then made a big production out of putting everything away.

"Hold on a minute," he said, putting a hand on her shoulder. "Are you in trouble?"

She winced. "Not trouble, exactly. I'm not the most organized bookkeeper. I told you I'm hopeless." She looked hot and embarrassed and uncomfortable. He kissed her nose.

"I've saved huge companies from bankruptcy, Bron. I bet I can help you, too."

"Really?"

"Sure. First we eat, then we do some 'boring accounting,'" he said, imitating her well enough that she giggled.

While she put the rest of the groceries away, he started cooking. "Oh, shit," he muttered. "I forgot to put fresh thyme on the list."

She opened a cupboard that was stocked with some dried spices. "No thyme. Will oregano do?"

"The recipe doesn't call for oregano," he said, wondering if he should run out to the local corner store.

Bron came up behind him and kissed his neck. "Be a devil," she said.

Okay, so maybe he was a little anal sometimes, he admitted as he tasted the pasta dish and found the oregano had done the job.

After dinner, she was so desperate to escape the accounting ordeal that she even volunteered to do dishes, but he shook his head. "Let's get you organized."

She made a revolted face, but she didn't refuse the help.

"So, where's this fridge you bought and forgot to pay for?" She didn't even have a place to live, what did she want with a fridge?

"That was for a girlfriend. She lost her job and then her fridge went. She'll pay me back when she can."

"You're a generous friend, Bron." She'd been generous with him, too. Giving him tours of the area, her time, and sharing her body with him. He was enjoying this trip more than he'd dreamed possible.

"Yeah, well, I'm not an organized one." She dragged her toe across the floor like a little kid. "I don't know how to balance my checkbook. Never can work it out, so then I don't know how much money I've got, see?"

"Do you want me to do that for you? Balance your checkbook and figure out where you stand?"

She thought about it and then nodded.

"You don't think it's too personal?"

"What, more personal than you sticking your tongue inside my body? I don't think so."

"Okay. Sure." Absurdly, he fought the urge to blush. She was right, they'd been intimate physically, why shouldn't he see her bank account if she was willing?

It didn't take him all that long to get her sorted out or to explain to her how to reconcile her account every month. "You'd find life a lot easier with a budget, which I can set up for you."

She made gagging noises, but, he noticed, she didn't turn him down. "As for the fridge, when that collector calls me tomorrow, we'll work out a monthly payment schedule you can live with. All right?"

She breathed a huge sigh of relief. "Yeah. Thanks. Really."

"You're welcome. Now, do I get a reward?"

She grinned at him in that way he loved that had his body already tightening in anticipation. "Yeah," she said. "You get a reward. I'm taking you shopping tomorrow."

His erection wilted along with his smile. "Shopping?"

"I can't stand it another minute. You dress like my dad."

Mark gazed down at his crisp navy Dockers and checked golf shirt. "I'm guessing he's not a really hip guy."

"He's all right for a fifty-five-year-old, but you're young. You need to start acting like it."

"I have two words for you," he said advancing on her.

Her eyes crinkled. "What?"

"No yellow." And then he scooped her up, giggling, and hauled her up the stairs to bed.

Mark wondered if it was some Australian courting ritual he'd never heard of when he began to notice the women of Crane glancing surreptitiously at his crotch. Even a few of the guys were doing it.

After checking to make sure he was zipped and hadn't inadvertently dropped something in his lap, he decided it was some kind of cultural thing and filed it away for future reference. He wondered if he was supposed to reciprocate.

He'd always understood Australians to be an earthy people, but he'd never heard of this crotch-checking business before. He'd have to ask Bron.

He'd feel a little strange telling her about the crotch thing, though, in case she thought he was coming on to other women. Which, surprisingly, he had no interest in doing. He'd gone out with her on the weekend more as a matter of form than that he really cared to meet any women. They'd shopped, and argued like crazy trying to find him clothes they could both live with, then they'd gone to some party or other, but he'd pretty much never left her side all evening.

He'd already worked out that if he was free to date other

women then Bron was free to date other men, and as far as he was concerned, it wasn't going to happen.

After almost two weeks in Sydney, he had to admit he'd struck out spectacularly in the slutting-around department. But, he kept reminding himself, there were no rules. If he wanted to bed the same woman every night—hell, every morning, early evening after they got home from work, and any snatch of time they felt like it, then why shouldn't he?

He was seeing plenty of Sydney, enjoying the challenge of work, and he'd formed a few friendships of his own. Bill had taken him fishing and they hadn't caught anything, but they'd drunk some beer and toured the amazing coastline around the city.

He'd gone surfing with Bron and a few of the guys from the office and been amazed at how much he liked the sport. He'd forgotten the thrill of being picked up and carried by a wave, the heart-pounding excitement mixed with fear as the wave curled above you and the world was nothing but a noisy blue tunnel.

And Bron! When he'd jokingly likened her to a mermaid, he hadn't been far off. Bron perched on a surfboard, her hair and body golden as she rode waves like they were hers to command, was a sight he'd never forget.

And surfing, he discovered, made her horny. Yes, he'd decided he was a big fan of surfing after all.

He was also learning some new customs. How to order a coffee, the correct way to order a beer; he'd even made half a stab at working out the rules of cricket, and tried not to fall asleep when he actually watched a game.

He really ought to ask Bron about this crotch-checking business, though.

But as it turned out, something new and far more unpleasant took its place at the top of his mind.

He'd endured the by-now familiar crotch glance, this time with the addition of a smirk from some young punk with blindingly bright board shorts, a goatee, hair decorated with sand, and a big honking earring. After the crotch-glance/smirk combo the fellow said, "G'day, ah'm Peet."

A quick glance at the list of people he'd requested meetings with clued Mark in that *Peet* must be Peter Moorehead, the company's in-house accountant, who'd been on holiday for the last couple of weeks.

"Hi, Pete," he said, shaking hands and coming away with more sand. These people must be hell on computer keyboards. They were certainly hell on the eyes of the unwary. "I need to ask you a few questions about how you do your tax accounting."

"Righto. Ask away." And to give the young guy credit, he certainly knew his stuff.

After half an hour, they'd gone from the general to the specific, and Mark asked, "And do you code different colors under the same product code?"

"Dunno, mate. You'd have to ask Cam's sister about that."

"Cam's sister?" His gut bubbled like an underground geyser at the mention of the man. He'd thought he was free of Cameron Freakin' Crane for the first couple of weeks he was here, and now it turned out he had a sister working here?

Well, whoever she was, he'd avoid her like the man-eating crocodiles he'd read about.

"Yeah. Bronwyn Spencer."

He felt like someone had just encased him in ice. Mark couldn't move, not even his lips; he couldn't so much as blink.

Unconcerned, Pete lifted a sandaled and rather hairy foot to his knee and picked sand out from under a toe ring the size of a plumbing fixture.

The resulting sandhill on the industrial carpet caused Pete to rub the sand into the pile with a crooked and wholly unapologetic grin. "Sorry, mate. The surf was beaut this morning. I didn't have time to shower before coming to work."

"Bronwyn Spencer is Cameron Crane's sister?"

"Yeah."

"Excellent," Mark said, pulling himself together with an effort and pulling his notes into a neat right angle with hands that hardly shook at all. "That's great, Pete. Thanks. I think we're done here."

"I thought you also wanted to know about how we file with the government?"

"Maybe later. Thanks." He rose, and with a shrug, his sandy friend rose also and shuffled out of the temporary office.

If Mark had ever been this angry, he didn't remember it. He'd been pretty near gutted by Jen's *sorry pal, it's over* long distance phone call, but that had been nothing like the crimson tide of anger that washed over him now.

He stormed out and in the general direction of where he'd last seen Bron. If he were being sensible, he'd go for a walk, calm down, and speak to Bron when he could see straight.

The hell with that. What he had to say couldn't wait.

Chapter Seven

"No. That's the wrong pink," Bron sighed, looking at a trio of samples from a supplier. "I want surfie-chick pink, not the color of something you take when your guts are churning."

"I'm not sure they understand the sort of color you have in mind," the hapless sales rep said.

"Well, it's bright, but not too bright; pink, but not too pink. Wait a sec. I've got a lipstick that shade, I think."

She scrabbled through her shoulder bag, past the extra set of keys to Cam's car that she thought she'd lost, a few crumpled ticket stubs from the train, a small flashlight she was pretty sure needed new batteries, a couple of squat colorful bottles of nail polish, and, in the bottom, a selection of lipsticks.

"There you are," she said in triumph. "That's the color I want. Here, you can take it."

"I'm not sure we can do this shade, Bron."

She leaned back and held out her hand. "No worries. Harry Welsdon has been begging for a chance to quote on our jobs. I'll see if he wants to give it a go."

When her current sales rep didn't hand back the lipstick, she knew she had him.

"I'm not saying—"

He never finished whatever it was he wasn't saying, for

the door opened as though a cyclone were on the other side of it and in stormed Mark, looking a little like a natural disaster bent on destruction himself.

"What are you—"

"Sorry to interrupt," he managed, "but I need to see you right away, Bronwyn."

Without giving her any time at all to decide whether to ditch her meeting right when she was about to get exactly what she wanted, he walked up to her and took her arm. "It's really important."

"Okay." Mystified at both the heat in his hand and the wild expression in his eyes, she wondered if he suffered from some mental condition no one had bothered to tell her about. A second glance showed that his eyes weren't wild; they were perfectly sane, just blazingly angry.

Her stomach sank. Oh, she was going to kill Fiona. Her little white lie about his package seemed to have got back to him.

Deciding that the last thing she wanted was an audience when he blew, she said, "Okay, Joe. See what you can do with the color and let me know. Can you find your own way out?"

"Yeah, sure."

Letting Mark pull her out into the corridor, she tried to think of the closest place she could drag one steamingly irate man where, when he blew, he wouldn't be overheard by too many people, keeping the embarrassing damage to a minimum.

"Where are we going?" she asked, realizing that he was still dragging her.

"I'm taking you to lunch," he said from behind clenched teeth.

"It's ten-thirty in the morning."

"We won't be eating." And with that he dragged her past a startled-looking Fiona. *Traitor.* Even as she was frog-marched past, she managed a pretty lethal glare in blabber-mouth's direction.

The morning sun was bright and merciless, and, naturally, she had no purse or sunglasses with her. It was too hot to walk this fast, but Mark didn't seem to notice.

Okay, he was angry. He had a right to be, and her justification was weak at best.

They sprinted past a pub, closed at this time of the day, with some tables and chairs set out on a brick patio. She dug her heels into the sidewalk like a stubborn hound and this time she did some dragging, pulling Mark into the relative privacy of the patio area.

She could berate him for no doubt bruising her arm, and she could act innocent of starting such malicious gossip, but she was, at heart, honest. She'd done a stupid thing, been caught out and it was time to apologize.

God, she hated apologizing. "Mark," she said, drawing the first full breath since he'd grabbed at her in her office, "I'm sorry."

"Sorry?" he hit a high note that couldn't be good for him, and startled a lorikeet into squawking and flying out of the tree above them. "You've made a complete fool of me. How could you do that?"

She squirmed where she stood. How could she have let the office think those things about him? "I was just trying to protect you from Fiona. She's a maneater," she said, feeling how feeble a defense that was for undermining his manhood. Oh, boy, was she in trouble. "I'll go back in there and tell her that you've got a donkey dick."

Instead of looking appeased he merely looked confused. "Would you please stay with the subject at hand?"

A blush of mortification began at her baby toe and started to work its way up. Was it possible they were talking about two different things?

"Could you tell me specifically why you are so angry with me?"

"You didn't tell me you were Cameron Crane's sister!" he thundered.

This is what he was so pissed off about? "The subject never came up."

Instead of appeasing him, this only made him more furious. "You don't have the same name. Why would I ask?"

"We're half-sibs. It doesn't make any difference. I'm an adult. My actions are nothing to do with Cam."

"It makes a difference to me. My behavior was completely unprofessional. I seduced—unknowingly, mind you—I seduced the sister of the man who hired me."

"Not to burst your bubble, mate, but I seduced you."

"Well, that's it. I'm sorry, but it's over. I thought . . . I never intended to—I mean I didn't want—"

And suddenly it was as though the anger did some complicated atomic switcheroo, for she was now as blazingly furious as the man in front of her had been a second ago.

"Oh, I know what you didn't want," she shouted back. "You didn't want *me*. Or at least not only me. You wanted to shag every girl in the city. And now you're all full of righteousness because I'm related to Cameron Crane so you're giving me the flick. Fine. But don't fool yourself, because you're not fooling me. You're getting rid of me because your precious Jennifer Talbot is coming over with Cam and you don't want her knowing you've been having it off with his sister."

"Jen has nothing to do with this," he yelled.

"She's got everything to do with it. What are you planning? To win her back?"

There was a painful silence. Mark looked so hurt and confused a part of her wanted to kiss him better, and he was so blind to what was right under his nose she wanted to haul off and smack him.

That was her trouble, she realized. She'd been literally under his nose the entire time he'd been here. There'd been no wooing, no romance, no effort at all required. She'd wanted him, he'd wanted her. They'd gone to bed. From the first moment she'd known he was special, but she realized he'd never had a similar epiphany. And whose fault was that? She was there every bloody minute. She'd stopped seeing other men because she was only interested in Mark.

Well, no more.

"Don't worry. I'll move my stuff out today and clear the way. Maybe you can win back the woman who dumped you for another man. Maybe you'll even want her. All I know is, I was wrong about you. I thought you were special, but you're not. You're pathetic. You're just so pathetic."

For a second they stared at each other. He was angry, hurt, confused, and so bloody, completely useless she couldn't believe it. And she was so hurt that he thought of her as disposable that she felt tears threaten.

"Bronwyn . . ."

Bron didn't cry. And the thing she most especially didn't cry over was men. Before such foolishness could emerge, she turned on her heel and stalked back the way they'd come.

Only this time she was alone. She was almost at the Crane building when he yelled her name.

"Bron."

She ignored him and speeded her pace.

"Bronwyn!" Mark yelled louder, and she picked it up to a jog.

"Would you hold up a minute?" He caught her arm as she opened the door but she yanked it out of his grasp and stormed into reception. Her gaze hazy with anger, she focused on the woman sitting behind reception staring at the pair of them coming noisily through the door.

"Bron," he said urgently.

"Fiona," she said in a loud, clear voice, "I lied. Mark here is the eighth wonder of the world in the sack. Hung like a stallion, tireless, your kind of bloke."

There was a moment of deafening silence.

Then a voice she knew all too well. "What have you been up to this time, Bron?" asked her brother Cam.

She turned, hoping against hope that he was alone, but of course, he was standing with the altogether too-perfect Jennifer Talbot, who was looking not at Bron, but behind her where she felt Mark's presence.

"Oh, shit," she said, torn between trying to escape out the front door, blocked by Mark Forsythe looking like he was the last man standing after an attack by aliens, and going forward to hide in her office. That way was blocked by Cam looking like he wanted to wash her mouth out with soap.

Chapter Eight

"My office, Bron. Now."

Mark's reunion with the man who'd ruined his life wasn't a fortuitous one. Cameron Crane looked the same as he had the one time Mark had met him: scruffy, unshaven, cocky, and arrogant, but his usual expression of sleepy womanizing was replaced by the sort of look an irate father would give a delinquent teenager.

And Bronwyn, care-for-nobody, I-do-what-I-like-when-I-like Bronwyn, transformed into a sulky rebel before his eyes.

He couldn't let Bron take the responsibility for what was essentially his fault.

He'd let her stay in the corporate house against his better judgment, then he'd slept with her—and even if he hadn't known she was Cam's sister he had known she was a Crane employee and for that reason alone he should have kept his hands off. And, finally, he'd been the cause of her turning the reception area of Crane Enterprises into a burlesque show.

"Just a minute," he said, walking forward to face the man wearing the scowl.

"I'll deal with you later."

He was amazed at the primitive urge for violence that swept through him, but he knew that would only make things worse. Somebody had to keep a cool head around here. "I'd like a minute alone with you first."

"Get stuffed," said Bron.

"You'll be having that word with me," Jennifer said, and he realized she was part of this comedy-drama, too.

With a helpless glance toward Cam and Bron, both of whom ignored him as well as each other as they stalked, with a similarly athletic stride, to Cam's big office, Mark realized that Bron didn't want his help.

"Fine," he snapped and followed Jen.

She led him to the spare office he'd been using and paused in the doorway. "Oh, they've set you up in here?"

"Yes." She looked good, he thought. Her hair was a little longer than it had been the last time he'd seen her and the humidity was adding some curl he could tell she'd been at pains to eradicate.

She looked as slim and beautiful as ever. And he knew they had a lot to talk about, but right now he couldn't spare the time. He couldn't bear the thought of Bron being hauled on the carpet by big brother Cam, not when it was his fault she'd blown her top. "Look, I really need to get in there and explain."

"Bron's a big girl. She can do her own explaining. You need to do some explaining of your own. To me." She paused and he realized she was angry. Her jaw had a certain pinched look and the way she held her shoulders, he knew they were knotted with tension. In the old days, he'd have rubbed them for her.

"I asked you to take this project on because you are the best and I trusted you. How could you make such a spectacle of yourself?"

"I . . ." How had that happened? Why had a fun-loving, all-for-laughs party girl like Bron told everyone he'd been short-changed in the sexual equipment department? Come to that, there was something odd about how women had treated him every time she was around.

And why had she thrown all that stuff in his face about Jen? Looking so angry he'd thought she was going to cry?

Because she'd been right.

His entire strategy had been to get Jen back.

And now that he stood here with Jen in front of him, he realized he didn't want her back. The woman he couldn't stop thinking about was Bronwyn.

"I hurt her," he said, recognizing that while he'd been trying so hard to live a wild, carefree existence, an incredible woman had given him back something he'd lost. And he'd hurt her.

"You're sleeping with her."

Jen's gaze clouded, and he watched her lean back against the wall as though she needed the support.

"Yes. I'm sleeping with her." He tried a smile and it wasn't nearly as painful as he'd supposed. "It's surprising how much it hurts, isn't it?"

Jen nodded. "I guess I imagined it would take you longer to get over me," she said softly. "Even though I have no right."

"I'll tell you something. A little part of me will always love you."

She raised her gaze and her eyes filmed. She nodded. "Me, too."

"But we weren't right together."

She shook her head.

"Cameron Crane, for reasons that are a complete mystery to me, is the man for you."

"And Bronwyn?"

"Bronwyn will probably never speak to me again."

"Whoever the right woman is, she's out there. And she's special," Jen said huskily and opened her arms to him. He hugged her and realized that this, for him, was goodbye.

"That bastard better be good to you."

She hugged him hard. "He is. And I'm good for him."

He loosened his grip. "I've got to go. We'll catch up later."

For the second time that day he couldn't get to Bron's office fast enough. But when he got there, nothing but silence greeted him. The lights were off and, as far as he could tell, her bag was gone.

His next stop was the front desk, where he asked the goggle-eyed Fiona where Bron was.

"She's gone."

"You mean she won't be back until tomorrow?"

"She won't be back for two weeks."

"What? She didn't say anything to me about holidays."

Fiona shrugged and answered a ringing line.

He stood for a moment undecided, then turned on his heel. Cameron Crane had caused enough trouble in his life. It was time they got things straight, man to man.

Crane's door was closed, but it didn't stop Mark. He threw the door open without knocking and found Jen in there, perched on the edge of his desk and leaning over, whether to talk intimately or in preparation for a necking session, Mark couldn't say.

He took a step in and shut the door ungently behind him.

"Mark. What are you doing?"

He ignored Jen. "What did you do to her, you bastard?"

Cameron Crane didn't look any happier to see him than he was to see the boogie board king himself.

"She's my sister, and my employee, so why don't you piss off?"

"Cam!"

Still ignoring Jen, Mark took a step closer, and Crane rose from behind the desk. Mark was pleased to see that though the Aussie was stockier of build, he topped him by a good four inches.

"She may be your sister, but she's my lover, and I won't have you hurting her."

"Listen mate," the unshaven mug jutted belligerently his way, "I don't know what you were getting up to while I was away, but I'm back, and I look after what's mine."

Mark wasn't a back-alley-brawl kind of man. He believed in conflict resolution, in calm deliberation, in compromise.

But not here and not now.

At this moment all he wanted to do was ram his fist into that too-many-times-broken-to-count nose. He didn't even realize he'd fisted his fingers until Jen's voice splashed over him like ice water.

"Oh, for God's sake. Why don't the pair of you pull your dicks out and have a pissing contest. Just get it over with."

He was so surprised to hear Jen talk that way that he dropped his hand and turned to stare at her. He might have thought she'd picked up her coarse habit of speech from Crane except that he was across the desk with his mouth hanging open in identical shock.

"Now that I have the floor, maybe we can talk business for a minute. How are you doing with the accounting systems?" She fixed Mark with a look that said, *behave, or you'll be sorry.*

She ignored Cam completely, and her new boyfriend didn't say a word.

"I've done all the training necessary here and I've got everything I need," he said stiffly. "The rest I can do from home."

In fact, he'd planned to write a report and spend a couple more days making sure everyone he'd trained was up to speed. But now that Crane was back he felt no great desire to hang around.

Especially if Bron wasn't going to be here.

What Jen had coaxed out of him was the fact that he was done. He didn't need to stay here any longer.

He'd always loved how smart Jen was. He'd finish up today and then instead of heading home take a holiday himself. Hell, it had been in the back of his mind from the beginning.

He nodded. "I've got everything I need. I'll finish up and head out."

286 / *Nancy Warren*

"Great. I'll e-mail with any questions," Jen said.

"I'll be out of touch for a couple of weeks. I think I'll do some sightseeing while I'm here."

To give him credit, Crane wasn't as stupid as he appeared. "You hurt my sister, and you'll be sorry you were born."

Mark leaned in until they were nose to nose with the desk between them. "You hurt Jennifer, and you'll be sorry you were born."

Then, because he wanted to, and because it would annoy Crane, he turned and kissed Jen. Right on the mouth. "You take care."

"Good luck," she said softly.

"You, too." Why she'd choose an ape like Crane over him, he'd never know, but she had and was obviously happy.

And she'd done them both a favor, he now realized.

All he had to do was figure out what would make him happy.

He had a few ideas.

Bron shoved her beach thongs on top of a silk halter top, and didn't even pause to rearrange them. She didn't care what ended up where in her bags, what got gunked with sand, creased, or ruined, she didn't even care what she left behind, so long as she could get out of here.

She heard the front door slam and cursed, ramming the thongs down hard enough that she could close the bag. She'd get everything else later, when Mark was out of the country. Right now she was on a self-imposed stress leave.

That was a term a Yank like Mark would like. Stress bloody leave.

After a short but shattering interview with Cam, she'd actually quit her job, something she had never done before. She was just so mad she didn't care. Cam could blaze with the best of them, but just as she'd reached his office door he'd yelled, "Don't be daft. Take a couple of weeks off. Have a holiday."

She hadn't even acknowledged he'd spoken, but by the time she'd tidied her desk, made a couple of phone calls that had to be made or the company would suffer, and picked up her bag, he still hadn't come to grovel.

Which was annoying because she was ready to accept his apology, and even admit she'd been partly wrong. Not for sleeping with Mark of course, or with anyone else she felt like, but because she'd moved into the corporate house even though she knew Cam would have a fit if she'd asked.

But Cam didn't come to grovel sufficiently that she felt she could apologize, so she sucked in a breath and walked with her head as high as she could get it to the front door.

"Have a good holiday," Fiona said casually, even though her eyes were shining with all the pent-up excellent gossip she'd stored today. She should be good for years on today's fiasco.

"Thanks."

"Here's your holiday pay." Fi handed her an envelope.

Her brows rose, but the receptionist shrugged. "Never turn down free money."

Good advice if she'd ever heard any, especially as she was currently skint: semi-unemployed and homeless.

The envelope was still in her bag, unopened. If she cashed it, she'd do something stupid. What she needed to do was get a new place.

And some new attitudes.

And no more men.

"Bronwyn?" Why hadn't he given her enough time to get clear of the place? Even as her foolish heart leapt like a hooked fish, she scowled. Couldn't the man have worked to the end of the day like anyone else? If only to give her time to get her stuff out.

She bumped one of her big canvas bags against her thigh as she limped her way out of her room. She got to the top of the stairs and found Mark at the bottom staring up at her in a way that made her heart flip over just as it had the first time she'd seen him. It wasn't fair. How could he do that to her?

She said the first waspish thing she could think of. "Why aren't you with Jennifer?"

"Jennifer Talbot?"

"No. Jennifer Lopez."

A beat passed, and she felt him looking at her in a way he never had before. "Jen's with your brother, Cameron."

She snorted. "Does Cam know she was hugging you in the office?"

Mark didn't argue or deny or even look guilty. He smiled up at her. She wasn't sure if he was stupid, crook, or amoral. All three probably. "It was kind of a goodbye hug."

She continued to stare down at him. He continued to stare up.

"I hear you're going on holiday."

"That's right. I'm packing for Paris as we speak."

Mark slipped a folder out of his briefcase. "How about the Whitsundays?"

There was no doubt that the white folder looked like it came from a travel agent, but why would he be flashing it at her?

Since she didn't know the correct answer, she kept silent.

"Do you think you could come down? Or maybe I could come up? I'm getting a crick in my neck."

She sat down and pushed her bag out of the way.

Mark sprinted up the steps and sat beside her. Too late she realized she'd have been better to go down. By making him come to her, she'd ended up wedged against the wall of the landing, with his hip warm against hers and the familiar feel of his thigh and the brush of his shirt against her arm.

She wanted to throw herself in his arms and weep. Instead, she sat stiffly and pretended great interest in her manicure.

"Bronwyn, will you go to the Whitsunday Islands and spend your holiday with me?"

"I thought you were dumping me because I'm Cam's sister."

"I want to start over. I was stupid, foolish, misguided—"

"Tactless," she added, happy to help him abase himself before her.

"Definitely tactless," he agreed. "And you were . . . amazing. I came over here bruised and angry and really believed I only wanted to have fun; party and bed a different woman every night. And then I met you. And even when I tried, when we went out together, I didn't want any other women. I only wanted you."

"Really?"

He took one of her hands in his and she liked the warm current that passed between them. He kissed her knuckles, and she liked the soft brush of his lips and the tiny scrape of whisker as his chin hit.

"You were right. I think deep in my head I thought I wanted Jen back, but when I saw her today, all I could think about was you. I can see that she's happy. No idea why. What she sees in that hairy brute is a mystery to me."

A giggle from beside him reminded him this was her brother he was talking about. "Me, too," she agreed. "So you're saying you don't love her anymore?"

"I'll tell you what I told Jen. A little part of me will always love her. She's terrific. But she's not for me, and I'm not for her. I guess we were together so long we stopped realizing that we were friends more than lovers and destined to be better colleagues than spouses."

"Crikey. You worked all that out today?"

"I think I've known it for a while. I didn't want to face it."

"So now what?"

"I think your brother's an ass, you think your brother's an ass, let's say to hell with him, and take a holiday. I want some time to enjoy you and get to know you."

"You're not going to try and score with other women when you're with me?"

He winced. "How could I have acted like such a jerk? No. I promise."

"Well, okay. Then I won't have to tell my friends you're gay."

He stiffened alarmingly. "I thought I heard something about deficient equipment."

"That was at the office."

"I see. So you told your friends I was gay and your colleagues I was sexually deficient. Anything else?"

"I might have mentioned Viagra."

"Okay, that's it."

He hauled her to her feet so fast she squeaked. "What are you doing?"

"Obviously, I have to remind you that I'm not gay, all my impressive parts work, and medication will not be required."

"You're not mad?"

He shoved a shoulder into her belly so fast the air oofed out of her and hoisted her over his shoulder. "I am extremely mad. And you are about to be punished."

She sighed with pleasure, hanging on upside down to his waist as he walked her to his bedroom.

"The Whitsunday Islands are near the Great Barrier Reef," she said to his swaying butt. Nice butt. "We can go snorkeling and diving and see all sorts of things."

"The only thing you're likely to see is the ceiling of our hotel room," he warned her as he tossed her to the bed.

Chapter Nine

After he'd treated her like a disposable toothbrush for the first couple of weeks of their acquaintance, and she'd still fallen for him, Bron was helpless to resist Mark when he treated her like the most important woman in the world.

They flew to Brisbane and then changed to a smaller plane which took them to Hamilton Island, where a motor yacht ferried them to their island. She'd been to the reef once on a scuba trip, but she'd never been to the scatter of tropical islands that edged the Great Barrier Reef.

While uniformed waiters served them champagne and hors d'oeuvres, the sea sparkled around them and ahead she spied a half-moon of the whitest sand she'd ever seen.

The resort was populated with young, well-to-do couples, and there were few children. The entire place was geared to romance and hedonism. She'd never stayed at a resort as swish and dreamy as this one.

Perfect. Except that they seemed to be the only pair who weren't newlyweds.

"Are you honeymooners, love?" asked the woman handing out towels by the pool.

"Not yet," Bron said bitchily. "We're still practicing."

And practice they did, but still it seemed they couldn't get enough of each other.

Funny, tender, uncomfortably contorted or slow and

easy, it didn't matter. She couldn't get enough of him and Mark, it seemed, couldn't get enough of her.

He'd said nothing about going out to the reef, so she decided to surprise him with tickets.

After a dinner of fresh seafood they'd sat out and listened to the waves for hours, talking about everything from the politics of their two countries to first boyfriends and girlfriends to sports they'd excelled in and trophies they'd won, should have won, or lost ignominiously.

"Hey," she said when there was a lull, "I bought us a present today."

He glanced at her with a gleam in his eye she knew well. "Did it come from the sex shop?"

There was a well-stocked one in the main building, but so far they hadn't felt the need for any extra excitement.

"No," she said, and handed him the envelope.

The excited gleam in his eyes died when he read the tickets and the brochure she'd included. "Great," he said with enthusiasm so false she wished she'd discussed it with him first and hadn't surprised him.

"What's the matter?" she asked. "Did you once have a near-death experience with a sea turtle?"

"No."

"Allergic to coral?"

"No. But it's nice to know you're still using your gifted imagination to make me look foolish."

"Scared of sharks."

"N—" His eyes widened. "There are sharks out there? People pay to snorkel in shark-infested waters?"

She snickered. "If you worried about everything in our waters that can kill you, you'd never dip a toe in."

"I get seasick," he admitted as though it were a shameful secret.

"Oh, that's nothing to worry about. They hand out Dramamine and sick bags when you get on the boat."

He swallowed. "This is not inspiring me with greater confidence."

"Come on," she coaxed. "It's a once-in-a-lifetime opportunity."

"So was my appendectomy."

Of course, he went in the end. And while he didn't get sick, he did snore for most of the way after liberally dosing himself with Dramamine. Bron stuck with a ginger pill, since she had a strong stomach anyway.

And oh, wasn't it worth every minute on the open ocean to share that experience with him. The boat docked to a metal platform that floated in what appeared to be the middle of the ocean. There was no land visible anywhere, only a chop of waves at the reef.

Once she had Mark awake, he seemed quite eager so they suited up with face masks, snorkels, and flippers, and from the first moment they dipped their faces in, it was as though they'd been transported to another world.

Giant clams, their gaping mouths proudly displaying vivid red, green, and purple centers, giant sea turtles, quietly going about their business, mostly oblivious to those watching them, and fish of every color and description.

They held hands as they darted here and there pointing sights out to each other, pulling in this direction then that.

After hours of snorkeling, they took a break for the lunch the crew put together on the pontooned raft, and then reboarded the launch back to their island resort.

Mark, she couldn't help but note, was too busy reliving their adventure to remember his Dramamine pill, and since the return ride was fairly smooth, he made it home fine.

"Snorkeling makes me horny," he told her as he pushed her into the room on their return.

Since she'd been thinking more of a hot shower and dinner, she rolled her gaze. "Everything makes you horny."

"Only when you're around."

"I can't believe it's our last day," she said. Her wail was supposed to be theatrical, but underneath it was the knowledge that when this holiday was over, so was the best affair she'd ever had.

Mark would be going back across the world to San Francisco. Sure, she consoled herself, she'd see him the odd time. He'd still consult for Crane. Maybe she could convince Cam to send her over on a research mission. They could snatch a few weekends together.

But it wouldn't be the same.

Refusing to hurt, or at least to let him see how much she hurt, she said brightly, "What do you want to do for our last day?"

"Make love to you."

She giggled, but it had a wistful sound. "That's what we did yesterday."

"And the day before."

"And the day before that."

"Is there something you'd rather do?" he asked politely.

She gazed across at him, with a dab of shaving cream still sticking to his chin, a towel wrapped around his tropically tanned shoulders, and a pair of plaid boxer shorts. The whole package made her liquid. She grabbed the hem of her cotton sundress and stripped. It was all the answer he needed.

"We've only got an hour until the boat leaves," she said sometime later.

"Mmmm." And he nuzzled her belly and nibbled his way to her hipbone.

"Mark," she said later, waking from a deep and comforting sleep. "Mark!"

"What?" he mumbled.

"That's the boat whistle. We aren't even packed." She began pushing at limbs that seemed to twine about her like enormous choking vines.

"Coming in or going out?" he said with maddening calm.

"I don't know. Wake up."

"We're probably too late," he said, using precious remaining seconds to kiss her breast. "I love your breasts," he murmured.

"Do you have sunstroke or something? The boat is going to go without us."

"Yes," he agreed. "It is."

The man was beyond sunstroke. He was certifiably insane. "Don't you even care?"

"Not particularly. I like it here."

She felt his forehead for fever, but he pulled it away and kissed her palm.

"You can come here again," she assured him, wondering if maybe it was something he'd eaten.

"I want to spend my honeymoon here," he added, going back to her breasts.

"Well, you wouldn't be alone."

"I want to spend my honeymoon here next week," he explained further, moving from her left breast to her right. "You know, I'm sure each of your nipples tastes slightly different, but I can never work out why."

"What?" she shrieked.

"Your breasts. I think they taste different."

She smacked his shoulder. "Not that part, the other part."

He raised his head, and the expression in his eyes caused her heart to stutter. "They have a chaplain on call, and the wedding chapel's got some openings. We can get married today."

"Why would you want to marry me?" she asked, trying so hard not to sound like she was about to bawl her eyes out.

"Because I love you."

"But I'm completely hopeless. I'm terrible with money, and I get chucked out of flats, and make fools of people at the office, I'm not smart and smooth like Jennifer Talbot."

"You're funny, and sexy, and wildly creative, and I love you."

"Oh." She sniffed. She did not cry over men, she reminded herself. Okay, she could be catching a cold. One sniff did not a sob make.

"What about me?"

"You're funny too, kind of. And definitely sexy. But I don't know about the creative part. I think not." She paused for a minute. "Bloody brilliant with a calculator, though."

"That's why we're perfect for each other. You make my life crazy and exciting, and I can probably straighten out your bank account and keep you on track."

Maybe it wasn't romantic, but the idea of someone who could take care of all that stuff she was so hopeless about was definitely appealing. He was right about her, too. He could be plenty fun and creative with her around. Without her, he could end up a stick in the mud. She was almost willing to marry him just to get a crack at livening up his wardrobe.

"So will you marry me?"

"Are you sure?"

"Oh, honey, I've never been so sure of anything."

She sniffed again and blinked a few times. "I am not wearing one of those over-the-top white wedding gowns they sell in the clothes shop." There was a wonderful sky-blue silk, though, cocktail length and backless, she'd had her eye on. That would be perfect.

"You can wear anything you want if you'll marry me."

"Why would I do that?"

"How about you love me?" he asked with a gleam of challenge in his eye and as much love as any woman could ask for.

"How about I do," she said and rolled on top of him, naked and eager to get on with a whole life together.

Please turn the page for an advance

look at Diane Whiteside's

THE IRISH DEVIL,

coming next month from Brava . . .

Donovan & Sons was busier than usual, with men working hard to load a series of wagons. Viola's eyes passed over them quickly, seeking one particular fellow clad in a well-tailored suit. He could be found occasionally in a teamster's rough garb but only when driving a wagon. His clean-shaven face was always a strong contrast to every other man's abundant whiskers.

Her eyes lingered on a midnight head above broad shoulders, tugging hard on a wagonload's embracing ropes. The right height and build but red flannel? Then the man turned and Donovan's brilliant blue eyes locked with hers.

Viola gulped and nodded at him.

His eyebrows lifted for a moment then he returned her silent greeting. He strode toward her, still gentlemanly despite the dust. She was barely aware of his men's curiosity.

"Mrs. Ross. It is an honor to see you here." Her grandmother would have approved of his handshake but not his appearance. His black hair was disheveled, his clothing was streaked with dust, his scent reeked of horses and sweat.

And his shoulders looked so much more masculine under the thin red flannel than they ever had in English broadcloth.

She swallowed and tried to think logically. She was here

to gain his protection, no matter what distractions his appearance offered.

William smiled down at Viola, curious why she'd come to the depot. Probably for money to return back East.

"May I have a word with you in private, Mr. Donovan?"

Poor lady, she sounded so awkward and embarrassed. "Certainly. We can use the office," he soothed and led the way across the yard. "Would you care for some fresh tea or coffee?"

"No, thank you. What I have to say should not take long."

She must want a seat on the next stagecoach out of town, if the conversation must be fast. Buy her that ticket and she'd be gone in a day. Bloody hell.

William ushered her into the small room, bare except for the minimum of furniture, all solid, scarred, and littered with paperwork.

She accepted the indicated seat but was wretchedly nervous, almost fidgeting in her chair. He wanted to snatch her up and swear the world would never hurt her again, then hunt down Charlie Jones and his fool wife. William closed the wooden shutters on the single window, filtering out much of the light and noise from the bustling corrals, then settled into his big oak swivel chair.

"What can I do for you, Mrs. Ross?" He kept his voice gentle, his California drawl soft against the muffled noises from outside.

She took a deep breath, drew herself up straight and tall, and launched into speech. "May I become your mistress, Mr. Donovan?"

"What?! What the devil are you talking about?" he choked, too stunned to watch his language. He knew his mouth was hanging open. "Are you making a joke, Mrs. Ross?"

"Hardly, Mr. Donovan." She met his eyes directly, pulse pounding in her throat. "You may not have heard but my business partner sold everything to Mr. Lennox."

He nodded curtly. He must have been right before: she needed money. "I met Mr. and Mrs. Jones on their way out of town. I won't be doing business with them again," he added harshly.

"Quite so. But my only choices now are to marry Mr. Lennox or find another man to protect me. I'd rather be yours than an Apache's."

"Jesus, Mary and Joseph," William muttered as he stood and began to pace. Think, boyo, think. She deserves better than being your woman. Heat lanced from his heart down his spine at the thought of her in his arms every night. Marriage? No, she'd never agree to a Catholic ceremony. "There are other men, men who'd marry you," he pointed out hoarsely.

"I will not remarry. Besides, Mr. Lennox blocked all offers other than his."

"Son of a bitch." The bastard should be shot. "What about your family?"

"They disinherited me when I married Edward. Both families refused my letters informing them of his death."

How the devil could a parent abandon their child, no matter what the quarrel? His father had given everything to protect his children.

William's gut tightened at the thought. Condoms were helpful but not a guarantee. If she stayed in his bed long enough, the odds were good . . .

"You could become pregnant," he warned, his eyes returning to her face. Blessed Virgin, what he wouldn't do to see Viola proud and happy, holding his babe in her arms.

"I can't have children."

"The fault could be in the stallion, not the mare," William suggested, his drawl more pronounced. And this stallion would dearly love to prove his potency where another had failed.

And here's a sizzling sneak peek

at our new Brava anthology

HOW TO BE A WICKED WOMAN,

and Susanna Carr's "Wicked Ways."

What am I doing here? Peyton wondered as the man's groin invaded her personal space. It took all her willpower not to flinch, even as the musky scent of arousal and masculine sweat assailed her flared nostrils. She tried to maintain a casual pose, but every muscle in her body hummed with tension. Her hands clenched underneath her chair. Her rigid fingertips brushed against something gooey.

It's gum. She assured herself. *Please let it be gum.*

"Hey, I know you," the blond god said as he placed his hands behind his head and displayed his magnificent shaven chest. He rotated his hips to the restless beat. "You're my boss at Lovejoy's Unmentionables."

Peyton flashed him a tight smile. "That's right," she admitted. Is there no end to this night? Why did she think she would have gone unnoticed? Nothing else was going her way.

But who was he? She hadn't really been looking at his face. She squinted as the disco ball spun crazily, swirling white dots of light over everyone. "Bubba Joe from shipping?" she ventured a guess. "I'm sorry, I didn't recognize you . . . ."

"Yeah, that's because I'm incognito," he said and punctuated each syllable of the last word with short pelvic thrusts.

Okay. . . .

"You know this is my alter ego." He gripped the back of

her chair. She felt like she was caged in testosterone. "But call me by my stage name, Hubba Bubba."

"Did you come up with that all by yourself?" Peyton willed her arms to stay at her sides, although her elbows started creeping in.

"Nah. I ain't that creative. It was the nickname girls gave me in high school." He got off her and Peyton slowly let out a relieved sigh. It lodged in her throat as he turned around and straddled her again, this time clenching and unclenching his buttocks. His bare buttocks. To the beat of the music. In her face.

"So whatcha doing here, Miz Lovejoy?" he asked as he turned around again. "This ain't no place for someone like you."

Tell me about it. "Entertaining some business clients." Why wasn't this song over? She didn't remember it lasting this long. Wagner's operas were shorter than this.

"All these women wearing black?" He nodded his head to the women sitting at the table, flexing their fingers wildly as they hollered about what they wanted to do with his butt. "I though you guys just come back from a funeral or something."

No, it just felt that way. "They're here to relax." And to see if she was one of them. If she was willing to be a team player. She wasn't sure if she was succeeding.

"They could save Lovejoy's?" He did a cat stretch before dipping his spine. Peyton was momentarily entranced by the play of muscles until she realized he was rubbing his full erection against her black straight skirt.

Her knees knocked together. "We might reach an agreement that could bring us a lot of money," she replied hoarsely. Did everyone know about the company's financial troubles? "Nothing's definite yet."

Bubba Joe leaned in close until all she could see was his tight nipple. If she spoke, her lips would press against his slick skin. Peyton felt her cheeks turn a vivid red. "You want me to be real nice to them?" he whispered into her ear. His hot breath stirred the tendrils of her hair that escaped from her French twist. "Give them a private showing?"

Peyton winced. Oh, yeah. That's what she needs to do; make her employee stud for the night. "Thanks for the offer," she said graciously. "It's very generous, but I want you to come out alive."

He flicked a look at the group of women. His smile kicked up a notch, overflowing with confidence. "Don't worry, Miz Lovejoy, I can handle it."

It seemed like everyone could handle the evening but her. "I think it would be best if you didn't treat them differently. Why don't you go over there now?" She hoped the ah-ah-ahs from the speakers drowned out the desperation leaking in her voice.

He glanced down. Pointedly. Peyton reluctantly followed his gaze. Were the strobe lights doing something to her eyes or did those leopard spots seem bigger?

"You need to tip me."

"Oh. Oh!" She forgot about the dollar bill that was scrunched into her fist and probably stuck to the gum. Peyton tore it from under her chair and offered it to him.

Bubba Joe dipped his head next to hers. "No, Miz Lovejoy, I can't take the money. It's against the rules. You have to put it on me."

On him? He was her employee! Peyton's polite smile wavered. She cleared her throat nervously. "Of course." The heat emanating from his snug G-string scorched her hovering hand. She changed her mind and crammed the mangled dollar over the minuscule string on his hip, the farthest place away from any private parts. "I don't want to injure you."

"You couldn't. This is designed for protection from over-eager hands." His splayed fingers framed the leopard skin.

Peyton was at a loss. "Love the fabric," she finally said.

Bubba Joe smiled proudly. "Thanks. My mom made it for me."

An image of his quiet mother hunched over an industrial sewing machine popped into her mind. "She always does excellent work."

"I'll be sure to tell her you think so," he said as he strutted away. "See ya, Miz Lovejoy."

Peyton closed her eyes. Oh, God. She didn't want his mother to know she was anywhere around Bubba Joe's G-string! Her stress headache threatened to erupt into a full-blown migraine. Peyton shot up from her seat. She needed a break. She almost wished she smoked so she could have the excuse of escaping outside.

She sure couldn't get excited about this place. What was wrong with her? Why couldn't she be as enthusiastic as the other women in the crowd? They acted like they'd been trapped in a convent since puberty and were just recently released. She felt like if you've seen one half-naked man show off his package, you've seen them all.

As she waited in line for the bathroom, Peyton noticed the empty men's room. If she really wanted a moment's peace, that would be the place to go. She decided to take the risk of entering. Chances were she'd seen what was in there already displayed on the stage. The moment she stepped across the threshold, Peyton gagged from the stench. She clasped her hand over her mouth and nose and tiptoed her way through the debris to the row of sinks.

She pinched the edges of a coarse paper towel dangling from the chrome dispenser and blotted the sweat from her face. The humid June night managed to sneak its way into the strip joint despite the air-conditioners chugging continuously.

Peyton looked at the row of sinks and tried to decide which one looked the least infectious. Turning the faucet knob with her elbow, she ran tepid water over the paper towel and pressed the damp wad onto the back of her neck.

She closed her eyes and sighed with relief before blowing the wisps of hair that tickled her forehead. Peyton opened her eyes and looked at her reflection. She looked—boring.

No, that wasn't true. She wouldn't let it be true. Peyton straightened in front of the mirror. There was nothing boring about her. Her job wasn't boring. It was challenging and demanding. Her social life wasn't dull. She had a group of wonderful, interesting friends.

No boyfriend right now, but not because she was boring! Peyton straightened her shoulders and tossed the wet towel in the vicinity of the stuffed trash can. None of her ex-boyfriends ever had complaints in that area. She knew how to have fun.

Even in bed. Peyton snapped her jacket collar into its perfect position. She'd had plenty of amazing sex in her life. Fantastic. Unreal. Okay, she hadn't quite accomplished multiple orgasms, but she was beginning to think that was an urban legend.

And so what if she hadn't had any sex recently? She'd been busy. Peyton briskly tugged the edge of her suit jacket. Everyone thought she was so lucky to have inherited the family business. They didn't see the struggle behind the scenes. They didn't understand the fear of being the Lovejoy who'd lost it all.

Peyton watched her left eyebrow arch. Her mouth set into a determined line as she hiked her chin up a notch.

I'll show them. I'll show them all. Peyton Lovejoy has what it takes to turn around the company.

She ripped open her jacket like a first-time flasher. What she didn't have in content, her enthusiasm should have made up for with extra bonus points. She shrugged off her jacket and clenched it in one hand, her eyes intent on her reflection.

Peyton Lovejoy is not a dork or a loser. She is a wild, wicked woman who gets what she wants.

Her hair was next. The French twist had to go. She clawed out the pins with determined fingers and gave her straight brown hair a good toss. It didn't billow like the hair color commercials, but fell and landed onto her bare shoulders.

Peyton Lovejoy . . .

She made a face.

. . . has got to stop referring herself in the third person because it's really annoying.

She gave her appearance another once-over. With a sharp nod of approval, she swung her jacket over her shoulders with two fingers and strutted to the door, pausing only to kick a fragment of paper off her heel.

Watch out world, here I come.

She exhaled sharply and—stood still.

Who was she kidding? Peyton dipped her chin. She needed those women execs more than they needed her. "If I have to walk across town stark naked, I will do whatever it takes to save my family's company."

She blinked and looked around the skuzzy stall. Not exactly Scarlett O'Hara shaking her fist with the sun setting behind her in blazing red.

It didn't matter, Peyton decided. She was going to be a sexy young thing if it killed her. She was going to walk the walk, talk the talk. But how was she going to convince those women out there? They were the real thing and could spot a pretender.

Peyton paced the floor in front of the urinals, dodging sodden paper towels. She mulled over the problem before she opened her purse and grabbed her cell phone. She needed information and quickly. Peyton hit the speed dial. Accurate info because she didn't have the luxury to make any mistakes.

"Main Library Answer Hotline," the low masculine voice rumbled in her ear. "This is Mike. How can I help you?"